Pleasure
of the
CHASE

Ann Roberts

Bella
BOOKS
2016

Bella Books, Inc.
P.O. Box 10543
Tallahassee, FL 32302

Printed in the United States of America on acid-free paper.

First Bella Books Edition 2016

Editor: Katherine V. Forrest
Cover Designer: Linda Callaghan

ISBN: 978-1-59493-500-8

Other Books by Ann Roberts

Romances
Beach Town
Beacon of Love
Brilliant
The Complete Package
Hidden Hearts
Petra's Canvas
Root of Passion

General Fiction
Furthest From the Gate
Keeping Up Appearances

The Ari Adams Series
Paid in Full
White Offerings
Deadly Intersections
Point of Betrayal
A Grand Plan

Acknowledgments

Thanks to my friend LK for her knowledge of the auto industry and carparazzi. She planted the idea for the book and provided critical information that made the story plausible. I am honored to have Katherine Forrest serve as my editor for the fourth time. I always learn from her and the final product improves with her suggested changes. My wife was the first and most critical reader. Without her love and support, I'd never finish a book. Finally, thanks to all my romance readers who continue to take pleasure in all the chases I create. I am grateful for your support.

About the Author

Ann Roberts is the author of seven romances and the Ari Adams mystery series. She was honored to receive the Alice B. Medal in 2014 for her body of work. A two-time Lambda finalist, Ann's mystery *Point of Betrayal* received a 2014 Goldie for Best Mystery. Ann lives in Phoenix, Arizona, with her wife, and she is planning to retire this summer after three decades in public education. She hopes to devote more time to writing and learning to play her dusty ukulele. Please visit her website at annroberts.net or on Facebook at Ann Roberts – Author.

CHAPTER ONE

Verde Valley, Arizona

Just a hair to the right and the Jeep would've spun out, careened over the embankment and plunged into the Verde River. Fortunately, Parnelli "Nellie" Rafferty had learned from prior experience. She pulled the wheel ever so slightly, avoided the river and kept pace with the car in front of her.

Her prey was hard to miss: a black-and-white-spotted Toyota prototype, a vehicle not yet green-lighted for manufacturing. First it had to pass hot weather testing. Similar to the Chrysler Prowler, its rear was boxier, but she could see the sleek lines of a hot sports car beneath the camouflage. The engineers had taped pieces of Styrofoam to the car's frame before applying the black-and-white shell. The camouflage often distorted photos taken by industrial auto spies like Nellie.

She snapped the pictures car fanatics longed to see. As a freelance photographer, her goal was to scoop her competitors and sell the photos to the highest bidder, who would publish them prior to the manufacturer's planned launch. She didn't care which magazine bought the photos so long as someone did. Those in her line of work were referred to as the carparazzi.

Much like the paparazzi, the carparazzi had a love-hate relationship with the automakers. They hated when auto spies undermined months of their PR department's work, but at the same time, they loved them—when it was someone else being scooped. If consumers didn't like what the carparazzi revealed, they'd buy a different model from a competitor. In Nellie's mind, it all balanced out for each company's profit and loss column.

She checked the speedometer. Ninety-five in a fifty-five. That would be a hefty ticket if a highway patrolman happened to be parked behind the stand of chokecherry trees ahead. If she was going to get the shot, it needed to be in the next seven miles. When they hit Camp Verde, the speed limit dropped to twenty-five and a clear shot would be nearly impossible amidst the townspeople, other cars and buildings.

"Go big or go home," she said as she accelerated to one hundred.

The prototype's bumper was so close she could see the seams of the boxy hatchback. It was fake, another common trick of the manufacturers: add falsies to make the proto look like a different model or different brand. Normally she wouldn't chase a car to get a shot. It was too dangerous. But as she'd followed the vehicle, the diaper, the trade name for a back camouflage, had fallen off, exposing some interesting taillights that looked like fins. It was too tempting not to pursue.

And she loved to drive fast. Her Jeep's soft top had long ago been discarded after someone sliced it to ribbons. She assumed the vandal was an automotive engineer, angry that she'd exposed a model before it hit production. The vandal had done her a favor. She'd never known such freedom until she sailed down the road without the confines of a roof and windows.

Finally in position, she readied her camera around the windshield. This was the most suspenseful moment of the chase. The hot August wind blasted in her face. The desert landscape rushed past her. She held the camera and steered the Jeep with her knee, ignoring the pain in her back. It was a tricky and dangerous thrill ride not found in any amusement park.

There was a rumble and the prototype pulled away. She clicked madly, swearing all the while. She knew the photos would be fuzzy at best. She shook her head. She should've guessed a sports coupe would be designed for power.

"That's certainly impressive pickup," she said dejectedly.

She slowed to a legal speed and smacked the steering wheel. She hated missing the shot, but the first rule of spying was to know when to call it a day. She wondered if she'd get another chance to photograph the prototype. She'd heard through her sources that Toyota wanted a showstopper in next year's line, and the car leaving her in the dust would certainly qualify. Perhaps there would be a need for more hot weather endurance tests, and the prototype would brave the sweltering August sun again before it returned to the proving ground in little Wittman, Arizona, the place Nellie called home.

She winced and shifted painfully in the Jeep's custom-made bucket seat. She'd avoided back surgery despite an MRI that indicated two vertebrae needed to be fused together. At forty-eight, the last thing she wanted to do was go under the knife. Instead she'd had a friend who worked on Lamborghinis make special seats for her Jeep. The lumbar support guaranteed she'd be able to walk after a five-hour drive to Palm Springs or Nevada, two of the other hot weather testing sites.

Up ahead she noticed the prototype had also decelerated. She sighed and made a plan for the rest of her day. She'd stop at the Verde Brewing Company for lunch, and then she'd traverse the length of Maricopa County to a press conference in Mesa. The old proving ground formerly owned by Chrysler had been sold to the French carmaker, Argent. Nellie had a short but colorful history with Argent and its strong-arm security team. She wondered if they knew Phoenix was her home. In the space of a year it was customary for her to travel throughout the world to get the money shots. Another proving ground in the immediate area would afford her some easy money without the airfare and hotel bills.

Far ahead the prototype was a mere dot against the expansive desert landscape. Suddenly a helicopter appeared from behind the neighboring mountains and set down in the brush, its nose pointed toward the highway. She couldn't be sure, but she thought it had landed in front of the car and was waiting for it to pass.

"Okay, this is interesting." She gunned the engine and reached for her binoculars. "C'mon, c'mon," she mumbled as the road dipped and her long-range view momentarily disappeared. The road leveled out again and she raised the binoculars for a quick look. The prototype had pulled off the road. The driver exited the car and headed across the highway, probably concerned that something was wrong. He suddenly stopped on the blacktop and ran back to the prototype. He sped away just as Nellie pulled up.

Sitting next to the pilot was a woman with a camera. Her head was down and she was studying the images through the viewfinder, oblivious to Nellie's arrival amidst the noise from the swirling blades of the chopper.

"Shit," Nellie said with a scowl.

It was Jos Grant, a newbie member of the carparazzi who also worked as a photographer for a trade rag. She tended to stay in the Arizona area, unlike Nellie who'd hop on a plane and fly halfway around the world at a moment's notice. They'd never been formally introduced, and she'd only seen her from a distance at some of the carparazzi hangouts, like the Circle K in Wittman. She was certainly a looker, but Nellie had never seen her as serious competition since she refused to travel.

Only when the pilot tapped Jos's shoulder and pointed did she glance up and see Nellie in her Jeep. Surprise quickly shifted to amusement when Nellie held up her camera and smiled. Jos laughed and pointed at her own camera, almost sheepishly. Hers was a Nikon 8008 with a large zoom, probably a five hundred millimeter mirror lens. Not a bad choice for a beginner. Nellie heard she was around thirty-five, but from her looks she probably got carded every time she bought alcohol. She wore a pink tank top and white walking shorts that made her skin look coppery from exposure to the sun. Her blond hair was pulled back in a tight bun. She looked like she was ready for a set of tennis, not a ride in a helicopter.

Many of the other auto spies would be gloating and puffing up their chests at staging such a coup. But Jos adopted a look of concern and pointed at her own camera and then at Nellie, as if to say, "Did you get a good shot?"

Nellie shook her head, and Jos mouthed, "I'm sorry."

Nellie waved her off and pointed at the chopper's blades before offering thumbs-up. It was a great idea and it proved she'd done her homework. She knew the car would be too fast to tail, so she'd found faster transportation. Today it was Jos who deserved the money shot.

Jos replied to Nellie's thumbs-up with a smile that, despite the August heat, warmed Nellie in a very different way. If they'd been somewhere else, like a bar or a coffeehouse, Nellie would've attempted conversation and turned on her charm. But they were pantomiming across a state highway while a male helicopter pilot watched. Clearly not meant to be.

She set her camera on the passenger's seat and grabbed her shades from the visor. Although the possibility of a money shot was gone, she'd look cool as she drove away.

She turned to wave goodbye, but Jos was bounding toward her. Nellie immediately noticed her long, muscular legs and the freshly pressed shorts with their razor-sharp crease. Nellie couldn't picture her crawling across the desert floor to hide from engineers, at least not in those clothes.

Jos held out her business card. "I'm Jos. Jos Grant. I thought we should at least know each other's name since there aren't many women who do this—at least I haven't met them."

"Nellie Rafferty. Um, hold on. I know I have a card in here…" She scanned the console, tossing aside gum wrappers and old receipts.

"You don't need to find it. I know who you are."

Surprised, Nellie dropped the collection of trash. "Oh, really? And how is it that we haven't met before?" she said seductively. She leaned out the window, invading Jos's personal space. A hint of lavender surrounded her.

Jos didn't move or flinch. "Actually, we've sorta met. You cut me off on I-17 a few months ago when that Volvo go-out team headed to downtown Phoenix."

Nellie attempted to look penitent. "Sorry, I cut off a lot of people to get the shot." It was true. She remembered the morning. She'd waited for a week for the car to leave the proving ground. There was a lot of traffic, and Volvo had surrounded their new model of the xc90 with other cars to keep the carparazzi away. It hadn't worked. She'd been determined and *Car and Driver* magazine had been happy to give her a payday.

"I'm still a rookie. I haven't developed your cutthroat tactics," Jos said with a wink and a smile.

Nellie gasped. "Me?" She threw her chin in the direction of the chopper. "That certainly wasn't a rookie move. That was brilliant. Wish I'd thought of it."

Jos blushed and leaned against the Jeep. She gazed at the twin storage lockers behind the seats. "Wow. You've totally customized this baby. Look at all that room for your gear."

She smiled broadly, showing the dimples on her cheeks. Nellie's gaze strayed from Jos's light blue eyes to the crease between her large breasts. A bead of sweat had trickled from her neck downward past the scoop of the tank top. She suddenly yearned to see its destination. She blinked, realizing she hadn't responded to Jos's statement. "Yeah, they're bulletproof, hammer proof, you name it. My stuff fits and I still get great power. But it's not as fast as a helicopter," she added.

"He's a friend." Jos nodded over her shoulder at the pilot, who was tapping his wrist. She held up her index finger and turned back to Nellie. "I know we're competitors, but I'd really like to talk to you sometime since we're both based in Arizona. Are you on social media?" Before Nellie could answer, Jos's cell phone rang. "Hold on a sec," she said, pulling the phone from her pocket. "What is it, honey?"

Nellie leaned forward. She wanted to know who Jos was calling "honey." Boyfriend? Girlfriend?

Jos listened for another ten seconds and said, "No, you tell Grandma that cookies are not lunch, even if they have oatmeal in them."

Her child. She glanced at Nellie and mouthed, "Sorry." Nellie shrugged, as if this happened all the time.

"Bridget, I don't have time to argue. I've got a helicopter waiting for me. Cookies are not for lunch, not even if they're stuffed with broccoli, blueberries and all the other super foods. Even if you've done an ingredient analysis. Are we clear?"

Nellie couldn't help but chuckle as Jos signed off. "Ingredient analysis?"

Jos shook her head. "I'm sorry. My daughter has learned persuasive arguments need evidence."

"How old is she?" Nellie asked, impressed.

"Nine." Jos glanced at the helicopter and folded her hands as if begging. The pilot waved her off and she turned back to Nellie. "We were talking about social media."

"Uh, yeah. I don't do a lot with it."

"Well, maybe we could work an exchange. I'll show you how to make social media your friend and moneymaker, and you can give me some tips on using my camera. I'm still not great with the action shots and choosing the best settings. I'll be lucky if one of these pictures turns out."

"Hmm. That would be a shame. Uh, sure, we could get together." Nellie tried to sound enthusiastic, but learning how to use Facebook wasn't what she wanted to do with a woman like Jos.

"Great," Jos said. "Now that you have my card, feel free to call."

Nellie watched her return to the chopper. The back pockets of her shorts shifted left and right with the gentle sway of her hips. Nice ass. Great legs. As she stepped into the cabin, Nellie got a profile view of her chest. Tank tops were definitely an excellent wardrobe choice.

CHAPTER TWO

Mesa, Arizona

"The two of you have ten seconds to get your butts down here for breakfast!" Jos shouted up the stairs in the general direction of her children. The swift clonk of feet above her indicated Myles and Bridget were finally moving into overdrive.

She shook her head. They were so much like her ex-partner Colleen that it was hard to believe they'd both been adopted. As she finished topping off the cereal bowls, they barreled down the stairs and each took a bowl to the table.

Ten-year-old Myles was the oldest and walked with a limp, a result of neglect during his time in a Vietnamese orphanage. He'd contracted rickets and no one had treated it. Bridget was Cambodian and had been born with a cleft palate. Three surgeries later it was barely noticeable except for the tiny scars around her nose and mouth. At nine she was just starting to pay attention to her appearance and regularly asked Jos about concealer colors.

"What's the plan, Mom?" Myles asked.

It was his usual question. He loved structure and they reviewed the Plan of the Day each morning. He was fine if he knew what to expect, but he came unglued if the schedule deviated, as it often did with Jos's career. She tried to prepare Myles for the possibility that she could get a call any time and have to go to work. Still, it was impossible for a ten year old to expect the unexpected, and it was difficult for him to understand that if she missed the shot, she didn't get paid. Of course, Colleen had never understood, so how could Jos expect that of Myles?

"No, honey, tonight Mama C has you." She reminded him gently and used the term of endearment they had chosen for Colleen.

His gaze fell to the table and he sighed heavily, causing a small wave of milk to spill over the bowl's edge. "I don't want to go to her house."

She didn't need to ask why. Colleen had a new girlfriend, Kelly, whom she'd met at her law firm. Colleen was a senior partner and Kelly was a new associate. Kelly didn't seem to like kids and she didn't bother to hide her feelings. Myles was incredibly perceptive and knew where he stood with her. Colleen thought it was just a phase that would pass, but Jos worried Colleen was rationalizing the problem because she wanted the relationship with Kelly to work. Colleen was a mater, not a dater, and after their relationship had fallen apart eleven months before, she'd quickly gone hunting for the next love of her life. So far there had been three potentials who hadn't worked out.

The breakup had devastated Jos, and she'd pleaded with Colleen to keep the family together. Colleen hated Jos's constant absenteeism and had given her an ultimatum: quit gallivanting around the desert snapping pictures and get a regular job or find a new partner. She'd had an affair with one of their best friends to drive home the point. When Jos suggested they stay together but have an open relationship to quell Colleen's loneliness, Colleen had stared at her, slack-jawed, and told her she just didn't get it.

That was true. She probably didn't. Whereas Colleen was incredibly traditional, Jos was not. It most likely had something to do with her mother, who'd never married Jos's father and viewed raising her only child as an ongoing sociology project. Her avant-garde style of parenting trickled down to her grandchildren. Myles and Bridget already had attended a pro-choice rally, campaigned for their liberal state senator and learned to cook. Whenever Jos left them at her mother's house, she wondered if she'd be getting a call to bail them out of jail.

So it was no surprise to anyone that Jos was the exact opposite of Colleen when it came to dating. She wasn't looking, partly because her heart still carried a sliver of desire for them to reunite, but her brain told her they were done after nine years together, and that her desire was based on a need for parenting help. She hoped when she learned to parent alone, the idea of reviving her relationship with Colleen would finally be extinguished.

The image of Nellie Rafferty sitting in her Jeep came to mind. She was cute, with a pleasant face and warm brown eyes. When she'd put on her sunglasses, Jos's stomach had somersaulted. She'd changed from cute to sexy in two seconds.

Two weeks had passed since her helicopter ride, but she frequently replayed her exchange with Nellie. Her employer, *Auto Monthly*, had appreciated the pictures of the Toyota prototype and the helicopter story, but they'd loved the part where she bested Nellie Rafferty. Jos knew Nellie had been pissed. She got scooped and that didn't happen very often to the infamous Parnelli Rafferty.

Nellie was legendary in the auto spy industry. There were many stories of her risking her life to get the shot. It was rumored she'd paid off a window washing crew and been lowered from the roof of a ten-story building to snap a photo of a mini version of a Renault car sitting on an executive's desk. Another story claimed she'd once donned a nun's habit and gained entry to a convent that sat over an Italian proving ground. And supposedly she'd stolen the keys from another carparazzi's vehicle so he couldn't escape, causing him to receive a beating from several angry engineers. Jos imagined some stories were true and others urban legends. She'd been the only woman for a long time, an enigma who refused to work for one magazine. She had questionable ethics as Jos had personally witnessed, and she sold her photos to the highest bidder.

Jos smiled. Nellie wasn't what she'd expected. She seemed to admire Jos's ingenuity and didn't hesitate to flirt. Jos had liked it. Colleagues at *Auto Monthly* talked of Nellie's lesbianism. Apparently she'd bedded most of the top auto models. While Jos certainly wouldn't want a relationship with someone like Nellie, she appreciated the attention—and she wouldn't mind having a little fun.

"Why are you smiling, Mom?" Myles asked.

She took a sip of coffee and ignored his question. "Here's the plan, big guy. I'm dropping you off at Matt's house where you will commence playtime for approximately three hours."

"Um, you mean hang out," he corrected. "I'm not a baby."

"Of course. Hang out," she agreed. "Your sister and I will join the rest of the Girl Scout troop and go over to the Adopt-A-Highway stretch, where we will skewer garbage for an hour, thus earning a service badge." She looked at Bridget and they exchanged smiles.

"I want to pick up trash," Myles whined. "Why can't I go?"

"You're not a scout," Bridget answered.

Myles ignored her. "Why can't Matt and I go?"

"Honey, I promise that in the future you can come, but this is a service project for your sister's troop. Members only. But when you're seventeen I hope you're still this eager to pick up garbage."

Myles thought for a second and said, "I will be."

Jos looked at him skeptically. "I'm not so sure."

Her cell rang and she stepped away from the table since that was one of their rules: no talking on the phone at the table. It was Colleen.

"You're not canceling on me," Jos whispered, foregoing a hello. She knew how Colleen operated.

"No, well, maybe…"

"Colleen," she hissed as she headed into the kitchen where the kids were less likely to hear. "It's your weekend and the kids are dying to see you."

"We all know that's not true," she retorted. "They hate Kelly."

"They don't hate her. They just don't know her very well, and frankly, she doesn't seem to want to get to know them any better."

"She's just not a kid person," Colleen stated for what seemed to be the hundredth time.

Jos bit her tongue and chose her words carefully. "But you are. You have two kids. We have two kids. That's not changing."

"I know."

Jos could hear the gloom in Colleen's voice. Something was going on between Colleen and Kelly, and up until a few weeks ago, when Colleen would call and beg off taking the kids, Jos would jump in and save the day, offering to swap nights or weekends. Eventually she'd seen the pattern and realized she was enabling Colleen's behavior. She'd learned to be firm and immovable with her, but parenting three children was tiring.

"So, what time do you want me to bring them over?"

"Um…well, we're going to Prescott. You know, trying to get out of the August heat."

Jos shook her head. "Look, I don't have time to do this. I'm working later today so I'll leave the kids at my mom's house and you pick them up from there."

She hung up before Colleen could comment. Colleen and Jos's mother didn't get along. At these moments, when juggling the circus that was her life, she doubted her choices, one of which was keeping Colleen connected to the children. Jos was their legal parent since Arizona had not allowed lesbian couples to adopt when Myles and Bridget came into their lives. They'd talked about Colleen adopting them, but then their relationship fell apart. Still, Colleen had been their other mother for six years. When they split, they agreed to co-parent, but Colleen seemed to be distancing herself from the kids, as if the divorce from Jos was also a divorce from their children.

Once in a while she wondered if leaving the humdrum world of computer programming had been worth it. She hadn't intended to become an auto industry spy. It had just happened one day when she walked out of a fast-food joint and saw a ridiculously painted car. It was covered with huge swatches of black fabric. She took out her cell phone and snapped photos until a middle-aged man came running out of the building, yelling at her to get away from the car. He shook his finger and told her to delete the images, but the manager appeared and got in his face. She left and sent the pictures to a friend who knew about cars. He'd forwarded them to another friend, and eventually they wound up in the hands of *Car and Driver* magazine. When Jos received her first paycheck for the five little photos, she was hooked. For the first year, she moonlighted and kept her job writing computer code for a startup company.

In hindsight she realized that was the beginning of the end for her and Colleen. After a year, she left the day job and declared herself a full-time auto spy when *Auto Monthly* offered her a position as a staff photographer. Three months later came Colleen's ultimatum and cheating confession.

"Mom, make him stop!" Bridget cried.

Jos looked over at the table. Myles was flicking milk at Bridget. "That's enough, Myles. You're done. Now, go get a paper towel and clean it all up."

"But Mom, she started it."

"And I'm ending it."

She sighed, wondering when she'd started sounding like her mother. She glanced at the chalkboard and a phone message written there she hadn't seen.

"Hey, Bridge, who's Brent?" Bridget shrugged and took her bowl to the sink. "Did he say who he was with?"

"Nope. He just wanted me to let you know he'd called. He said he would try again."

"When did he call?"

"Um, yesterday while Gram was here."

"And his name is Brent," she confirmed. It was often like this with the children. She needed to review something at least two or three times to get the whole story.

Bridget tapped her chin with her spoon. "Mr. Brent."

"So, Brent is his last name."

"Uh-huh," she said as she ran upstairs.

Jos went to her phone. She suddenly remembered there was a voice mail she hadn't reviewed from the day before. She pressed speaker and set the phone on the counter while she multitasked, cleaning up from breakfast and wiping down the kitchen.

"Hello, Ms. Grant. My name is Mr. Brent." Jos raised an eyebrow. He'd left a message on her home phone and cell. "If you would be so kind as to call me back at your earliest convenience, I believe I have some information that will change your life."

Jos snorted and rolled her eyes. "Salesmen. Always salesmen."

CHAPTER THREE

Wittman, Arizona

The Girl Scout troop spaced themselves along the stretch of highway near Wittman, Arizona. Jos had adopted this section thirty miles north of Phoenix for a specific reason: it bordered the Toyota Proving Grounds. The shoulder sank about three feet, making it perfectly safe for the girls to pick up trash away from the busy highway. It also made an excellent blind for her to snap pictures of prototypes leaving the Toyota facility.

Three other adults herded the busy Girl Scouts while she adjusted her lens and waited. She promised the other mothers a generous donation to the troop whenever she snapped a moneymaking photo during one of these outings. In return she wasn't expected to provide close supervision. It might be that nothing came of this morning except seven service badges, but once in a while she got lucky. Her last photo had sent the troop to Waterworld for a day.

She glanced up and checked her lighting. It was only eight a.m. so the sun was behind her and they had an hour before the temperature became unbearable.

"Hey, Jos," a voice called.

Nellie Rafferty stood on the other side of the chain-link fence that ran parallel to the road, her camera around her neck. She was dressed in a tight T-shirt and cargo shorts, and her thatch of short brown hair had a messy hipster look. She either used a lot of hair paste or she'd just rolled out of bed. Either way it worked for her, especially since her eyes were once again hidden behind those sexy round aviator sunglasses.

"Rented any more helicopters?" she joked.

Jos laughed but knew it sounded ridiculous. She wasn't good at chatting with women she found attractive.

Jos glanced at the Girl Scouts before she wandered to the fence. "What are you doing here?"

"That's my question for you." She waved a hand behind her. "This is my place."

Jos sized up the area. "You live next to the proving ground?"

"I do." Nellie pointed at the Adopt-A-Highway sign. "And I guess you're Troop 305?"

"I am. We still have to get together and talk about social media and cameras," Jos said.

"That's right," Nellie agreed, but from her tone, Jos doubted she'd ever call.

She felt Nellie's gaze slide up and down her body, as if she was assessing her competition. "You know, I also tried to adopt this part of the highway but I was too late. I guess you beat me to it."

Jos leaned against the fence and said, "I guess so." She threw a glance at the vast parcel of property behind Nellie. She noticed a platform jutting from a strong Juniper tree. "But it looks like you have a pretty good setup."

She turned and pointed. "I do. Years ago my dad built that stand. It's just high up enough where it's covered by the limbs but I can still get a decent shot."

When she turned, Jos noticed a small tattoo at the base of her neck between her shoulder blades. It was a trinity knot from

Celtic culture. It symbolized mind, body and spirit. Jos imagined her lips brushing against it as they traveled up Nellie's neck. She blinked and realized Nellie was staring at her, grinning.

Flustered, she lifted her hand to her brow to shield her eyes. "I'm sorry. I was admiring your trinity knot."

"You know what it is?" Nellie's hand automatically touched it.

"Yeah, my mom's into spirituality. She knows about a variety of religions and cultures."

"That's cool," Nellie said. "My mom was from Ireland. It was part of her heritage. When she died, I had it done in her memory."

"Sounds like her passing was a great loss."

"It was," Nellie said, looking away.

Jos sensed she'd hit a nerve so she changed the subject. "How long have you owned this place?"

"My parents bought it in the seventies when the Toyota people came to town. The company didn't realize there was a patch of thirty acres adjoining their property because somebody at the surveyor's office screwed up the calculations. My dad figured it out before they did. They offered him an obscene amount of money to sell, but of course, he wouldn't take it. Have you heard of my dad, Willie Rafferty?"

"Of course."

"Would you like to meet him?"

"I'd love to meet him," she said, trying to contain her excitement.

Nellie pulled a baby monitor from her belt and held it up. "It's how I keep track of him," she said. "Dad? Dad, can you come around the hill?"

"Ten-four," was the gravelly reply.

Jos had thought it necessary to study the entire history of carparazzi. She'd downloaded hundreds of articles and read back issues of as many magazines as possible to develop a working knowledge of the players in the industry and the types of pictures the magazines preferred.

Willie Rafferty was old school. From the fifties through the eighties he'd snuck into the proving grounds and showrooms of the major manufacturers. From what she'd read, it seemed Willie balanced his desire to get the shot with a sense of ethics, which was why so many auto manufacturers had respected him. He'd worked for a time as an engineer for GM, but he missed spying too much and quit after a year on the job.

An old man wobbled over the hill, followed by a German shepherd. He was waving his hands and yelling, but Jos couldn't make out what he was saying. Nellie ran to him and pointed at the road. Jos guessed this was Willie, and Nellie was telling him about the children on the other side of the fence. She looped her arm through his and brought him over with the shepherd following behind.

He was probably in his nineties. A sun hat protected his balding head, concave jowls and bushy gray eyebrows. He wore a white T-shirt with a picture of a '64 Mustang. His blue walking shorts ballooned around his twig-like legs and were belted above his waist. He seemed quite frail and Jos guessed it was a struggle to keep his clothes from falling off his body. He kept licking his lips, as if peanut butter were stuck to them.

"Jos, this is my father, William Rafferty. Dad, this is Jos."

"Everybody calls me Willie," he said, tipping his hat. "Glad to meet you. Are you here for the meeting?"

Jos looked at Nellie who shook her head slightly. "Um, no, Willie, I'm here with the Girl Scouts. We're picking up trash along this part of the highway." She motioned to the busy nine-year-olds behind her, but his eyes focused on the camera around her neck.

He leaned closer to the fence, a devilish grin on his face. "You takin' pictures of the protos?"

She couldn't hide her surprise. Nellie chuckled and said, "He can spot 'em anywhere." She touched her father's shoulder. "Dad, Jos is also carparazzi. Like me."

"Nah," he said. "Two women shootin'? Really?" He eyed Jos shrewdly. "So, you're the competition?"

Jos couldn't hide her surprise, and she couldn't tell if Willie was pleased or upset until he clapped and said, "Hot damn!" Then she laughed.

"Yeah, Dad, it just ain't like it used to be," Nellie deadpanned. "Thank God."

"Did you enjoy being an auto spy, Willie?" Jos asked excitedly.

He met her gaze and Jos could've sworn the fog behind his eyes cleared. He cracked a grin. "Ms. Jos, I was the best."

Jos looked at Nellie. She was nodding with pride. "He's telling the truth. You can look him up."

"I have," Jos said and Nellie looked pleased.

Willie lifted a finger. "I got stories—"

"And today we're not going to tell them," Nellie said. "It's too hot for you to be out here for very long." She reached over and patted the German shepherd's head. "This is Chevy, my dad's service dog. Okay, let's get out of the sun." She tried to lead him away but he wouldn't budge.

"I've got to stay here," he argued. "Get the shot."

"Dad, there's no shot today. I thought there might be, but neither of us got anything. Right, Jos?"

"Right," Jos said with disappointment.

Willie's gaze bounced between them. "What about the meeting?"

"It's canceled," Nellie said. She whipped out her cell phone and tapped the screen several times. "See? It says so right there."

He read it and his face settled into a troubled look. "Did somebody tell Ralph?"

"Yes, Dad. I called Ralph."

Willie scratched his head and stared out at the road. "Well, we'll go wait for him at the house in case he shows up. And don't forget you're taking me to bingo today."

"I won't, Dad."

He looked at Jos with a grin. "I play bingo at the senior center. Win a lot of games."

"I'll bet you do," Jos said.

He turned to go, remembered his manners and tipped his hat. "Pleasure to meet you, ma'am. C'mon, Chevy."

"You too, Willie," she called as he walked away with the dog at his side. Nellie's gaze stayed with him until he disappeared around the hill. "I take it he has dementia?"

She nodded and held up the phone. "He's been talking about meetings for the past few months. I finally had one of his old friends send me a text saying the meeting was canceled. I just keep showing it to him when he asks."

"Who's Ralph?" she asked.

"I have no idea."

Jos felt a tug on her elbow. When she looked down, Bridget was standing next to her. She said to Nellie, "Guess it's my turn." She smiled at Bridget. "What's up?"

"Mom, Tamicka doesn't believe this is an igneous rock." Bridget held up the stone for Jos to examine.

"Bridge, you're interrupting. I was talking to Ms. Rafferty."

Bridget looked puzzled. "You didn't look like you were talking. You were just looking through the fence at the old man."

Jos felt her cheeks go red. She didn't want to have an argument with Bridget in front of Nellie. "Well, we were. So what do you say to Ms. Rafferty?"

"I'm sorry for not realizing you were talking, Ms. Rafferty. Who was that man?"

"That was my father, Willie."

"His shorts are too big for him."

"Bridget!" Jos proclaimed.

Nellie laughed and said, "You're right. Sometimes when people get older they lose a lot of weight and their clothes don't fit so well."

"That happens to my brother, Myles. He keeps outgrowing his clothes."

"What's your name?"

Bridget lifted her chin and said proudly, "I am Bridget Linnelle Grant."

Nellie squatted to Bridget's eye level. "That's quite a name. Can I see your rock?"

"Sure." Bridget held it up and turned it around.

"Well, you are correct. Can you tell me how you knew that?"

Bridget took another minute to recite the qualities of an igneous rock. Jos watched Nellie, who never took her eyes from Bridget's face, completely engrossed in her story. She couldn't help but compare Nellie's interaction with Bridget to Colleen's interactions. Colleen had no idea what to do with the little girl who loved science and being a girly-girl at the same time. Colleen related much better to Myles, who shopped in the boys department and liked watching sports.

"Is this your ranch?" Bridget asked.

"It is," Nellie replied.

"Do you have any horses?"

"I do. I have two."

"Do you have any kids?"

"Bridget! We don't ask those questions of people we hardly know." Jos's reprimand was halfhearted since she wanted to know the answers as well.

Nellie waved her hand. "It's okay." She looked Bridget in the eye and said, "I don't have any children. I travel a lot so it's easier to stay by myself."

Bridget contemplated this for a moment. Then she said, "So, you don't have a girlfriend or boyfriend?"

"No. Sadly I don't."

"Neither does my mom."

"Okay, that's it," Jos said. She set her hands on Bridget's shoulders, spun her around and gave her a little push back to the group. She watched her reclaim her trash bag and inform Tamicka that it was indeed an igneous rock. The lady at the fence said so.

Jos knew her face was red when she turned back to face Nellie, who was grinning from ear to ear. While she wasn't a raving beauty, she was cute and had a smile that undoubtedly charmed women throughout the world.

"I should apologize for my nosy child. I'm sorry she asked you such personal questions."

Nellie shrugged and leaned against the chain link. Jos was completely aware of her nearness.

"This is how I see it. I don't care if people ask me personal questions. I've heard 'em all. That's how it goes when you're almost fifty. Besides, there was a side benefit to your daughter's lack of tact."

"What was that?"

Nellie didn't answer right away. They stared at each other, their sunglasses hiding the thoughts behind their eyes. For a few moments the chatter of the Girl Scouts and the roar of the cars zooming down the highway were forgotten.

"I'm glad your daughter asked me those questions because I learned something too."

"What?" Jos whispered, leaning as close to Nellie as she could.

"You're available."

CHAPTER FOUR

Beatty, Nevada

The call Nellie had been waiting for came the next day at nine a.m. Her contact had told her weeks ago that Honda was planning a photo shoot for its brand-new, yet-to-be-named SUV. She'd learned the shoot was happening the next day, Monday. So Nellie hit the road for Beatty, Nevada.

Beatty was the gateway to Death Valley, one of the most popular hot weather testing areas in the world, especially among many of the Japanese manufacturers, Toyota being the exception. The Japanese were the most secretive about their new releases, often loading cars into huge trucks, driving them to the locations and then loading them back onto the trucks for return to the manufacturing facility once the test or photo shoot concluded.

Catching a photo of a Honda prototype was never an accident. Nellie would never see one randomly parked outside a fast-food joint or motel. She had to know exactly where the event was occurring. In this case, she'd learned the new SUV would be photographed for its promotional launch off SR 90 past Salt Creek. At the beginning of her career, before people knew who she was, she'd blended in with the other attendees at various events and snapped a few pictures with her tiny Minox camera. Now most of the manufacturers recognized her, and she was forced to hide in the desert shrubs across the road. She didn't mind, although her back did. Still, a stationary target was always preferable to one moving at eighty miles an hour.

Over the years she and Willie had culled together a network of informants in various parts of the world. Her contact in the town of Beatty was Caress, the bartender at the Sourdough Saloon. Caress had heard two of the engineers talking about the shoot, and although they spoke in whispers, her hearing was exceptional.

Caress lived up to her name, and Nellie enjoyed her comfort anytime she visited Beatty. She cracked a smile remembering how good Caress could make her feel, physically and spiritually. No one loved women—all women—the way Caress did. Nellie shifted in the Jeep's bucket seat, already horny and still a few miles away.

Her thoughts drifted to the chance meeting with Jos Grant. For the last year she'd wondered who'd bested her and received the Adopt-A-Highway stretch right outside the Toyota Proving Grounds. Periodically Nellie would stroll out to the highway, hoping to see the adopter and quell her curiosity, but she'd never seen anyone until last weekend. The sign that went up had been somewhat cryptic: Troop 305. A Google search yielded nothing. There was no way to contact the adopters and possibly convince them to transfer the rights to her. Jos had to have known someone who worked at the Department of Transportation, someone who filed her paperwork the minute the stretch became available. Nellie guessed that if Jos showed up in that pink tank top, female and male workers would've fallen all over themselves to make her happy.

Nellie had wanted the Adopt-A-Highway stretch for a cover story. Although the blind Willie built on their acreage had yielded many good pictures over the years, standing on the side of the road inches from a new car would definitely be better. But to linger on the highway for any length of time meant she needed a good reason. Adopting the highway would've given her that reason when Toyota security questioned her, which certainly would've happened the first time a proto turned onto the highway.

She laughed, thinking about Jos and her horde of Girl Scouts. She remembered Jos's blush when her daughter divulged she was single. Her rosy cheeks matched her rich red lips, perfectly kissable and soft. Nellie was a toucher. It was her form of flirting. She'd squeeze a shoulder, play with a lock of hair or boldly invade a woman's personal space if the possibility of a kiss existed. The chain-link fence between them had tempered her urges, a good thing since she wasn't interested in anything serious, especially with a woman who had at least two children, Bridget and a brother named Myles.

Still, there had been a spark between them. It seemed odd to Nellie that they'd never met before, yet in the past few weeks they'd run into each other twice. Perhaps fate was sending a message. Other than the single embarrassing moment caused by her daughter, Nellie had felt at ease with Jos. She pictured the two of them riding her horses, Smokey and Blue, around the ranch, laughing and talking.

She shook her head as an odd thought came to her. "A friendship?" She didn't have any female friends, only lovers and contacts. The few times she'd attempted to be friends with a woman hadn't gone well. She either ruined it by constantly breaking promises because of her job or she seduced the woman and altered the relationship permanently. "Hmm," she thought, thinking of Jos. "Maybe I will call her."

Yet as she made the turn to Beatty, she felt her urge growing. Caress was less than five miles away. Nellie equated driving with sex. Her libido was the ignition, and it never took much to turn her on. Knowing what her partner needed was the same as shifting gears. She had to know when. The hum of the engine was the parts working together. That was the formula for great chemistry in bed. Her mind drifted to Jos's rear end as she'd boarded the helicopter. The gentle sway of her hips suggested she knew how to find the right rhythm. She looked down at the speedometer. She was going ninety. She eased up on the gas and took a long sip of water. She needed to cool down.

She pulled up in front of the Sourdough Saloon. Two vehicles sat in the lot. One of them was Caress's old Cadillac. She'd always said a big woman needed a big car. The inside of the saloon was a fire marshal's nightmare. The walls and ceiling were plastered with dollar bills and car parts from every manufacturer in the world. It was customary for new visitors to leave a calling card in the form of a signed dollar bill, and carmakers routinely donated a part of a new model to be displayed. Grilles, fenders and doors took up every inch of wall and ceiling space. Her gaze settled on the light blue Mustang door, her favorite.

Caress was behind the bar drying glasses, laughing with Jake, an old-timer with an ancient face and an expensive cowboy hat. Most women who weighed three hundred pounds wouldn't wear leather pants and a matching leather vest without a blouse underneath, but Caress was not an average woman. Leather was her regular attire, and her enormous cleavage was often a topic of gossip among bar patrons, gossip that Caress encouraged and fueled. She flirted with everyone, male or female, but they all knew she was a lesbian, one who didn't shy away from giving her lover of the moment a boob grope or a slap on the ass in public. Consequently, Caress's tips had topped four figures regularly— enough to buy a new house.

When she saw Nellie, she stopped her story in mid-sentence and flew around the bar. The crushing hug was followed by a sizzling kiss, which only heightened Nellie's awareness of her physical needs. When Caress cupped her left buttock, she sighed.

"I guess you missed me." Her voice was breathy and smooth.

It was like that with Caress. Her genuine magnetic smile attracted people. Some wanted her sexually and others just wanted a hug. Her spiky maroon hair and a connect-the-dots tattoo of a giraffe on her left breast were often conversation starters. When a female stranger asked about the unusual tattoo, if Caress fancied her, she would hand her an erasable marker. While the woman drew, Caress often made suggestive jokes. If the woman found the game seductive, they usually went home together. Nellie had found it seductive.

"When can you leave?" she whispered.

Caress smiled. "Anytime, honey. I was waiting for you. Jake's on today," she said loudly. The cowboy lifted his glass in salute and downed the rest of his whiskey before returning behind the bar.

"Let's get out of here," she said, once again reeling Nellie in with her smile. "You haven't seen my new place."

Caress's house sat at the base of Bare Mountain, affording her a gorgeous sunset every night. She'd furnished it with lavish antiques and European-styled furniture. While Nellie didn't know much about the Victorian or Baroque periods, the place reminded her of a fancy hotel. Stuffed chairs with low arms and sofas with balloon backs and intricate millwork filled the large house. Most prominent was her art collection. Sculptures, oil paintings and ceramics all celebrated the naked female form. The decor sent a clear message: prudes and conservatives need not enter.

"Come see my newest acquisition."

She led Nellie into a sitting area and made a sweeping gesture toward a painting of three naked women lounging in a river, playfully enjoying each other's company. Caress had displayed the painting in an ornate wooden frame with gold trim. Nellie was familiar with the artist but couldn't remember his name.

"It's Renoir's *The Bathers*," Caress said. "Of course it's a print, but I felt it worthy of a glorious frame."

"I like it," Nellie said.

"I love it," Caress said. She spun in a circle, her arms outstretched. "What do you think of my tribute to womanhood?" Nellie's gaze flitted from the Renoir to a sculpture of a woman's vagina. She struggled for words and Caress's ever-present smile vanished. She set her hands on her hips and faced Nellie.

"I can't believe you're uncomfortable. I'm incredibly disappointed. All women are beautiful, inside and out. There is nothing more gorgeous than the female form. And our beauty doesn't come from a tube, an expensive cosmetic or a plastic surgeon's knife. We've allowed the patriarchal society to create the definition of beauty, which is why we have anorexic skeletons parading down runways wearing tiaras, sporting boob jobs and bleached teeth."

"Hey, I would never disagree with that," Nellie said. "I'm just a little taken aback. Remember, my family was somewhat conservative. All that Irish-Catholic upbringing and Mass every Sunday."

Caress frowned. "I'd forgotten that you weren't given much freedom to celebrate your body."

She slipped behind Nellie and turned her to face the Renoir. "Look at those fresh, young faces. Completely free. Enjoying each other. Look at that woman's upturned breasts."

She continued to curate the painting but Nellie's mind was elsewhere. Caress unzipped her shorts, worked the buttons on her shirt and unhooked her bra. All the while she whispered in Nellie's ear. At some point she'd stopped talking about the painting and started telling Nellie how beautiful she was. By the time she was done, Nellie's clothes barely clung to her. She desperately wanted to shake them off. Desire overwhelmed her and she closed her eyes and moaned. Caress laughed and turned her toward the full-length mirror, opposite *The Bathers*.

"Open your eyes," she commanded.

The naked Renoir women, like voyeurs from another time, watched through the reflection while Caress slowly disrobed her. As her clothes fell away, a sense of freedom overtook her. Caress kissed and nibbled her exposed flesh, opening her mind to the possibilities that awaited.

Caress took her hand and led her through a door to the bedroom. Pastoral images of naked women looked down on them from the ceiling. A large armoire sat across the room and purple drapes with gold sashes framed the patio door that led outside.

The centerpiece was the four-poster bed. Fringed throw pillows were piled against the dark wood headboard. Four handcrafted poles at each corner spiraled toward a purple canopy that matched the drapes. Tied to each pole was a gold silk scarf. Caress grabbed the closest one and wrapped it around her naked torso. At some point while Nellie gaped at the bedroom's splendor, Caress had disrobed.

"I love the feel of silk against my body. Don't you?"

"Uh-huh," Nellie managed. She admired the wave of gold against Caress's lily-white flesh. She looked regal.

"Let's get in bed." Caress dropped the scarf and went to the bedside. Three small steps extended from the frame. She climbed up and lounged against the pillows. The brocaded purple comforter had been turned down, revealing plum-colored sheets. Caress patted the bed and Nellie bounded into the space, her eagerness obvious.

"Oh, you need to slow down, sweet pea," Caress cooed. "I'm gonna take you all night."

Lying side by side, Caress offered soft kisses and traced a line down Nellie's side with a single finger. Nellie pressed against her, the desire for a complete connection overwhelming. Caress's largesse engulfed her. The kisses descended past her jawbone. Caress's fleshy thigh slid between her legs, stroking her already tender need. Adept fingers massaged her nipples. Nellie's body, like a motor revving, waited to explode from the starting line. Teeth nicked her neck. She knew what was coming. Her body undulated. The high-pitched engine squealed as the orgasm ripped through her. Caress bit her neck as she came. Hard, but only once. It was her form of branding.

The afterburn rolled through her. Caress unwrapped herself and the air-conditioning immediately chilled Nellie's skin, wet and sweaty from Caress's love cocoon.

Caress admired her handiwork, a hickey that Nellie imagined would stay with her for days. "That's definitely going to leave a mark."

"You always do," Nellie laughed.

"You love it and you know it."

That part was true. Sex with Caress was like driving full speed through a forest, anticipating the next turn and what lay ahead.

She remained still as Caressed moved around the bed shackling her to the four poles with the scarves. "You're now my love slave," Caress proclaimed.

Nellie gazed at her beautiful smile, but Caress's attention was focused much lower. She was exposed, vulnerable, and she flexed her muscles to test the silk bonds. They were taut. She lay at Caress's mercy. She heard a drawer open and she lifted her head. Caress held a plume. She stroked it against her own face before dancing it across Nellie's breasts and belly.

Nellie fell back against the pillows. She closed her eyes, imagining a long highway. With each flick of the plume, Nellie shifted gears until the gas pedal pressed against the floor and she was one with the Jeep, flying down the road. The plume tickled her inner thighs. She groaned, anticipating where the feather would go next. She lifted her torso, begging to be satisfied. The Jeep's red speedometer needle hugged one-twenty. The chassis shimmied, or was that her?

"Please!" she begged.

Caress complied and Nellie moaned, struggling against the taut silk. She thrashed about to free herself but the scarves held her in place. Again and again Caress dipped the plume between her legs, pleasuring her until she couldn't take it anymore.

"Stop, stop," Nellie cried. Tears streamed down her face, her body quaked and she was drenched in sweat. She collapsed on the pillows and closed her eyes.

She knew what came next, the reason Caress was named Caress. Each limb was unfastened from its silk bond. Nellie smelled the vanilla body oil before she felt it on her skin. Caress started with the tips of the fingers on her left hand, working her way toward Nellie's shoulder, kneading, stroking—caressing. All the while she sang, "The Nearness of You" in a chocolaty voice. She moved from one limb to the next until Nellie's arms and legs seemed languidly detached from her torso. She was drenched in oil and Caress's song had ended.

"Enjoying this?" Caress asked in a voice with a tender lilt.

"Uh-huh," Nellie managed. "Keep going."

Caress drizzled oil over her belly and breasts. When she was completely greased, Caress moved on top of her. She held her enormous frame up with her forearms and Nellie slid her right leg between Caress's thighs. Caress dipped her head and caught Nellie's right nipple between her teeth. She licked it to attention and then moved to the left. All the while, she rode Nellie's leg, her orgasm growing, eventually driving her to distraction. She threw her head back and Nellie watched her face carefully. As with driving, it was all about control. When she moaned, Nellie flexed her leg and pushed her over the edge. After the waves of pleasure had subsided, Caress fell next to her and wrapped her in a strong hug.

As Nellie dozed off, right before she crossed over from daydream to sleep, she saw the Jeep coasting down 89A toward Jerome, Arizona, through the trees. The leaves were changing to a rich orange and gold, announcing Nellie's favorite time of year. She glanced at the passenger's seat and realized she wasn't alone. Next to her was Jos Grant.

CHAPTER FIVE

Nellie awoke before the sunrise and crept to the bathroom. She checked the hickey on her neck. The purple and red circle was too high to cover with the collar of a shirt. She'd have to apply makeup, because she certainly didn't want to explain it.

She dressed hurriedly and offered a fleeting glance at Caress before leaving. She was sleeping, a smile on her face. Nellie knew she loved Caress in a special way, but neither of them wanted a relationship. It was perfect how it was.

She headed west toward Death Valley, one of the most popular hot weather testing sites in the world. It was a place of extremes, where temperatures averaged one hundred fifteen degrees. The aptly named Furnace Creek held the record for the hottest day ever—one hundred thirty-four degrees in 1913. Death Valley was also the lowest and driest location in the Western hemisphere, dipping two hundred and eighty-two feet below sea level.

It was one of the most underrated national parks in America, but Nellie enjoyed its amazing topography and eclectic sites.

Over the years she and Willie had traveled throughout the park. They'd taken Badwater Road to the Devil's Golf Course, a large salt pan that extended for forty miles. Weather had sculpted the salt formations into a rough, uneven surface that "only the devil could play golf on." Of course, they'd visited the Racetrack, a dry lakebed containing ancient boulders moving in random, erratic patterns. One of Nellie's favorite memories from her teenage years was seeing for the first time the eerie pathways formed in the geometric mud bubbles of the playa by these large, mysteriously wandering rocks.

Armed with a sun hat and several bottles of water and covered in sunscreen, she hoped to set up before the Honda entourage arrived with the vehicle. Her plan was simple. She intended to hide across the road with her camera and its powerful zoom lens. Sometimes the manufacturers would put up screens to hide the car, but because this location was on a highway, such screens were illegal and would create a hazard. When the large moving van that carried the SUV arrived, the driver would open the back and the SUV would slowly descend an extended ramp. It would be the only time when a group of people didn't surround it. For a few seconds, while the car was suspended above the Honda employees, it would be a sitting duck.

She slowed as she approached the photo site, a level patch of dirt and sand with several cacti in a semicircle. Other manufacturers had used the same background for their desert shoots. She U-turned and went back four-tenths of a mile to a dusty path she'd found years ago. As far as she knew, she was the only spy who'd discovered this cutoff.

Like many places in the desert, tumbleweeds and wild vegetation disguised the mouth of the path. With one eye on the road, she grabbed her tattered journal from the passenger seat. This was her version of a bible. It had belonged to her father and he had passed it to her. So far she'd only studied the parts she needed, but she knew she should read the whole thing with Willie's help before he didn't remember his life at all.

She'd added a few dozen pages, and now it contained every secret, every informant's contact numbers and every trick she and Willie knew, such as this path's location. Over the years Willie had been offered outrageous amounts of money for the journal, and at least one carparazzi competitor had attempted to steal it from him. Nellie always kept it locked in one of the footlockers, except during a job. When she was out in the middle of nowhere, she had a more accessible hiding place.

She leafed through the section on California and found the directions. She was looking for two side-by-side saguaros. She saw them on the left and quickly turned between them.

She chugged along for two-tenths of a mile. A cloud of dust surrounded the Jeep and she struggled to see beyond the nose. She came to a clearing and turned around. This was where she'd leave the Jeep. No one would see it from the road, and it wasn't too far from her hiding spot, making a walk in the summer heat bearable. A critical part of auto spying in the desert was finding a good hiding place for the spy's vehicle. Engineers and security noticed the cars around them.

She glanced at her watch. It was still twenty or thirty minutes before anyone from the PR team was scheduled to arrived. She checked her phone. Cell coverage was incredibly spotty in Death Valley, but she saw that she had a message from Gary, a friend at *Speed* magazine.

"Hey, Nellie. Have you heard about Argent? I'm guessing you have, but if not, we'd pay big for a shot of whatever they've got going that's motivating this move to Phoenix. Just wanted—" She suddenly lost the connection. It was like that in Death Valley.

She didn't have a good relationship with Argent. In the last ten years they'd released three new models. Nellie had scooped their PR department each time, splashing a spy photo of each vehicle on the cover of different trade magazines. At their home base in France she'd heard that engineers walked around with her picture on their clipboard or tablet.

"They'd probably shoot me on sight," she muttered.

Gary's offer was tempting but it would be risky. She imagined that several of her competitors would arrive in Phoenix soon to scope out Argent. And there was Jos, the woman who'd scooped her. She smiled every time she thought of the helicopter. It was genius.

She could say no to Gary. That was the joy of freelancing. She'd tried working for someone else and found it wasn't for her. She wanted to set her own hours and didn't want to fly thousands of miles because a boss told her she must get a shot of a particular vehicle. There were actually cars she had no interest in following, like the Yugo of the eighties. It was that way with women as well. Some of her relationships had been more serious than others but none had been permanent.

She checked her watch. It was time to go. She reread the journal entry before returning the book to its hiding place. She grabbed her camera and a small backpack and headed across the road.

From her vantage point she had a perfect view of the area. The desert floor was low and no tall cacti or bushes grew near the road. Her sciatic nerve burned, a side effect of the problem with her lower back. She hoped they started soon, or she'd be sitting on an ice pack during the drive home. She watched a few cars whizz by but the highway was mostly empty. It was summer in Death Valley, not a great time to vacation.

A few minutes later a large orange semi rumbled around the bend, the words Special Automotive Transport on the side. It rolled past the shoot site and parked on the shoulder. A white sedan pulled up behind it and two men got out. They retrieved their equipment from the trunk and started to set up. The photographers. She knew at least two or three other vehicles would arrive, effectively blocking the site from anyone who wanted to see the car. That was why it was so critical to get the shot while the car was still on the truck.

The truck's driver and passenger emerged from the cab and greeted the photographers. Ten minutes later two other cars arrived and three men and a woman joined the group. The engineers. Now everyone was waiting for the most important people, the model or models and a vice president-type who was in charge of the shoot.

Another fifteen minutes passed. Nellie's water was half gone and the sun was creeping higher. "They need to get started.

They're going to lose the light," she murmured. "And I'm not going to be able to stand up."

She looked through the lens at the dismayed photographers who continually looked to the sky. They were worried as well. Finally a limo pulled up. A man in a gray suit offered a hand to a woman wearing a short black cocktail dress. They could finally start. The truck driver pulled out the ramp and raised the truck's back door.

"Here we go," Nellie whispered.

Jos watched Nellie jog across the highway to wherever she planned to hide to get the shot of the Honda SUV. When she was out of sight, Jos opened the Jeep's passenger door and scrounged through the debris on the seat. Where is it? She checked the glove box, which only contained a few maps and a pen. There was nothing but trash on the floor and napkins between the seats.

"Maybe she has it with her." But Mr. Brent, her contact, had said it was always in the car. She checked the two large lockers behind the seats. Both were secured with padlocks. She looked about the Jeep and the mess around her. A thought suddenly occurred to her. She opened the glove box again. It was too tidy. It should've been stuffed with junk. It didn't match. She withdrew the maps and pen and felt along the edges. She found a cloth tab and tugged, revealing a false back. Behind it was the journal, an old composition book that had to be as old as her. She opened to the first section, a list of contacts in the auto industry dating back to the 1950s when Willie worked for GM.

She pulled out her tiny camera and held it over the first page. She froze, her conscience breaking through and demanding a few seconds of her time. She liked Nellie. A lot. But she knew if the roles were reversed, Nellie wouldn't hesitate to do this. Nellie did whatever needed to be done to get information, like sleeping with the bartender from the Sourdough Saloon. The image of Nellie and the large woman kissing and groping in the parking lot compelled Jos to start snapping.

* * *

Nellie positioned the camera and pressed the shutter. She'd learned the hard way not to wait for the appearance of the car. She only had a few seconds to capture the shot, and if she waited until she saw the bumper, it was often too late.

She heard brakes squeal just as the car descended the ramp. The truck driver and photographers started shouting, and she guessed she'd been seen, but they were moving away from the prototype and not in her direction. She kept snapping. Down, down, down, came the large SUV. It had beautiful lines and screamed power.

"Get her out of here!" she heard a man shout.

She raised her head. No one was looking in her direction. Their attention was focused on a white Honda Accord, the cause of the squealing brakes. It had stopped on the opposite shoulder across from the truck. As the engineers charged across the highway, the Accord pulled away, and for a split second she saw Jos Grant's distinctive profile.

"Shit!" Nellie hissed.

The Honda team headed back to the truck and continued their preparations while the man in the suit yelled at the engineers. He kept pointing his finger to where the Accord had stopped. Nellie actually felt sorry for him. Once the pictures hit the newsstands, he'd probably lose his job. Either Nellie or Jos was about to steal his glory.

Nellie checked her watch. It was a race. If Jos had managed to capture a few decent shots, she'd be searching for an Internet connection, just as Nellie was doing right now.

She pulled a firewire from her pocket and hooked up the camera to her phone, praying she'd find a signal. While she watched the phone search for a connection, she observed the desert foliage. It seemed a bit surreal and silly that a decrepit forty eight-year-old woman was sitting amongst creosote bushes in the middle of nowhere. While she waited she stretched out her back to alleviate the pain.

No Connection appeared on the screen. "Shit."

She jumped up and jogged back to the Jeep, keeping her head down, hoping the Honda people weren't admiring the desert landscape across the road. She knew what she needed to do. She had to get back to the Sourdough Saloon and Caress's computer. She kept her phone open, her gaze flitting between the long stretch of highway and the small screen. She might catch a pocket of service as she approached Beatty.

She pulled out her binoculars and saw a white dot in the distance. Jos. She wondered who was feeding info to her. Did she have a large network of informants? "This is becoming a habit," Nellie murmured to herself. She wasn't used to competition, and really, Jos wasn't playing as if she were in the same league. Fifteen years ago it would've been Nellie screeching to a stop in front of a prototype for a quick snap. But she'd learned most of those photos turned out blurry. It was much better to be stealthy and calculating.

As Beatty came into view, she automatically decelerated. A stand of trees marked the town line. The white dot disappeared into the trees and Nellie grinned. She knew what was coming.

Sure enough, as she approached the trees she saw the flashing blue and red bubble lights. Herb, the police chief, loved to sit on the side of the road with his speed gun. The white Accord sat in front of his police car.

She pulled up beside Herb, who was lecturing Jos about Beatty's strict enforcement of all laws. "Hi, Herb," she said.

He acknowledged her with a salute, and she grinned at Jos, who didn't look amused.

She continued to the Sourdough. Although it wasn't open, she pounded on the front door, knowing Jake would be there setting up the bar. He glanced out the window and she held up her camera before he let her in. She offered a "Hey, Jake," and barreled toward the office and Caress's computer.

Five minutes later when the pictures were uploaded and sent, she exhaled. She'd been holding her breath. Her heart was pounding and she needed an ice pack desperately. Fortunately, Caress kept some in the kitchen freezer for her.

I'm getting too old for this shit, she thought. She found Jos's number and sent her a text with one word: Done.

She scrolled through her messages. There were three missed calls from Mai, the Navajo woman who lived with Nellie and Willie. She was studying nursing at Arizona State with an emphasis on geriatric care. Nellie knew she'd lucked out when she found Mai, who cared for Willie on a daily basis.

"Nellie, call me as soon as you can," Mai said in the first message. "Your father is very angry that you went to the photo shoot and didn't take him. He's asking that I call so you can explain yourself. He says you knew he was supposed to go with you. It was in the contract. Please call back."

She slumped in the oversized office chair. Leaving the phone message was a deescalating technique Mai used with Willie. For the past six months, he'd grown uneasy and nearly inconsolable every time Nellie left for a job. He'd convinced himself he was supposed to go with her because they were a team. When he discovered she was gone, Mai would call and say the same message. It seemed to work and Willie calmed down once the call was placed. Of course by the time Nellie arrived home from her travels, Willie had completely forgotten he'd ever been agitated.

She checked the other two messages, which were basically the same. It worried her that Mai had to call three times.

A text popped up and she grinned.

You beat me this time. Herb's serious about his speeding, isn't he? See you next time. And I'm still waiting for my invitation.

CHAPTER SIX

Mesa, Arizona

Jos insisted on driving Myles and Bridget to school the next day. She hated being away and always missed them terribly. Part of her contract with *Auto Monthly* stated that any out-of-town shoots were optional and she had the right to refuse. Since Phoenix was already home to two proving grounds, and Argent was opening a third, she was in a position to negotiate.

Her personal rule was five hundred miles. She would never be more than five hundred miles away from the kids. She would travel to neighboring California and Nevada, but at this point in her life, she'd never fly across the Atlantic to Cologne or up to the tar sands of Alberta. Nellie Rafferty could have those assignments.

Sitting in the parent drop-off line, a form of slow torture, she thought about the journal. Her conscience was in knots. She'd missed the shot and that meant she'd left Myles and Bridget for nothing, but a part of her was glad Nellie had bested her. It made it okay that she copied her journal. No, it wasn't okay. It just was. Business. That's what it was. Auto spying was all about getting the upper hand. She had two kids to feed and she'd use whatever tactics were necessary to get the shot.

"Mom, what's a threesome?" Myles asked from the backseat.

She nearly tapped the car in front of her before she slammed on the brakes. Both kids jolted forward and laughed.

"What? Where did you hear that word?" She looked through the mirror at Myles, who continued thumbing through one of her auto magazines.

"Kelly," he said absently. "She was talking about it on the phone."

"Does it mean having three pets?" Bridget offered. "They have a dog and a cat. If they rescued another dog, there would be three animals."

Jos inhaled and nodded. "Yes, that's it exactly, hon."

The answer seemed to satisfy Myles who made no comment. Jos made a mental note to discuss the conversation with Colleen. Kelly clearly didn't understand the "kids have big ears" concept.

Once the children were safely at school and she was out of the wretched drop-off line, she headed back up U.S. 60. She wanted to see if there was anything happening at the new Argent Proving Grounds. Argent was the second most successful French company after Renault, but the industry gossip suggested Argent was about to make a move. She rationalized she needed to see it, rather than going home and perusing the printouts of Nellie's journal pages.

"If you don't feel guilty, why are you avoiding it?" she asked the empty van.

Mr. Brent, the stranger who'd left a voice mail on her phone and the man she'd dismissed as a salesman, hadn't given up easily. And he'd actually had information that changed her life. He'd described the journal and what it contained. Somehow he'd learned that during a job, Nellie tended to keep it hidden in the glove box. He made it clear he had no interest in acquiring it, but since he was a fan of Jos's work, he thought she might want to obtain a copy to level the playing field. Those had been his exact words.

When she mentioned it to her editor at *Auto Monthly*, Andy waved his hands and plugged his ears before he said, "You are not fucking telling me this. We would never stoop so low." Then he removed his fingers from his ears and whispered, "But if you were to get your hands on it, I imagine you'd improve your status in the industry significantly. Many spies tried and failed to take it from Willie."

That was his diplomatic way of suggesting that she steal the information. "No, I didn't steal it," she muttered as she turned onto the 60. "Nellie still has it. I just have access to it now. That's all. I'll read it later."

The Argent Proving Grounds were forty miles east of Phoenix. To get there, Jos motored through Mesa, the largest community in the east valley. Miles and miles of identical tiled roofs lined the highway and disappeared at the Apache Junction border. Every winter AJ was inhabited by thousands of snowbirds who filled a multitude of RV parks. Since it was August, the traffic was light.

Seven miles later she saw the high walls built to keep carparazzi out. For the last decade passing motorists surely had wondered what was there. Now the Argent logo was everywhere, and a ten-foot sign with the company name sat next to the road. Jos had seen the press conference where the incredibly good-looking CEO, Jacques Perreault, unveiled the enormous sign and officially announced the opening of the Argent Proving Grounds.

High above the buildings sat a saucer-shaped structure. She'd heard this was the dining room. It slowly turned, allowing guests to have a three hundred and sixty degree view of the facility. With typical French flair, Perreault wanted an impressive location for schmoozing his board of directors and potential clients. Thus, the C'est La Vie restaurant was born.

She drove half a mile past the main entrance and noticed a dirt road on her right. This was undoubtedly the employee entrance. She turned and followed the curve around the structure. She could see a gate and a guard shack in the distance. She stopped and pulled her binoculars from the passenger seat. Indeed, there was a person in the shack.

"Uh-huh," she said.

She headed back to the highway and pulled onto the shoulder as if she were a distressed motorist. It was a perfect scouting location since she could see both entrances. She seriously doubted Argent was ready to transport any test vehicles to Mesa so soon, but sometimes car manufacturers did the unthinkable.

After twenty minutes her minivan was an oven. She flipped on the ignition to run the air conditioner and grabbed a bottle of water from the cooler. She held it against the back of her neck and pictured Nellie Rafferty's colorful trinity knot.

"I wonder if that's her only tattoo," she whispered. "Maybe there are more."

Her thoughts grew lascivious. She imagined a heart above Nellie's left breast and a butterfly just below her waistline. Jos would hook a finger underneath her boxers, for she was certain she wore boxers, and tug, revealing the land between Nellie's legs.

She sat up and took a deep breath. Her heart was racing. Despite the AC blowing full blast, she was smoldering. She stuck her face in front of the vents and closed her eyes. Once her body temperature had stabilized, she leaned back in her seat. Why was she thinking of Nellie? Granted, she had rock star status in the carparazzi world, so did that make Jos the equivalent of a backstage groupie?

She was sexually frustrated. That much was true. It had been a long dry spell since Colleen left. Her mother and others had tried to set her up on dates, but she'd refused, claiming she was too busy. Was she too busy for Nellie?

"I don't think so," she whispered.

She thought of Nellie squatting down at the fence, listening to Bridget with respect. She was obviously great with kids. She was cute and funny. "Why haven't you called me?" she mused.

Someone tapped on the window and she jumped. A security guard motioned for her to roll it down.

"I'm so sorry, sir," she blabbered. "I was very tired and I just pulled over. On my way back from Globe. I've been visiting my aunt."

"Have you?" he asked cynically.

"Why, yes. And who are you?" She offered a hard stare. He wore an Argent patch on his sleeve and the word SECURITY was embroidered on the front of his polo shirt. "You're not a police officer," she added haughtily.

He held up his clipboard. Attached to the large silver clip was a picture of Nellie and Jos's staff photo from *Auto Monthly*. "You wanna stick with that story?"

Jos faced forward and threw the car into drive. "I was just leaving."

She drove for several miles before the shock of the encounter diminished. She'd heard stories about spies having their cameras taken by burly security personnel. Some spies had been chased, and one had his nose broken when a guard callously pushed his camera into his face while he was shooting a picture.

She'd made a habit to stay far away from those encounters, but she paid a price for her timidity. Andy had urged her to take more chances and put herself out there. "If you want the money shot, Jos," he said, "then you have to earn it."

Something suddenly occurred to her. She dialed Andy's cell and was preparing her voice mail message when he answered. "Oh, hi. You actually answered."

"What's up? I've got thirty seconds before my godforsaken fucking team-building exercise starts. Do you know what those are, Grant?"

She stifled a laugh. She couldn't picture Andy, a man who wore shirts from the 70s and food-stained ties, tossing beanbags or passing an apple under his chin. "Uh, yeah. We did them when I was in computers."

"Yeah, well I don't do them, Grant. Fucking ridiculous having adults play kiddie games. We've got a fucking magazine to run here!" He sighed heavily. "Sorry. Just then I wasn't using my fucking sensitivity training. I apologize. This call is about you, not me. Please continue."

"I was just out at Argent, sitting on the sixty. You're not going to believe this, but a security guy confronted me. He had a picture of Nellie Rafferty, but he also had my picture on his clipboard. How weird is that?"

"I'm not surprised," Andy replied. "Grant, you're making a name for yourself and Argent knows you live in the East Valley. That helicopter story made the rounds, and your pictures gave us the number one spot this month. People are gonna be gunning for you, not the least of whom will be Nellie Rafferty. You need to remember that. Okay?"

When Andy said okay, Jos knew he wanted to end the conversation. She had more to discuss. What did it mean that she was making a name for herself? How would people gun for her?

She rolled all of her thoughts together and simply said, "Okay."

"No, not okay," he said. "Grant, you need to go home and think about what leverage you have moving forward. Capisce?"

"Yeah," she said. He was acknowledging the journal and encouraging her to use it.

"What?" He was almost shouting. This was Andy's version of a pep talk.

"I got it!"

"Fucking right," he said and disconnected.

She headed home, determined to read the pages of Nellie's journal. It might not be the moral thing to do, but it was good business. Yes, it definitely was.

CHAPTER SEVEN

Wittman, Arizona

Two proving grounds existed in Wittman, Arizona, the Toyota Proving Grounds and the Arizona Proving Grounds, home of Ford and Volvo. They sat on opposing sides of Patton Road about ten miles apart. In between was a county island, a large swath of unincorporated land surrounded by the cities of Phoenix and Surprise. Since it was unincorporated no fire trucks came to put out fires, inhabitants hired their own private water companies and the Maricopa County Sheriff's Department was responsible for law and order—except budget cuts meant there was very little of either. The people who chose to move to Patton Road lived off the grid, knowing they were on their own and that help would be slow to come if they ever had an emergency.

When the Arizona Proving Grounds were built in the 80s, Willie Rafferty thought it a good idea to befriend the citizens of the county island. Since Patton Road was the primary artery to Interstate 17, Volvo, Ford and later Toyota drivers passed the private properties as they headed out for their test runs.

Several of the citizens became Willie's informants, and Nellie continued the Rafferty relationship with them, often bringing staples like toilet paper, aspirin or peanut butter in exchange for information or a roadside seat as the prototypes zoomed toward the highway. Nellie's favorite Patton Road landowner was Justin Juniper.

She doubted that was his real name since his five acres were covered in juniper trees and that seemed a far more logical basis for his moniker. A fellow Vietnam veteran, his best friend, Julio, had died in his arms. Julio's last words were, "Don't forget Christmas." Consequently, Justin honored Julio's wishes by covering the cacti, tumbleweeds, plants and juniper trees in garlands and other holiday decorations. Every day was Christmas at Justin's house. Over the years people brought him their discarded lights and blowup yard figures, which he added to the ever-increasing display. Patton Road drivers marveled at the sight and often slowed to five or ten miles an hour to sightsee. During the designated holiday season, traffic was bumper to bumper. It was quite a spectacle, but a bit unnerving to see the baby Jesus cradled by two arms of a giant saguaro.

Justin took his job as carparazzi informant quite seriously. In the 90s he'd acquired sixty-five wooden pallets, and he built a twenty-foot scaffold next to the highway with a toilet at the very top. He'd sit up there for hours, eating peanut butter and drinking cold coffee while he watched the cars from the proving grounds come and go. Depending on his needs, the toilet seat cover was up or down.

Nellie found him perched on the scaffold bright and early, his binoculars pointed toward the west. He wore a wide-brimmed sun hat, cargo shorts and a Hawaiian shirt with sunglasses around his neck. Next to him was a large bottle of suntan lotion. Nellie sensed he'd just lathered up, as she could smell the coconut oil from her vantage point on the ground.

"Hey Justin," she called.

He pulled the binoculars from his face and cast a glance downward. He smiled. "Hello, Nellie."

"Just wanted to check in. I'm hearing Volvo's new v60 might've arrived for hot weather testing. Can you confirm or deny?"

Justin frowned. Nellie had noticed in the past two years his memory was starting to fade, so she'd bought him a journal, which he took pride in using. As he flipped through the leather-bound book, his index finger scanned the many entries. She'd come to realize that he noted everything he saw or heard, not just auto sightings. Interspersed with the comings and goings of the proving grounds were notations of visits by the sheriff's department, recently blooming flowers, birds nesting in cacti and road kill. If it happened on Patton Road, most likely it was captured in Justin's log.

"Ah, yes. Source is good. Two days ago what appeared to be the v60 passed at oh ten hundred."

"When did it return?"

He scanned more entries and flipped a few pages before he shook his head. "Didn't see it. Either it went through the back gate or I was otherwise engaged. Family brought me a giant Santa that day." He pointed east, and Nellie gazed at a giant deflated Santa that appeared to be hugging a cactus.

"Looks good," she said. "Did you see the Volvo yesterday?"

He checked the last entries. "Nope. Sorry I'm not more help," he added.

"No, you've been very helpful, Justin. You've confirmed the car's being tested. And with our first August monsoon last night, I'm guessing the driver crossed the Hassayampa Wash and went through the back gate before the flooding happened. Anything else for me?"

He tapped the journal. "Someone else has been out here, Nell, talking to the islanders."

The hairs on her neck stood up. She and Willie were the only people who had ever bothered to meet the county island inhabitants. Most of the carparazzi wouldn't know to talk to them. Their land was too scary and carparazzi made them naturally suspicious. Then she remembered the helicopter.

"Would this be another woman by chance?"

He nodded, surprised. "Yes. How did you know?"

She tried to control her anger. She didn't want to upset Justin. *How in the hell does she know about the islanders?* She cleared her throat and said calmly, "Because she's local. Her name is Jos Grant."

He snapped his fingers. "Yup, that's her. She brought me a sleigh with reindeer!"

He pointed behind Nellie but she didn't bother to look. She just smiled, biting her tongue. It wouldn't do her any good to tell Justin to stay away from Jos. She'd just have to share.

She checked her watch. It was only nine fifteen. Since there'd been a violent monsoon the night before, the Hassayampa was impassable. The drivers couldn't go out the proving ground's back gate, so she guessed the Volvo might make an appearance. If they were testing today, they would need to use Patton Road.

"Do you mind if I camp out by the road, Justin? Maybe the Volvo will show up this morning."

"Go right ahead," he said. "The more the merrier."

She blinked, confused. "What do you mean?"

"Ah, well, after Jos gave me the sleigh she asked the same question. You might see her out there."

"Great."

Nellie parked the Jeep at the westernmost point of Justin's property. He owned a long strip of five acres shaped like a thin rectangle. No one in his right mind would ever purchase such an odd-shaped property to make a home, but Justin wasn't in his right mind. All he wanted was to display his passion for Christmas for the passing motorists and honor his promise to Julio.

She grabbed her binoculars and checked the ribbon of highway to the west. No signs of the Volvo. When she looked toward the east, she didn't see another vehicle.

"Maybe she's not coming."

She opened a footlocker and took out her tripod and camera. As she finished setting up, she heard the crunch of gravel nearby. She groaned. A silver van pulled up behind her about fifteen feet away. The back window rolled down and she saw Jos's silhouette rummaging around as she set up her own tripod and lens.

When Jos squatted down next to her tripod, she saw Nellie leaning out over the Jeep's hood staring at her. Nellie was trying to send a message. She hoped she looked intimidating. When Jos flashed a smile and waved, she knew she hadn't succeeded. She found herself smiling back.

What the hell?

She turned away from Jos, completely flustered. The woman was invading her world and she was smiling at her, inviting her to the chase. It was as if she wanted the competition, which she didn't. Of course, other members of the carparazzi frequented Arizona, but Nellie had home turf advantage. She knew the terrain, the locals and the sun. She'd learned from Willie the sun could be your best friend or a menacing enemy. Using the right aperture was critical, which was why her Arizona photos were the ones most often picked by the trade magazines. And now here was the competition showing up and practically sitting in her lap.

Suddenly the image of Jos crawling into her lap filled her mind. She wondered how her lips would taste. What sort of tongue action would ensue? She blinked. "Get a grip, Rafferty. You're losing your edge." She frowned. "Then why am I smiling at her? I should've flipped her off."

"Flipped who off?" a voice said mildly.

Nellie jumped. Jos stood on the highway next to the Jeep, holding two plastic bottles of orange juice. "You scared me," Nellie spat, struggling to hang on to her anger. She wanted to stay pissed, but the sight of Jos in tiny nylon running shorts and a top that looked like a sports bra conjured a completely different emotion.

Jos's smile vanished. "I'm sorry I scared you. I just thought you might like something to drink," she said. "Orange juice is your favorite, right?"

She held it out and Nellie took it. She really was thirsty. "Um, thanks. How did you know I liked orange juice?"

The smile returned and Jos leaned against the Jeep. In the morning light, Nellie could see toned muscles in her arms and shoulders, like those of a rower. Her hair was piled on her head in a messy bun with a clip holding it all in place.

"I told you last time we met that I've read up on you and your dad extensively."

Nellie snorted. "Don't believe everything you read. Half of it's wrong and another fourth is just flat-out untrue."

Jos looked at her thoughtfully. "That still leaves the last fourth. Is that the slice of truth?"

Nellie chuckled. "I suppose it is. I just haven't seen it reported yet."

"So does that mean you won't do anything to get the shot?"

Nellie tried to focus on her beautiful face, but from her vantage point standing in the Jeep above Jos, her gaze constantly strayed to Jos's abundant cleavage.

"Nellie?"

"Huh? Sorry. What was the question?"

Jos laughed. "I asked if you'd do anything to get the shot?"

She jumped out of the Jeep and joined her on the road. "Well, not anything, but I'm not afraid to go to extremes."

"So does that mean the story of you dressing up as a nun and sneaking into a convent is true?"

Nellie adopted a wry smile. "Guilty."

"What about the time you were rumored to have stolen a sheriff's car? You chased a proto, flashed the lights, and forced it over just so you could take pictures?"

Nellie raised a hand and said, "I had permission to take that car. Nothing was stolen."

They both laughed. Nellie decided she liked Jos's laughing face. It was open and bright. A strand of hair hung along her cheek, and Nellie gently pushed it behind her ear, her fingers grazing Jos's soft skin. They were close enough to kiss but Nellie had no idea if that was the move to make. She could read a woman's desire in her eyes, but Jos's eyes hid behind her Raybans. Jos finished her orange juice and ran her tongue across her lips. The action was so sexual, Nellie couldn't resist.

"You missed a spot," she lied. Her thumb brushed the corner of Jos's mouth and she cupped her chin, guiding their lips together for a first kiss. Their mouths fit perfectly and sent a shiver down Nellie's back. Her tongue explored Jos's mouth until she sighed. Nellie immediately stepped away. "I'm sorry."

Jos shook her head. "I'm just out of practice. It was really nice. Thank you."

"You don't have to thank me." Nellie looked at her sheepishly. "I lied to you. You really didn't have any orange juice on your face."

Jos laughed again. "I know. I'm glad you lied."

A thought occurred to Nellie. "How did you discover Justin?"

Jos's face fell. "I read about him," she said casually, but Nellie noticed she looked away. It also looked like she was blushing. *She looks ashamed. Now who's lying?*

"I don't think you did. I've never mentioned him to the press. Neither has Willie. In fact we're the only carparazzi that have ever talked with the county islanders. Until you. How is that?"

"You must have said it in an interview," she insisted. Looking completely flustered, she glanced west and mumbled, "Good luck with your photos."

Nellie watched her walk back to the van, the nylon shorts clinging to her firm butt cheeks. She wondered what it would be like to slowly peel off those shorts. She imagined Jos sunbathing in the nude next to her, wearing only sunglasses. She'd lean over and kiss her and Jos would make that little sigh again.

A car zoomed by and she jumped. Fortunately, it wasn't the Volvo. "Get a hold of yourself, Rafferty. This woman is the competition. Her van is parked on top of you. How are you going to get the better shot?" And how the hell did she find out about Justin. That was a question for later.

She checked her watch. It was nearly ten. If the Volvo were following the same schedule, it would arrive soon. She jumped back in the Jeep and glanced at the van. Jos had situated herself behind her camera. She was ready. Nellie glanced up at the sky, confirming the aperture setting she'd chosen.

Lighting. That's it.

She grabbed her binoculars and gazed down the highway. The Volvo was nowhere in sight. She still had time. She unlocked the other locker and pulled out a high-powered UV flood lamp. The battery pack still had half its juice. She only needed it for a few seconds. She set it in the passenger's seat, certain Jos was watching her every move. She hunkered down with her tripod and the binoculars.

A few cars continued to speed by, and she thought of Justin sitting on his throne, making his journal entries.

At ten after ten a black vehicle approached from the west. As it came closer, Nellie could see it was in "Full Batman," meaning it was completely covered in Polystrong fabric to hide its true shape. Simple changes usually dictated a "sock" over the hood or a "diaper" over the back. Sometimes bulges were added to disguise the new design, but Full Batman meant many changes.

It was still a hundred yards away. Nellie whipped around and put the floodlight on the hood. She dropped behind the camera's viewfinder and started snapping pictures. Just as the car drew close enough for the money shot, without taking her eye away from the viewfinder, she stretched out her left foot and pressed the floodlight's foot-controlled switch. She smiled as the car raced by, imagining the enormous blur of white that would fill each and every one of Jos's frames. And since the camera was on a tripod, there was no way to pull it off quickly and catch a side shot from another of the van's windows.

She quickly dismantled her own tripod and returned to the front seat. She pulled the floodlight off the hood and turned over the ignition. She wanted out of there in case Jos emerged from the van carrying a baseball bat or worse. She doubted a woman who shared orange juice and kissed her would actually assault her, but she'd faced the wrath of many during her years in the carparazzi.

As she pulled away, she glanced through the van's back window. Jos sat there, dejected. Nellie couldn't see her face clearly, but she pictured Jos's smile and what her face would look like without it. She didn't like what she imagined. Happiness was her energy, her life force. She felt the kiss again. Jos had been tentative, and then when Nellie pressed for more...

And you played a dirty trick on her, Rafferty. You took away her smile.

She smacked the steering wheel and yelled, "Stop it! What's wrong with you?" By the time she turned onto the highway and headed for home, her edge had returned. She remembered that Jos had deceived her. She needed to determine how Jos knew about Justin Juniper. More important, she'd gotten the shot, one that would probably make her a lot of money. It was business. Yes, it was.

CHAPTER EIGHT

Wittman, Arizona

"Dad, do you remember the lady we met a few weeks ago out by the highway?"

Willie looked at her quizzically and shook his head. She knew he didn't remember meeting Jos, but it was a polite question, one she would've asked had he not been suffering from dementia. So she asked it now, determined to maintain a level of civility in their relationship. There wasn't much else left except his stories. And she hoped that when Jos arrived, he'd be coherent enough to tell a few. She knew Jos would appreciate them.

After their kiss on Patton Road, Nellie had investigated Jos and her life in the carparazzi. She'd had a few big scoops, like the day she'd chartered the helicopter and got the Toyota shot, but she was committed to remaining local. Like Nellie's own mother who stayed home with Nellie and her three sisters while Willie traveled the world, Jos remained tethered to Phoenix by her two adopted children. Nellie found Jos's devotion to her kids admirable, especially since it meant more out-of-state paydays for Nellie. Nevertheless, Jos's standing in the auto world increased with each money shot she acquired. Since they were both locals, Nellie decided it was better to keep the competition close. She wasn't sure if that decision was rooted in good business sense or the burning desire to kiss Jos again. She'd thought about their kiss many times over the past week. She found Jos's business card in the Jeep's console and finally invited her over to swap expertise about social media and photography.

Jos had sounded genuinely happy to hear from Nellie. There wasn't a hint of resentment or anger regarding Nellie's trick with the floodlight. When Nellie mentioned it at the end of the conversation, hoping she sounded somewhat remorseful, Jos had said, "Hey, business is business. I get it. No worries."

Nellie deliberately scheduled Jos's visit on a Tuesday morning. Willie would be at his fullest mental capacity and Mai would be available to help. She'd coordinated specifically with Mai's school schedule, but Monday night, Mai announced she'd forgotten about a special lecture she was required to attend Tuesday morning. Nellie would be on her own with Willie.

She'd thought about calling Jos and canceling, but the desire to see her outweighed the possible difficulties that might arise because he was completely unpredictable. Jos would just have to understand whatever embarrassing things he said or did during the visit. She had kids. Of course she'd get it.

Nellie had been especially attentive to his daily routine in the hopes she could prevent an outburst. While mornings were usually good because his mind was sharp, if he struggled to do something mundane, because he was ninety-three he'd become incredibly frustrated with himself and the day would unravel. Nellie really couldn't decide which was worse: when Willie's short-term memory failed him or when he couldn't forget the man he used to be.

She checked her watch. Jos was due any moment and he was still on the toilet with Chevy sitting obediently in the corner of the bathroom.

The doorbell sounded at exactly ten. "Punctual," Nellie murmured. She peeked through the bathroom door at Willie. "Dad, don't get up, okay?"

"Okay," he replied gruffly. She knew he hated it when she helped him with toileting.

She backed out of the hallway, her eyes never leaving him, and rushed through the living room to fling open the door. Jos was bent over, smelling a red rose from a bush that grew next to the house. Nellie was momentarily speechless, her gaze fixed on the curve of Jos's bottom.

"These are beautiful," Jos said.

"Yeah," Nellie managed.

Still bent over, Jos turned her head and grinned. "Everything okay?"

Nellie blinked. "Uh, sure. Please come in."

Jos stepped over the threshold and into the foyer. On her shoulder was her camera bag. She faced Nellie with a shy smile that telegraphed her nervousness. She looked toward the living room and said, "This seems like a very nice home."

"Thanks. My mom picked out most everything. It's old but comfortable."

Jos's gaze found the colorful knitted throws on the tan couch and matching loveseat. "Did your mom make these?"

"She did. She loved knitting."

Nellie pictured her mother sitting on the couch, holding her knitting needles. Jos examined the throw with the eye of someone who knew how to do it. "My grandmother knitted. She tried to teach me but I wasn't very good."

A crash and a bark made them jump.

"Shit," Nelly cried, rushing to the bathroom. She'd been so lost in thoughts of her mother that she'd forgotten about her father. They found Willie sprawled over the lip of the tub, tangled in the shower curtain, the spring-rod lying on top of him. Chevy was whining nearby.

"Dad, are you okay?" Nellie asked as she removed the rod.

"I don't know," he whimpered. "I fell."

"I see that." He'd stood and pulled up his pants, took a step, lost his balance and fallen to his left, the shower curtain absorbing most of the impact. She leaned over him to check for cuts or contusions. Seeing none, she lifted his right hand and rotated his wrist.

"Does this feel okay?"

"Uh-huh. Who's that?" he asked, staring at Jos.

Jos offered a little smile and knelt beside him. "Hi, Mr. Rafferty. I'm Jos. We met out by the highway a few weeks ago."

"Ah, the competition," he said. "I remember you."

"Good job, Dad," Nellie said, smiling at him.

Jos chuckled. "I suppose that's true, but right now I'd like to help you up. Would that be okay?"

"Sure."

Nellie craned her neck to check both sides of his body. "I'm worried about your left shoulder. Jos and I are going to lift you out of the tub and set you on the toilet, okay?"

"Okay."

Nellie and Jos wrapped their arms around his middle and lifted. He was so thin they got him upright on the first try.

Nellie squatted in front of him. "How does your shoulder feel?"

"Fine," he said, looking away.

Nellie knew he was embarrassed. If Jos weren't here, she'd chide him for not following her directions. "Are you good to stand?"

"Yup," he said.

Nellie and Jos helped him up, and after a few steps he hobbled down the hallway to his favorite chair in the living room on his own. Nellie fetched a tray of lemonade for the three of them. Awkwardness and tension filled the room and she wasn't sure what to say. Willie was embarrassed and angry and wouldn't look at them. Jos sat timidly on the couch, her hands in her lap. Nellie didn't know what to do.

"Mr. Rafferty, I noticed some of your pictures in the hallway," Jos began. "You got some amazing shots."

He laughed and the mood changed. "For every shot, there's a story. And please, call me Willie." He stuck out his hand as if they hadn't already met in the bathroom.

"Nice to meet you, Willie. I'm Jos." She rose from the sofa, greeted his handshake and sat next to him. She offered Chevy a head scratch and was rewarded with several tail wags.

Nellie felt the tension drain from her shoulders. Jos was a natural charmer.

She glanced at Nellie before she asked, "So were you the one who named your daughter Parnelli?"

He nodded. "I was. Had three girls and wanted a boy. Thought if I had the name picked out I might get my way." He sipped his lemonade and added, "I met Parnelli Jones at the Indy 500. Damn fine man." He slowly turned to Jos and said, "I didn't get a boy but I got something better."

Nellie grinned at her father. It was his favorite story and the one he always told first. "Tell Jos about the time you snuck into the GM plant in Detroit."

"That was something." He gulped down most of his lemonade and wiped his chin with the back of his hand. "Happened in 'fifty-eight. That was GM's fiftieth anniversary. I'd heard about the special edition cars they were making, including the golden anniversary Cadillac." He whistled for effect and said, "It was a beaut. So I checked out the place. Climbed the fence and walked in with the engineers." He laughed and took another sip of lemonade. "I followed them around for a piece. Then they went one way and I went toward the showroom where the cars were displayed. Right there on the middle turntable was the Caddy, all by itself, no one around. I started snapping pictures with my little camera. Ran into something…can't remember what it was, but it made noise. I looked over my shoulder and two heads popped up from the front seat—two women. And they weren't fully clothed."

"What did you do?" Jos asked.

Willie finished his lemonade. "Can I have some more, honey?" he asked Nellie.

"Not yet, Dad. We'll just have to keep going to the bathroom. Finish your story. You'd seen the girls pop their heads up."

"Uh, yeah. So they were eyeballin' me and I was eyeballin' them. Couldn't tell who was more frightened, but this look passed between us. A look that said, 'I won't tell if you won't.' So I hustled out of there and nobody chased me."

As Jos laughed, Nellie urged, "Tell her what happened when you went to work there six months later."

"I saw one of the ladies again on the first day. She was really pretty with red hair. A knockout I'd never forget. My new boss introduced her to me and her eyes got big as saucers. I just acted dumb, like I'd never seen her before. Worked there for a year and we never spoke of it."

"Why did you leave GM?" Jos asked, smiling at his story.

He offered a sad smile in return and said, "I wanted to take pictures of cars more than I wanted to build them."

He reached with a shaky hand to set the glass down on the end table, and Jos jumped up and grabbed it just as it slipped through his fingers. She set it on a nearby TV tray as Nellie rushed to her side.

"Thanks," she said fervently. She looked at Willie. "I think that's enough stories for now. Lean back and I'll turn on your program. It's almost time for *Password*."

"Okey-dokey."

Nellie reclined him and put a blanket over his legs. Once he was situated and the TV turned to his favorite old-time channel, she motioned for Jos to follow her out to the den. Through the doorway she could still see and hear him, but she could have some privacy with Jos. If anything happened, Chevy would start to bark.

"Thanks again. He just doesn't realize he can't do everything he used to do."

"No worries. With two kids I've developed great reflexes."

They both laughed and the conversation stalled. Jos gravitated toward the framed photos on the walls, pictures of the Rafferty family that went back three generations. Nellie provided a little narrative for some of the photos of her sisters, but mainly she stood by quietly, her hands in her pockets. She felt uneasy and she didn't know why. The women she'd brought to the ranch for sex had never bothered to look at the pictures. Once they were alone it was all about finding a place to have sex. But Jos wasn't like them.

"So, I have to ask," Jos said meekly. "That story Willie told about seeing the two women in the car..." She paused and searched for the question, the one Nellie had been asked by other lesbians or tactless reporters.

"You want to know if my dad was as cool about me being a lesbian as he was when he found those two women together in the Caddy."

She nodded. "It was 1958. I think how he handled it was extraordinary. Was he that way with you?" Her voice faded away at the end of the question, as if she was afraid of Nellie's response.

"Yes," she said plainly. "He was just as cool. He said he'd suspected when I was in high school. I'd look through his auto magazines, and he figured out I wasn't staring at the cars." They both laughed and she went on. "He was completely okay with it, probably because he knew two guys who were lovers. One was an engineer and the other was carparazzi. They both were married to women and they were miserable. When I came out to him, he told me their story and shook his head. He said, 'Parnelli, I don't ever want you to be that unhappy.'" She glanced at Jos who seemed to be absorbing the story.

"What about your mom? She was Irish. Was she Catholic, too?"

"Wow, you've got a good memory." Nellie was impressed and flattered.

Jos shrugged and her face turned red. "I really liked your trinity knot."

"Oh," Nellie said seductively. "Maybe I'll show it to you again."

"I'd like that," Jos said in a voice just above a whisper.

Nellie felt the mood shift. Jos was only a few feet away. She could easily wrap her arm around Jos's waist and scoop her up for a kiss. It was so tempting, but instead she coughed and said, "Yes, my mom was Irish-Catholic. She loved me but we didn't speak of it. She let me live my life and I didn't throw it in her face. That was our compromise."

Jos cocked her head to the side and her gaze slid upward, in thought. "So is that why you've never had a serious relationship?"

She quickly focused her expression when she realized what she'd said. "I mean that's what I've read. I have no idea if that's the truth," she blabbered.

Nellie opened her mouth to make a witty retort and suddenly closed it. She looked away and said nothing. She'd never thought of those two things being related. She didn't have time for relationships. She was always traveling. Of course, there had been a few women she cared for deeply but those liaisons had never gone anywhere. Why was that?

Jos cleared her throat and pointed to her desk. "Is that your laptop?"

Nellie sighed in relief at the change in topic. "Uh, yeah, it's kinda old."

"Kinda?"

Nellie could hear the playful disapproval in her voice. Jos slid into the desk chair and logged on. She started clicking buttons and opening screens Nellie had never seen. "How do you know so much about this stuff?"

"Computer programmer in my last life." She pointed at a graph with different colors. "Okay, so your memory is practically used up. You've got so many pictures on this thing that it can't operate properly. You need to remove whatever you don't need and put it all on an external drive. Social media will require a significant amount of space so we need to move some stuff first."

"Yeah, I just haven't gotten around to doing it." Nellie opened a drawer and pulled out an external drive still in the store packaging.

Jos chuckled. "Well, no time like the present." She started to work and Nellie stared at her legs. The shorts ended above her knee, and Nellie had a great view of her sculpted calves. She wore a crop top with a scooped neck, exposing enough cleavage to make Nellie's imagination swirl. She closed her eyes and envisioned Jos in a low-cut teddy that barely covered her buttocks.

"Stop staring and pull up a chair." Jos hadn't looked at her, but she wore a grin. She knew what she was doing to Nellie and liked it.

Nellie felt her cheeks flush. Caught. She pulled up a chair and scowled. "Okay, Ms. Bossypants."

Two hours later under Jos's supervision, Nellie had moved hundreds of pictures onto her external hard drive and written two pages of notes about how to use social media. Jos had learned more about her camera, specifically how to capture moving images and what aperture to use at certain times of day and night.

"Let's take it outside so you can try," Nellie suggested.

"Sure," Jos said. "Will your dad be okay alone inside?"

They gazed into the living room. Willie was asleep in his chair while the old *Concentration* game show provided background noise. Chevy was next to him, sitting at attention.

"He's out for a while." She grabbed the baby monitor and clipped it to her belt. "The other end is on the TV tray. If he wakes up, I'll hear and see him. And if something happens, Chevy will bark."

Jos stared at the tiny screen. "These things just get more advanced every year. The one for my kids didn't have a screen and it wasn't two-way audio either."

"It's weird how we enter and leave this world pretty much the same way." She started to get choked up and her gaze fell to the floor. She fought to control her emotions. Jos was practically a stranger.

Jos squeezed her arm. "Hey, I'm sorry if I upset you."

"You didn't, really. I know what's coming eventually." She tried to hold back the tears but a giant drop slid down her cheek. Jos caressed her face and wiped it away. "He's just so important to me," Nellie managed to say.

"Of course," Jos said.

Nellie pulled her into an embrace and said, "I'm glad you're here."

Jos returned the hug and Nellie inhaled the sweet, clean smell of lavender soap. For a few seconds, she wished away the pain of her life—her dad's condition, her growing discontent with the spy industry and her loneliness. She let Jos be the antidote for everything.

Jos said, "This feels good."

A sliver of Jos's belly and back peeked out of the crop top. Nellie stroked the soft skin and Jos sighed. She looked into Jos's light blue eyes. They were so unique. Almost opaque. Nellie leaned closer and gave Jos a choice—step away or kiss.

Jos's cell phone chimed and they broke apart. Nellie fiddled with her camera while Jos talked to one of her children. This time it was the boy, Myles. She reassured him that he was staying with her that night, and he finally allowed her to hang up. She looked at Nellie, embarrassed. "I'm sorry. That was my son. He has some issues with planning."

"It's just the two kids, right?" Nellie hoped she sounded inquisitive but not judgmental.

"Yeah, just two. The short version of the story is that I adopted them, thinking I'd be with my partner forever. But we're not together now. We're trying to co-parent, but frankly, that's not going so great."

Nellie leaned against the desk, her hands in her front pockets. She'd stepped over the line with a woman who had two children. "That must be rough."

"It is." She shook her head. "How about we move to light-hearted topics. Can we go outside?"

"Sure."

They went onto the deck and Nellie turned on the misters. Jos wandered over to Nellie's favorite spot and stared toward the west. Nellie said, "That's where we watch the sunsets."

"It's beautiful. I'll bet the lighting's just right." She paused and gave Nellie a serious look. "And I'll bet you never need to use a floodlight."

They both laughed and Nellie said, "Hey, it was business." She started down the steps. "C'mon, I'll give you a tour and then we can take pictures."

"Sounds great."

"Let's start over at the shed. I think you'll like what you see there."

They followed a path to a large, nondescript wooden building, its dark green paint blanched from years of exposure to the sweltering Arizona sun. There were no windows and the shingled roof looked new. Anyone walking the property would dismiss it as a storage facility and nothing more, which accounted for the bored expression on Jos's face as they approached.

Nellie flipped up the cover of a small black box on the front door, revealing a keypad. Suddenly Jos seemed much more interested. "What's in here?" she asked.

"A whole lotta hay for the horses," Nellie joked as she punched in a long code.

They heard a click and the steel door popped open an inch. She gazed into Jos's dancing eyes, focused on the sliver of light eking out and what waited inside.

"Ready to see something cool?" Nellie asked.

She wanted Jos to look at her. Suddenly it became very important that Jos acknowledge her before she opened the door. Nellie needed to feel in control. Jos tore her gaze away from the slight opening and stared at Nellie.

"Show me, please," she whispered.

Nellie swung the door open and Jos slowly walked inside.

CHAPTER NINE

It took several seconds for their eyes to adjust from the harsh sunlight to the prevalent darkness in the shed. Before them were six vintage automobiles, each one bathed in the glow of its own single pendant light, automatically turned on with the opening of the door. The tableau always reminded Nellie of a stage with six spotlights.

"Wow," Jos managed to say.

She drifted to the nearest car on her right, a 1966 cherry-red Ford Mustang. She circled it and turned to the car behind the Mustang, a 1960 light green convertible Thunderbird. She leaned toward the dashboard, her hands clasped as if in prayer. Nellie grinned. Only someone with a true appreciation of cars knew not to touch.

Jos meandered among the other four cars, giving each one the attention it deserved. She proclaimed the 1969 black Dodge Charger amazing. She squealed with delight at the sight of the 1964 Cadillac Eldorado and she gazed at the wide steel grille of the 1949 dark green GMC pickup truck. She sauntered back to its tailgate and peered into the bed. She glanced at Nellie and back at the bed. She knew what Jos was thinking. How many women have lain in the back of this truck? The number was too high to count.

Jos smiled but said nothing. Having circled back to the front of the shed, she turned and faced the last car, Willie's prized possession. Sitting before her was a silver-blue 1963 Corvette Sting Ray convertible. She stood there, frozen, hardly breathing.

"Can I sit in it?" she blurted. Her eyes pleaded with Nellie.

"Of course. But take off your shoes."

Jos flipped off her sneakers and carefully opened the door. She slid into the driver's seat and moaned. She set her hands on the wooden steering wheel at ten and two. Nellie watched her drink in the car—the shiny buttons on the radio, the blue leather console, the dials on the dash and the silver knob gearshift. Jos closed her eyes and leaned back in the seat.

"This is heaven. I have so many questions for you, but right now I just want to enjoy the feel and smell of this leather. It's like a cocoon."

"It is indeed," Nellie agreed. "And it suits you."

Jos blinked. "Really?" She batted her eyelashes. "Do I look good sitting here?"

"Yes," Nellie managed.

She was tingling and her need was overwhelming. She tried to push it down, telling herself yet again that Jos wasn't right for her. Jos was the competition. Still, the sight of her molded inside the Corvette caused a reaction Nellie couldn't control.

"Take my picture," Jos announced. She slid the camera off her arm and handed it to Nellie.

Nellie exhaled, grateful for the distraction. Jos shifted in the seat, one hand draped over the steering wheel and the other hanging over the door. Her megawatt smile nearly melted Nellie.

"Got it," she mumbled.

Jos looked around. It was obvious she was struggling to take it all in. Car enthusiasts were like that, but Nellie had met very few who were women. Often she'd been disappointed when she brought a woman to the shed. They thought the cars were pretty but they didn't ask questions. They accepted the little car museum tour as foreplay before they climbed into the old truck's bed and got naked.

"Do you ever drive these?" Jos asked expectantly.

"Of course," Nellie said. "We're just very careful about when we drive them."

Jos gazed out the Corvette's windshield. Nellie imagined she was picturing herself cruising down a highway, gunning the engine. Nellie kicked off her shoes and climbed into the passenger seat. They stared at each other, admiring how they looked in one of the greatest classic cars of all time.

"My dad bought this for my mom," she said. "Of course, he really had to fix it up. He bought all of these at auction, and they were in really sad shape. Each one was a project and one of us girls helped him. I got to help with the Mustang and the Charger."

"They're spectacular," Jos said.

"My dad believed that the greatest thing in the world was a beautiful woman in a sports car." She paused before she added, "I'm inclined to agree." Their eyes met but Jos didn't respond. Feeling like she needed to fill the silence, Nellie added, "Maybe sometime you can come by when Mai is here and we can go for a ride."

Jos smiled. Her gaze flitted about the dash. "Oh, I'd like that."

She gripped the silver gearshift and Nellie covered Jos's hand with her own. She stroked her fingers, absorbing the quiet of the shed.

"You know, my dad didn't want to invite you over," Nellie said quietly.

Jos looked hurt. "Really? Why?"

Nellie leaned over the console until their faces were inches apart. "He says you're the competition, which, I suppose is true." Jos looked away, unable to meet Nellie's gaze. "But I'm inclined to trust you," Nellie continued. "Can I trust you, Jos Grant?"

Suddenly Jos closed the distance between them and kissed her. This time, Jos's lips tasted like strawberries. One kiss wasn't enough. Their lips met again, eager and hungry. Tongues touched. Heat radiated between them. Jos shifted in the bucket seat and Nellie took full advantage. She slid her hand underneath Jos's shirt and cupped her breast. Jos emitted little sighs of encouragement between the kisses. She wanted more and Nellie shoved her concerns aside. Her hand slid to Jos's back and she unhooked her bra. Jos giggled and playfully pushed her back in her seat. They faced each other. Nellie knew she wore a stupid grin. The past didn't matter. Nothing mattered except her want. Her eyes begged and Jos complied.

She slowly pulled her shirt over her head and slid out of her bra. Half naked, she leaned back in the driver's seat and turned her chin toward the hanging pendant light. She looked like a model. She stroked her large breasts while Nellie snapped photo after photo. Nellie set aside the camera so she could suck on Jos's glorious nipples.

As if reading her mind, Jos shot her a penetrating look and said, "Do something."

"Nellie!"

They both jumped at the booming voice. Nellie fumbled with the baby monitor attached to her waistband. "Sorry, I didn't realize this thing was set on ten."

"Nellie! Where are you?" her father's raspy voice cried.

"Get dressed," Nellie cried. "We've got to go. He'll try to get up on his own."

Jos threw on her clothes as fast as she could and they scurried back to the house. Whatever spell the shed had cast over them was gone.

"Nellie!" he cried again.

"I'm coming, Dad," she said into the monitor. "Don't move."

The frustration in Willie's voice was obvious. She glanced at Jos's worried expression. She suddenly wished she hadn't invited her over. These things were private. She was the competition. *What was I thinking?*

They burst into the living room just as Willie took his first step away from the chair. He wobbled and they caught him before he fell.

"Geez, Dad, you've got to wait for me to help you."

"I called you. You weren't around. I need to go to the bathroom. Damn it, I don't need you." His eyes whirled in confusion. At these moments he looked frail and helpless. "I can go to the bathroom myself."

Nellie closed her eyes, holding back her tears.

"Nellie, do you have a walker?" Jos asked.

"No," Willie snapped. "Costs too much money."

"Dad, that's not it." She looked at Jos and said sheepishly. "It's only been in the last month that he's struggled with walking." Flustered and embarrassed, she just wanted Jos to go.

"Well, we have one from my mom's back surgery. I'd gladly loan it to you."

"No, that's okay," Nellie said automatically. "I'll get it done this week."

"Why not borrow mine until it comes? It's just sitting in a closet."

Willie nodded and shook his finger. "I like the way you think, young lady." He looked at Nellie and said, "This one's a keeper, not like those others you parade through here to see the truck." He toddled off to the bathroom, talking about the '49 GMC truck and mentioning several of Nellie's previous lovers by name.

Jos lowered her gaze to the floor. Nellie could tell she wanted to burst out laughing. Once in a while the old Willie appeared. Still, he didn't really know Jos the way Nellie did. She didn't want to be indebted to Jos. She never should've invited her over. She just wanted her to leave. If he only knew...

"Thanks, but don't worry about it. I'll get it ordered this week," she finally said.

"It's not a big deal—"

"I'll order it. Thank you," she snapped.

Confused and clearly hurt, Jos said, "Uh, sure, but let me know if you change your mind." She glanced at her watch and said, "I should get going." She grabbed her purse and camera bag from the table and headed for the door. Nellie followed behind her but stopped short of crossing the threshold.

Jos hurried down the driveway, already scrolling through her cell phone messages. No doubt she needed to check in with one or both of her children. They had to be like little weights tying her down. When Nellie heard Jos's van pull away, she shut the door and leaned against it before she collapsed to a sitting position on the floor.

The morning had hardly gone as she'd planned. Willie seemed totally infatuated with Jos, even though she was the competition. *I was infatuated with her too.* She never could've predicted her desire for Jos would be so uncontrollable. When they were sitting in the Corvette...If Willie hadn't started screaming, she imagined they would've wound up in the back of the pickup. One thing was certain: they wouldn't have had sex inside the Corvette, no matter what. Nellie wouldn't have lost that much control of her libido.

She put her face in her hands. She'd snapped at Jos who was just trying to be nice. *But she isn't nice.* "No, but I like her," Nellie muttered. "And she's so damn introspective." She thought about Jos's question regarding her mother. Had she deprived herself of lifelong happiness just to keep the peace with her mother? If that was true, then Willie had to have had something to do with it, but she couldn't remember. She'd always done whatever he said. He was always in control of their relationship. He was her hero.

"Put it in perspective, Rafferty. She's just a woman."

Control. She thrived on control. It's what made her a great photographer. Her emotions remained in check and she always knew when to walk away. She was a master at control and subterfuge. She'd gone so far as to create a list of questions that would help her understand where Jos was weak and most vulnerable. She'd planned to engage in subterfuge and trickery during Jos's visit. Then Jos had ruined her plan. Or rather, her libido and Willie's needs had ruined her plan.

"What's the matter, Nell?" Willie said, returning from the bathroom.

The question surprised her. She checked the time. It wasn't quite one o'clock. He still had two hours left before his thoughts fell apart like crumbling clay. Coherence and short-term memory sloughed off his brain by late afternoon, leaving only the deepest of memories. Sundowning was what the doctors called it. She helped him to the chair and dropped onto the couch. She knew she wouldn't have too many more years with him. She intended to make the most of these conversations.

"I'm sad, Dad. Sometimes people just aren't who they seem to be, you know?"

Her father started to laugh before he launched into a story about a time he'd donned a disguise to gain entrance to a private party for the DeLorean. He'd met Michael J. Fox, who was there promoting his new movie *Back to the Future*. Nellie nodded and smiled. She'd heard the story many times, but in each retelling he added a new detail, probably because each day he rebuilt his memory and didn't always include the same pieces. Lately she realized the stories were getting shorter as more details were lost and there was less to assemble.

So she kept smiling and laughing in the right places. By employing the subterfuge she'd meant for Jos, she didn't let him see her worry. But with him her motivation was compassion, whereas with Jos, she had no compassion for someone so treacherous.

Jos had found and read her journal. She knew it. And she'd probably copied it. Nellie didn't want to think about the implications of a second journal, but that wasn't what bothered her the most. She'd shared her personal life with Jos, let her into her home and shown her the shed. She'd given her a chance to come clean. She'd tested Jos and she'd failed. Despite all of Nellie's efforts, Jos hadn't fessed up to what she'd done.

CHAPTER TEN

Mesa, Arizona

Jos's two-hour drive home was ample time to process the highs and lows of the morning. She felt emotionally drained, so much so that before she jumped on the interstate, she pulled into a drive-through Starbucks for a triple-shot espresso. She needed the caffeine jolt to clear her head.

Nellie's one-eighty reversal from flirty interest to ice queen surprised and angered her. Perhaps it had something to do with Willie. Maybe she was upset that he'd interrupted them.

"I know she's not as sexually frustrated as I am," Jos shouted while she waited at a red light. "She's certainly getting some from that bartender in Nevada!" She smacked the steering wheel. The caffeine rush felt good.

She glanced at the car in the next lane. The female driver eyed her nervously and her son in the backseat stared at Jos. The light changed and she waved goodbye, a ridiculous smile on her face. *Maybe a triple espresso is too much.*

Once she merged with the flow of traffic, she took a deep cleansing breath. She was clearly at her sexual tipping point. Nellie had awakened a sleeping Amazon. "I'm going to need to do something about this soon."

She decided she was pissed and hurt. Why had Nellie turned into such a jerk? Had she said something offensive? She didn't think so. Was she not reverent enough when she saw their collection of cars? She thought she was. What the hell happened? If Willie had continued his nap, she was positive Nellie would've finished undressing her, and they would've wandered over to the bed of the '49 pickup. They certainly wouldn't have risked staining the beautiful Corvette's original leather with their natural juices.

"I would've insisted!"

So what happened? She was into Nellie and Nellie was certainly into her. What did she do? For a fleeting moment she thought about the day in Nevada. She'd broken into Nellie's Jeep.

"No, breaking in is too strong a term," she said, pointing a finger. "When your car is just a big open space, can it really be broken into?" she asked the moving traffic around her. "People who have convertibles or…" She couldn't think of a term to describe Nellie's Jeep. "Topless. That's it. A topless car." She wondered what Nellie looked like topless. "Mmm," she grinned. She'd seen the outline of an undershirt beneath her thin white T-shirt. Nellie had small breasts and Jos wondered if she bothered to wear a bra.

She sighed. "Note to self. Never order anything stronger than a double espresso."

Was it possible Nellie knew she'd copied her journal? How? Jos had taken a photo of the glove box before she removed its contents, ensuring that she'd return everything to its exact same spot. No, there was no way.

Besides, much of what she read was of no use to her. The journal began in the late 50s and she guessed most of the people Willie mentioned were dead. Several sections were illegible. She guessed he often wrote while he was driving, sitting at red lights or waiting in traffic. She imagined there were passages neither he nor Nellie could decipher.

There were some recommendations for favorite lookout points to see prototypes that might be useful. And she'd gathered there was drama between GM and Willie around 1960, but she'd stopped reading that section. It took too long to discern his script. Of course, the passages about the county islanders had led her to Justin Juniper, but then Nellie had ruined her chance at the shot by flashing the floodlight. That was most likely karma turning around and slapping Jos in the face for stealing the journal.

"I didn't steal it!" she shouted at her conscience. "Quit saying that."

The pages Nellie had added to the journal were much more useful. In addition to noting great spots for spying, Nellie had listed her various contacts. Many were women, and each one had stars by her name. Nellie's lovers. Since Caress the Bartender had three stars, and Jos had personally witnessed the chemistry between them, it all added up. But what didn't add up was Nellie's behavior that morning. It was as if they'd stepped away from the chase for a while. She liked that. She liked Nellie touching her. Maybe Nellie was trying to play mind games with her in the hopes Jos would let down her guard.

"Fine," she hissed. "You want to try and manipulate me? You don't know who you're dealing with." She glanced in the rearview mirror. Red and blue flashing lights. She looked at the speedometer. Eighty. "Shit."

Jos arrived home and tossed the speeding ticket on the desk with the other one from Nevada. She stood in the middle of her living room, unsure of what to do next. Colleen would be dropping off Myles and Bridget in less than an hour and she'd resume mommy mode, which required all of her attention. It dawned on her that Colleen's absentee parenting, coupled with Jos's own devotion to the children, equated to huge sexual frustration. She didn't have any time to think about sex. She worked and she took care of the kids. End of story.

She picked up the hefty stack of printouts: the pages of the journal. She still had a few more sections to read. She could hunker down and use the hour productively. Then she closed her eyes and pictured Nellie peeling off her T-shirt and dropping her cargo shorts. She probably wore boxers that matched her undershirt. She tossed the pages back on the desk and went upstairs. She had forty-five minutes to herself and she intended to use it.

She locked the bedroom door in case the kids came home early, stripped off her clothes and stretched out on her bed. She put on her headphones and grabbed her iPod. Diana Krall's sultry voice set the mood.

Her fantasy started in Nellie's study. Jos had worn the crop top on purpose. It was too low and too high in all the right places. Nellie's gaze flitted between her exposed belly and her deep cleavage. They slid into an embrace and a long kiss. Nellie's thumbs traced the waistline of her shorts, stroking her belly until she sighed. Down, down, she pushed her shorts and panties until Jos wiggled free of them. Nellie wasted no time undressing her completely.

Nellie squeezed her buttocks and whispered, "I want you. I want you bad."

"I haven't been with anyone for almost a year."

Nellie's gaze traveled downward, past her belly to the tiny bush of hair between her legs. "That's just wrong. We're gonna change that right now."

Before she could protest, Nellie was on her knees, planting butterfly kisses on her abdomen. She was so wet. She clutched Nellie's head and moaned in delight as Nellie's tongue disappeared between her legs, sucking and licking while she squeezed Jos's buttocks.

The orgasm rolled through every nerve in her body until she cried. It was a primal scream that came from deep inside her. "Please, you have to stop," she panted. Yet she undulated with every flick of Nellie's tongue. She shifted gears. The feeling intensified. She wanted it fast. Frenzied. Faster and faster until she exploded. The orgasm drove her out of the fantasy. She opened her eyes.

Colleen leaned against the armoire.

"What the hell?" Jos spat. "Are the kids here?" She threw off the headphones, jumped off the bed and started to dress.

"No, no, they're not," Colleen replied hurriedly. "I couldn't even make it down the street without the car getting stopped by their friends. They're over at the Smith's house. I thought it would be okay. I really need to talk to you."

Jos pulled on her shorts without her underwear. "What the hell are you doing sneaking in here?"

"I knocked but you didn't answer. I saw the van so I figured you were out back. I used my key. Yes, I know it's only for emergencies, but I wasn't going to leave without telling you where the kids were. Then I heard noises from upstairs. I swear to God I thought it was the TV." She took a breath but Jos said nothing. "I called your name three times. Then I saw the bedroom was locked, so I knocked again." She paused and said, "By the way, I think your noise canceling headphones really work."

Jos ignored her dry humor. "So you just let yourself into the bedroom with the key above the doorjamb."

"I heard a scream. I needed to make sure you were okay. How was I supposed to know what you were doing? You never did that when we were together." Her tone carried a wistful sorrow.

Jos continued to glare at her. She was embarrassed and also perturbed that the afterglow of her orgasm was interrupted. "When you saw what I was doing, you didn't think to excuse yourself? Maybe leave a note on the kitchen table?"

Colleen bit her lip and looked away. "Yes, I probably should've closed the door and gone back downstairs. Indeed, that's what I should've done." She took a step toward Jos, her eyes downcast. When Jos said nothing, she took a second step into her personal space.

They hadn't been physically close in nearly a year. Jos inhaled Colleen's spicy perfume. She always smelled amazing.

She always looked amazing. Her highlighted brown hair fell just past her shoulders and curled at the bottom. Her creamy skin was free of wrinkles and she looked Jos's age, thirty-five, not forty-five. Jos had been shocked to learn she was ten years older. She gazed at Colleen's blue eyes. When they'd made love, Jos stared into her eyes. It was hypnotic.

She wore a tailored suit to work every day with a complementing silk blouse. Today's choice was a dark gray suit and white blouse. She looked conservative and Republican, which explained why she had leap-frogged over other associates in her law firm to become a partner at thirty-three. Only her four-inch heels suggested what the rest of her appearance did not. Colleen was a wild woman, complete with a few X-rated tattoos strategically placed in very "liberal" locations.

And the two of us together…

Colleen slowly lifted her gaze until their eyes met. Jos was transported back to a different time, before Colleen's affair, before carparazzi, even before the kids. They went out every night, never hesitated to have sex in a public place and still got up and went to work the next morning.

"Yeah, that's what I should've done but I couldn't," Colleen whispered. She kissed Jos's cheek. When she didn't object, Colleen kissed her jaw. Her lips hovered near her mouth. Jos felt her heart beat faster. There was still time to end this. She tried to summon up the anger that had driven them apart, but it was nowhere to be found. All she felt was longing.

"Were you thinking of me?" Colleen asked.

"Yes," she lied. There was no point in mentioning Nellie.

They stood motionless, Colleen waiting for direction from Jos, but Jos was tired of being in charge. As if sensing her need, Colleen's lips worked their way down her neck to her ample cleavage. Her fingers grazed the waistband of Jos's shorts just long enough to unzip them and send them to the carpet. She pushed Jos backward until they reached the bed, pulling her top off in the process. They fell on the bed and giggled. Colleen sat up and quickly discarded her clothes. She was curvy. She carried the extra weight that came from a demanding career that didn't allow regular gym time. It didn't matter. She was incredibly attractive. She slipped her leg between Jos's thighs and circled an arm around her waist. Their breasts and lips automatically collided.

"We don't have much time," Jos whispered. "The children—"

She gasped. Colleen's magic fingers entered her and she forgot to finish her sentence.

CHAPTER ELEVEN

Milford, Michigan

Lucky's Place was the closest bar to the General Motors Proving Grounds. It had enjoyed decades of steady patronage from GM employees and auto spies who'd traveled to the quaint village of Milford since the grounds opened in 1924. Located on General Motors Road, Lucy Lucky had inherited the bar from her father Lyle, whose father Lowell had built it after inheriting the land from his grandmother Lois.

When he opened the bar in 1940, Lowell Lucky had tacked a wooden sign to the door proclaiming, "What's said at Lucky's, stays at Lucky's." This was his way of promising the GM Corporation that he wouldn't divulge any secrets shared by GM personnel after they'd had a few drinks. It also let the auto spies know he couldn't be bought. Decades later when an advertising firm created a strikingly similar slogan for the city of Las Vegas, the Luckys debated whether or not to sue, but no one could prove the ad executive who adopted the phrase had ever set foot in Lucky's Place.

Much to Nellie's dismay, granddaughter Lucy still displayed the sign prominently and believed its credo. Nellie tried to pry information from her each time she visited, and each time Lucy laughed and merely freshened her drink. Sometimes she'd take Nellie home to her bed, but their pillow talk gleaned little useful information.

So Nellie was completely surprised when Lucy called in the middle of September and asked if she was planning a trip to Milford any time soon.

"Should I be?" she asked.

"Yeah, you should," Lucy said. "A woman's been asking questions about you. I thought you'd want to know."

Nellie immediately thought of Jos. "Who is she?"

"Somebody I haven't ever seen before. She wanted to know where you lived, how often you came here, if you knew my dad. That kind of stuff. Of course, I didn't tell her anything."

"Is she still there?"

"Yup, I'm looking at her right now. Good looking too. Sleek black suit. Blond hair pulled back in a bun. Definitely your type."

Not Jos. Good. Nellie's mood improved and she grinned. "Are you jealous?"

"Always," Lucy joked. "Why don't you get your ass up here?"

Nellie glanced at her dad. He was sitting in his chair talking to Chevy, who actually seemed to be listening. "I don't think so, Luce. Lots of people ask about me. You know how it goes. She's probably another spy."

Lucy gasped dramatically. "Another female in the carparazzi?"

"Hey, there's one right here in Phoenix," Nellie replied. She closed her eyes and the memory of Jos half naked in the Corvette came flooding back like it was yesterday and not a month ago.

"Well, you need to send her my way," Lucy said, her voice thick.

"Not a chance," Nellie replied. "You're my informant."

"No, I can't be bought. Look, I think you should come check this out," Lucy said adamantly. "There's something off about this woman. I don't think she's another spy and I don't think she's a reporter."

"I don't know. I'd have to leave my dad again."

"How is Willie?" Lucy's question was full of love. She'd known him since she was a teenager in the late seventies. He'd been the one to introduce Nellie to Lucky's Place and Lucy.

"It's getting harder," she managed to say before a knot formed in her throat.

"I understand. Hold on a sec." Her voice fell to a whisper and Nellie heard a door shut. The clamor of the bar vanished. Nellie assumed she'd slipped into her office. "To sweeten the deal, I'll tell you there's a very special run occurring on Black Lake. They're testing the new Camaro. All sorts of new features and a tweak to the body style. Nobody knows about this, Nel. You'd have the scoop."

Nellie felt a tingle down her back. She could certainly use a great payday. She'd had no luck finding out what Argent had planned in Mesa. She glanced once more at Willie. He'd fallen asleep sitting up. Chevy's head was on his knee. She hated leaving him, but Lucy must have been very concerned to break her code of silence. She'd never given Nellie a scoop. In fact, they'd slept together two nights before the secret testing of the Acadia, GM's premiere crossover vehicle, and Lucy had said nothing.

"I'm surprised you're telling me this," Nellie said.

"I've always had a soft spot for you, Nel."

Nellie chuckled and said, "Not that soft."

"True. Just get up here. You could bring Willie," Lucy suggested.

"That would be a disaster." Nellie shuddered at the thought of Willie navigating security. He'd probably get pulled aside by TSA and they'd wind up in one of those interrogation rooms. "When's the test on Black Lake?"

"Friday. Three days from now."

"I'll try."

Nellie dismissed the idea immediately. She needed to stay with her dad. Then Mai announced her Thursday class had been canceled and if Nellie needed to be anywhere, she was happy to give up her day off and earn some extra cash.

Nellie wondered if it was a sign. Lucy had never given her a scoop, and if GM thought they'd kept the Camaro testing a secret, they wouldn't be looking for carparazzi. They might not put up screen barriers, dress the car in camouflage or minimize drive time.

And she loved going to Black Lake, which wasn't a lake at all. It was sixty-seven acres of black asphalt, the largest flat surface in the world. Since it was free of obstructions, drivers pushed the vehicles to the limit for high-speed tests, knowing it was one of the safest courses on earth.

For Nellie, it was one of the easiest places to photograph, too. Willie had seen to that.

"Hey, where are you going?" he asked on the way to the bathroom.

She looked down. She was holding her empty duffel bag and her camera case was over her shoulder.

* * *

Nellie landed in Lansing by noon the next day. She'd made sure to rent a silver Chevy Malibu since she was heading into GM country. The drive was only an hour and by three o'clock she was cruising through Milford. Historic Main Street housed all of the major businesses that had been there for decades. Tourists from nearby Dearborn and Ann Arbor regularly spent the day shopping or enjoying the local eateries.

She turned onto General Motors Road and headed toward the proving ground. She passed Lucky's Place, determined to get a shower before she went to hug Lucy. The proving ground was outside of Milford on what used to be vacant land, but urban sprawl had gobbled up the empty fields. GM now found itself with some unwanted neighbors, including Willie and Nellie.

A high-end subdivision had been built adjacent to the north end of the proving ground. Initially GM was relieved because private homes ensured carparazzi would no longer be camped out on the hill that overlooked Black Lake. For years GM had been required to take extraordinary measures to thwart the auto spies who had a fabulous view and routinely brought picnic baskets along with their camera equipment.

What GM hadn't known was that the builder had sold a parcel of land to a condo company. A handful of the condos overlooked Black Lake, and Willie had learned about the sale of the land and the sale of the units before anyone else. While Lowell Lucky refused to divulge GM secrets, he had no qualms about sharing town gossip with his best friends, including Willie Rafferty. Over the years GM acquired the other four condos that faced Black Lake, just not Willie's. Even when he was offered ten times what it was worth, he still said no.

Nellie punched in the gate code and meandered between the units until she reached three sixty-eight. The third floor meant an extra set of stairs, but it also meant a better view. Upon entering she made a face. The air was incredibly stuffy. They paid a local to clean every few months, but the condo had a distinct stale smell found in places that were unoccupied.

She opened the back patio door and inhaled the fresh air. Great air quality was one of the things she loved about small towns. Phoenix had some of the worst air in the world, and it didn't help that one and a half million people refused to get out of their cars and use public transportation. She bent over and did some stretches. Her left leg burned, a result of sitting for hours on the airplane and in the rented Malibu.

She gazed toward the proving ground. Her face fell. "Are you kidding me? Son of a bitch!"

Six pine trees lined the perimeter of the GM property. It was obvious they had been planted to obstruct the view from the condos, most specifically Nellie's condo. If she owned the southern or northernmost condo, Black Lake would be visible. But those were the ones GM had purchased.

As it was, the pine trees weren't tall enough yet to ruin every shot, but considering how quickly they grew, she imagined the condo balcony would be useless to the Raffertys within another year. GM wanted them to sell and now they might as well do it. Nellie imagined they wouldn't get a dollar over fair market value.

She kicked the air, so angry she could spit. She tried to remember how long it had been since she'd been to Milford. She was rather certain Willie had come with her, and it was probably his last road trip. She scrolled through her calendar. She couldn't find the dates quickly, but she was guessing it had been almost two years.

She glanced at her watch and called him. It was probably too late in the day for him to remember anything, but she might as well try. Mai answered and handed the phone to him.

"Hello?" His voice quaked as if she'd awoken him from a nap.

"Hi, Dad. Hey, I'm up here in Milford, and I'm trying to remember when we last came to the condo. You know, the one that overlooks Black Lake?"

"Oh, yeah. I remember that place."

"Dad, when was our last trip? Was Lowell Lucky still alive?"

He laughed. "Ah, Lowell. He was a character."

"Dad, GM planted a bunch of pine trees in front of our condo. I can barely see the lake now."

"Hmm. Probably Eastern Pines. Pretty tree."

Nellie closed her eyes. She wasn't getting anywhere.

"Are you meeting with the Chrysler people?" he asked.

She exhaled, trying to control her temper. "No, Dad, not Chrysler. I'm in Milford where GM is."

"Good. We need to meet with them. Try for next week. Make sure Ralph is there. He told me we needed to get him through the door. He said—"

"Sure, Dad. I'll let Chrysler and GM know. Gotta go. I gotta figure out how in hell I'm going to get around these trees."

"What trees?"

"See you soon, Dad." She hung up. "Shit."

She was as angry with herself as she was with GM. She resisted the urge to be angry with Lucy. There was no way she could've known that GM had planted the trees. And the maneuver was probably long overdue. Nellie and Willie had speculated for years about the countermeasures GM would take since they wouldn't sell.

She took a quick shower and got ready to visit Lucky's. There was the other matter of the mysterious blond woman. As she headed downstairs toward the parking lot, she decided she wanted a closer look at the trees. She turned around and ventured to the condo's front. Each building had a small yard that extended to a wrought-iron fence that surrounded the entire complex. A drainage ditch and a tall chain-link fence clearly divided the GM facility from the condos. Every ten feet a sign warned potential trespassers that the fence was electrified, and the coil of barbed wire at the top ensured no one hopped over when the electricity might be off. A ten-foot-high concrete wall surrounded Black Lake and prevented gawkers from standing at the fence and taking pictures.

The six trees had been planted between the chain link and the ten-foot wall. She guessed they were about eight feet apart, but eventually they would grow together like an enormous shrub. She pulled out her camera and focused the zoom lens. She took several photos at different angles, walking back and forth along the fence perimeter. When she positioned her camera at the point where the trunk rose from the ground, she noticed the fresh soil. At first she thought she had to be wrong, but as she focused on different trees, she saw the same rich, brown dirt.

The trees had been planted very recently. She couldn't help but take it personally. It was as if GM were deliberately singling her out, preventing her from photographing the Camaro.

She stormed to the condo office, determined to speak with the manager. Her fierce expression surprised the young woman sitting at the reception desk, whose smile quickly evaporated into a look of concern.

"May I help you? Is something wrong?" Her nametag read Marjorie, but Nellie thought she looked more like a Heather or a Jennifer.

Nellie took a breath and smiled, which seemed to put Marjorie at ease. "I hope so. I'm the owner of condo three sixty-eight. I noticed the GM people planted a row of trees right in front of my unit. Would you know when that happened?"

Marjorie shook her head. "No. I could ask Dan, the groundskeeper. He might've noticed."

"That would be great."

"Let me make sure I have your number in our system."

She went to her computer and tapped on the keyboard. She verified the contact information and said, "Oh, we have a letter for you."

"A letter?" They didn't receive mail at the condo. Lucy checked their P.O. Box once a month.

Marjorie disappeared and returned with an envelope. "Here you go. I'll call you after I speak to the groundskeeper."

"Thanks," Nellie said.

She waited until she was in the Malibu before she examined the letter. It was certified and dated August twenty-fourth, just a few weeks ago. Inside was a sheet of GM letterhead with one typed question in the middle of the page.

Do you like our trees?

CHAPTER TWELVE

Milford, Michigan

Jos had never ventured to Milford, Michigan, but it was becoming apparent that the bigger paydays would be farther away. Mr. Brent, the man who told her about Nellie's journal, urged her to make the Milford trip and enticed her with the promise of a hefty check. She'd debated whether she ethically could go, but she called Andy, who reminded her there was a clause that stipulated she could freelance as long as she met her obligations to *Auto Monthly*.

"You can do whatever the fuck you want with your life, Jos," he said. "That's what my self-esteem training class taught me. Just curious—how much they paying? I hope it's good because Milford's about as boring as it gets."

She didn't want to reveal an exact amount since the pay equaled a month's salary at the magazine. All she said was, "Enough," which seemed to squash his curiosity. He'd been in a hurry to get to his yoga class.

She'd only be gone three days, but to Bridget and Myles it seemed like an eternity. She almost called Mr. Brent back and declined, but then she fast-forwarded to the future. She saw her kids as college students in need of tuition.

The assignment was a photo shoot at Black Lake. Next year's Camaro model was undergoing high-speed testing. Mr. Brent had a contact with an ideal vantage point from which she could take photos.

"When you arrive on Thursday, you'll need to pick up a package. Go to Lucky's Place. It's a bar not far from the proving ground. Ask for Lucy. She'll give it to you, as well as the contact address. That's where you'll go Friday morning."

The whole scenario was a bit too cloak-and-dagger for Jos's liking, but she kept thinking about the paycheck. How could she turn it down? He'd assured her there was nothing illegal in the package, and he'd laughed when she asked about the contact. He promised she wouldn't be murdered.

So after she checked into the Best Western, she drove to Lucky's Place. It was Happy Hour and the bar was packed almost entirely by men, many of whom wore dress shirts and neckties loosened at the collar. Work was over and this was their reward.

She scanned the crowd looking for women. One female in a booth across the room downed a shot while her male counterparts stared and laughed. It was clear she loved being the center of attention. Two other women stood off in a corner and spoke in whispered tones, clearly avoiding the overwhelming presence of testosterone. Her gaze settled on the bar and the end stool—Nellie Rafferty.

"Unbelievable."

They locked eyes just as Jos turned to leave. Nellie looked shocked to see her but beckoned for her to come over. She waved back and fought the crowd to the empty stool beside her.

"I thought you only worked close to home?" Nellie said flatly.

Jos could tell she wasn't happy to see her. "This landed in my lap. I couldn't refuse."

For some reason, Nellie glared at the bartender who was chatting up another customer.

"Something wrong with your beer?" Jos asked warily. She noticed Nellie hadn't touched it.

"Nope."

The bartender, a thin brunette with long curly hair, sidled up to Jos. "Welcome to Lucky's. What can I get you?"

Nellie leaned over, pointing at Jos. "Wait. You don't know her?"

Jos and the bartender looked at each other. "No," Jos said. "What's wrong with you?" She made no attempt to hide her exasperation. She was done catering to Nellie Rafferty, regardless of her status in the carparazzi.

"Yeah," the bartender agreed. "What's wrong with you, Nellie? You've been a sourpuss ever since you got here." She turned to Jos, adopted a friendly smile and stuck out her hand. "I'm Lucy Lucky. Nice to meet you."

"I'm Jos Grant, and I think you might be holding a package for me?"

Lucy nodded in recognition. "Why, yes I am. I'll go get it and then take your drink order."

She disappeared and Jos turned to a pouting Nellie. She'd managed to down most of her beer in the last thirty seconds and was staring at the little bit left in the glass. Jos focused on her lips, downturned into a frown. She fought the urge to kiss her and turn her expression into a smile. She couldn't control her attraction but she could control how she reacted.

She cleared her throat and said firmly, "What's going on? Why are you upset with me?"

Nellie sat up straighter and asked, "Why are you here? I'm assuming you know about the testing tomorrow on Black Lake?"

Jos nodded. "Yes."

"I thought I had an exclusive. How did you find out?"

"A guy called and told me." She shook her head. "That doesn't matter. I want to talk about what happened at your house."

Nellie eyed her suspiciously. "No, tell me about the guy. Does this person have a name?"

Jos sighed. Nellie was all business. She debated how much she wanted to say. "I'm not sharing my sources with you. It's not like you're giving anything up."

Nellie mumbled, "Oh, I think I already have."

"What?"

Nellie looked away. She took a deep breath, as if she was collecting her thoughts, and leaned closer to Jos. "Okay, I'll share. My source is Lucy and she doesn't give out information very often. I got the impression GM had kept tomorrow's test highly secretive and I had an exclusive. So, who's your guy?"

Jos shrugged. "I don't really know. He calls himself Mr. Brent. He's never told me anything else."

"He's given you information before?"

"Yes," Jos hedged. There was no way she could explain Mr. Brent without mentioning the journal.

Nellie swirled the remains of her beer, deep in thought. Lucy reappeared with a medium-sized package wrapped in brown mailing paper. An envelope was attached to the front with Jos's name on it.

"Here you go. What can I get you?"

"A Heineken is fine," Jos said.

Lucy smiled. "You got it." She pointed at Nellie and said, "Figure out what the hell is wrong with Grumpy," before she left.

"What's that?" Nellie asked sharply, her gaze fixed on the box.

Jos leaned forward and got in her face. "I'm not telling you anything. You're treating me like crap. This is a continuation of when I left your house last month and you were so rude to me."

"I wasn't rude," Nellie argued.

"You call groping my breasts and then practically dismissing me without a goodbye not being rude? It felt like you just wanted to feel me up and throw me out after you got a quick thrill."

"That's not true," Nellie snapped.

"Then explain it to me."

Nellie struggled for the words. There was something she wanted to say but wouldn't. Jos sensed Nellie knew she'd been wrong but she didn't want to admit it.

Nellie opened her mouth just as Jos's phone rang. She glanced at the display and rolled her eyes. There was nowhere quiet to go so she put her finger in her right ear to drown out the noise. "Hi, honey. What's going on?"

"I don't want to go to soccer," Myles said sadly. He said something else but she couldn't hear it.

"Honey, I'm in a very noisy place so you'll have to really speak up. What's the problem with soccer?"

"Coach…"

She couldn't hear him but it really didn't matter. Myles had complained about his coach since the season started. He maintained that the coach had it in for him. "He's always yelling at me," he'd said repeatedly.

"I know it's not ideal, Myles. But sometimes we have to learn to get along with people who aren't like us." She stared at Nellie as she uttered the last sentence. Nellie scowled and motioned for another beer when Lucy came by to deliver Jos's Heineken.

"I don't want…"

"Myles, I can't hear you. Now you need to go to soccer and when I get home we'll figure it out. Maybe we should go sit down and talk to the coach."

Nellie shook her head. She clearly thought that was a bad idea.

"He called me a name…"

Jos didn't hear the rest of the sentence, but she heard that part. "What name did he call you?" She looked at Nellie, whose eyebrows were raised.

"Called me…"

She cursed under her breath. She couldn't hear anything. "Look, honey, go this once and tell Mama C to keep an eye on things, okay?"

"It's not Mama C who's taking us. It's Kelly."

They'd finally gotten to the real problem. "Okay, sweetie. I'll text Mama C and hopefully she can go, or she'll tell Kelly what to do. It's the best I can do right now, Myles. Remember when we talked about giving each other a break when we're doing everything we can? I'm fifteen hundred miles away right now. I'm trying to solve the problem, but I'm far away. Do you get that?"

"Yeah," came his small voice. "Okay. Love you."

He hung up and she sent the text to Colleen. Fortunately, she responded right away and promised to take the kids to soccer. She also asked when Jos was returning so they could plan another afternoon tryst.

Jos ignored that part of the text and thanked her for going to soccer. She didn't know what to do about Colleen. Since that afternoon a month before, they'd slept together twice more and now she was completely confused.

She felt Nellie studying her but she didn't care. She took a long sip of the beer and put the cold glass against her forehead. It felt so good. She had a headache.

"What position does Myles play?"

The question surprised her. She had to think for a moment before she said, "Forward."

"Is he any good?"

"Not really, but he tries. He's got a limp from a childhood illness at the orphanage so it's hard for him."

"Not that you asked me, but any coach who would call a kid with a physical or mental challenge a name is an ass in my book," Nellie commented.

Jos smiled. She couldn't help it. She couldn't stay angry with someone who was defending her child. "I'm not sure what to believe. The truth is probably somewhere in the middle but I'm not there to figure out where the middle is. I'm here. In Michigan." She gestured to the lively crowd around her. She knew she was about to cry when Nellie's hand slipped against the base of her neck.

Strong fingers massaged her scalp. She closed her eyes and drifted away. She saw an island surrounded by water. She was sunbathing on the beach, sipping a Cosmopolitan and watching Myles and Bridget play on the shore. Someone was holding her hand. Colleen? She turned and saw Nellie beside her. She wore a black one-piece with black board shorts. All black. She looked good enough to kiss, which they did, several times while the waves lapped the shore.

"Better?" Nellie whispered in her ear.

Jos blinked. "Yes."

Nellie kissed her cheek. "You're a great mom. The way you talk to those kids is going to make them independent problem-solvers."

Jos closed her eyes, willing the tears away. She wished they were on that beach. Just the four of them. Maybe it would be easier to say if she didn't look at her. She rested her hand over Nellie's and said, "I copied your journal."

"I know," she whispered as her hands slipped away.

It took a few seconds for the comment to register. Jos swiveled around to explain but Nellie was gone. She'd headed to the front door. A tall blonde wearing a skinny black dress had entered and Nellie was confronting her, hands on her hips. Jos could tell Nellie wasn't happy. The blonde crossed her arms and listened until Nellie was done. Then it was her turn. When she took a step closer and whispered in Nellie's ear, Jos's heart started to pound. She debated whether to jump off the stool and barge in on their conversation. That's what Nellie would do. But her legs wouldn't move. She just wanted to go home.

How could Nellie know? When did she find out? It explained everything, how she'd gone from hot to cold, why she hadn't called in the last month. Jos wondered if there was a way to make it right. "But not now," she whispered.

She tore her eyes away from Nellie and the blonde and studied the package. She had to remember why she was over a thousand miles away from her children. The box had no identifying information but the envelope was addressed to her. She pulled out a simple white card and found an address in block letters. 2759 E. Dove Street. Under it was a code: #547832 – 9 a.m. She guessed the package needed to be delivered there. To access the house she'd need the code, which was either for an alarm or a gate into the community.

She tapped the address into her GPS and glanced over at Nellie and the blonde. They were still talking, or rather, now the blonde was talking and Nellie was listening. It was obvious from her gestures and Nellie's defensive posture that the blonde was trying to convince her of something.

The address on the GPS was close to the GM proving grounds. In fact, it appeared to be practically on the property. She guessed the package was Mr. Brent's payment for Jos's bird's-eye view of the Camaro's testing on Black Lake.

Her gaze returned to Nellie, whose stance had softened. She had her hands in her back pockets. Then she laughed. The blonde smiled before she turned on her heel and walked out the door with Nellie following.

Jos shook her head and nursed the rest of her beer. Lucy ambled up beside her. "Want another?"

"No, thanks." She tried to muster a smile but it wouldn't come.

Lucy looked around. "Where'd Nellie go?"

"Out the door with some tall blonde."

"Oh. That's the woman who's been looking for her."

Jos looked up. "Really? Why? Is she Nellie's mail order bride?"

Lucy laughed. "Not in a million years. Not Nellie. She's a player, through and through." Lucy leaned closer. "I should know."

Jos couldn't hide her surprise. "Oh. Were you a couple...?"

"You wanted to say one-night stand, didn't you?" Lucy teased.

"Uh, no, I—"

Lucy waved her off. "The answer is somewhere in between. We've been casual lovers. If she's in town and we're both in the mood, then we hook up." Lucy glanced at the front door. "I'm thinking this time we won't." She scanned the length of the bar, which had filled with more patrons. "Let me know if you want another."

Jos nodded and twirled her empty bottle. She swiveled the stool around to watch the crowd. While many were her age or older, she guessed this was just a Happy Hour stop on their way home to their real lives that included family and love. For her, this was it, at least for tonight. If she wanted more money, there would be a lot of nights like this. She thought of Nellie's rating system in her journal. Maybe that's why Nellie took casual lovers, to stave off the loneliness.

Jos knew she'd screwed things up with Nellie. She missed Myles and Bridget. She'd spent nearly a year alone now and had entered a profession fraught with isolating competition. She looked around and owned her feelings: *I'm alone and I don't like it.* If she were honest, she missed Colleen, or at least what Colleen represented—a partner.

"I'm not going to find that here," she mumbled. She pulled out her wallet and searched for some cash to pay for the beer.

Lucy saw her preparing to leave and darted over. "No, no. Your tab is covered, and that includes a sweet tip for yours truly. The person who left the package handed me a hundred-dollar bill." She pointed at the one empty glass. "I'd say at the rate you drink, you're a freebie for about a year."

"That person wouldn't have been a Mr. Brent, would it?"

She leaned over the bar and turned away from the other patrons. "He didn't give his name. I've seen him around here so I know he's local in the auto industry. One of those movie star-looking types." She touched Jos's arm and said, "Normally I try to stay uninvolved with all the spy drama, but let me give you a little advice. Step carefully. There's some funny things going on and I'd hate to see you go under the Suburban."

Jos looked puzzled so she added, "Honey, you're in GM country. We don't throw people under the bus. We throw 'em under the Suburban."

CHAPTER THIRTEEN

Milford, Michigan

The blonde's name was Felice, and she was the most female female Nellie had ever met. She had to be a model with such finely chiseled features and straight hair styled in a blunt cut at her jawline. Only a model could walk in four-inch heels with such grace. Nellie followed her outside and watched her bottom sway from side to side as they headed to a waiting limo.

The driver opened the back door and Felice motioned for Nellie to climb in. The privacy window between the front and back was up and Nellie felt slightly claustrophobic. Felice joined her, perching on the edge of the seat but showing no regard for personal space. Their knees touched when Felice crossed her legs, and a burst of floral fragrance filled the air.

Felice gently set her hand on Nellie's knee. Her manicure was perfect, and Nellie imagined her long ox-blood red fingernails could cause serious damage in a catfight. That's what she reminded Nellie of—a cat. Her movements were fluid and graceful. There was nothing awkward about her. The tiny black cocktail dress, black hose and black stilettos made her milky white skin look even paler. Only the slash of red lipstick and dash of rouge provided any color. Her dazzling green eyes needed no assistance, and her skin was so youthful Nellie doubted she'd seen her twenty-fifth birthday.

The vehicle pulled out of the crowded parking lot and headed toward the proving ground. "Where are we going?" she asked.

Felice tilted her head slightly and offered a picture-perfect smile. "We're not going anywhere," she said. "We're taking a drive to talk in private."

Cloistered in a dark moving car, away from the noisy bar, Nellie heard a slight accent, but she couldn't place it.

"What are we going to talk about?"

"I've been sent to provide an invitation. Someone would like to speak with you."

Nellie laughed and said, "They could've just called me."

"No," Felice disagreed. "Phone call is not appropriate."

Nellie finally pegged the accent. French. "Do you work for Argent or Renault?"

Her fingernails gripped Nellie's knee and slowly climbed up her thigh, digging into the skin under her cargo shorts. The touch was gentle but threatening, and completely erotic. Nellie bit her lip.

"They said you were smart. Jacques Perreault wants you to come to France and meet with him as soon as possible. What do you think?"

Argent. Of course. She'd wondered how they would react when they realized their first American proving ground was practically in Nellie's backyard. Since Nellie had scooped them three times before, they had to be worried. Felice was their response. Send a gorgeous model to seduce the lesbian auto spy. Felice stroked her thigh, watching Nellie's reaction. She was practically sitting in her lap and her other hand was headed for Nellie's zipper.

Never one to be dominated, Nellie took Felice's chin between her thumb and forefinger. "I think, little girl, you are out of your league." Nellie removed her hands and placed them back in her own lap. "Now, why don't you tell me what this is all about?"

Felice's lip quivered slightly. She studied her hands, as if they'd been burned. It was obvious she wasn't accustomed to rejection.

"Hey, I'm not angry, but I'm way too old for you."

Felice looked at her with a wry smile. "You have no idea what you're talking about," she said dryly, no longer hiding her thick French accent.

Nellie knew what she meant. It was typical for executives to pass around the young models. She imagined if she surfed the Argent website long enough, she'd find Felice lying on the hood of a sleek sports car.

"It's not that I don't find you attractive," she said kindly.

"Then what?" Felice had tears in her eyes and she blinked several times to prevent her mascara from running. "Did I do something wrong?"

Her voice had a desperate tone and Nellie frowned. "Look at me." She shook her head and continued to stare at her lap. "Okay, at least be honest with me. Argent, specifically Jacques Perreault, has a reputation for ruthlessness."

She looked up and shrugged. "I don't understand that word…"

"He's not nice to people," Nellie said. "I'm wondering if you're going to be in trouble if I don't agree to meet with him. Is that true?"

She gave a slight nod. Nellie sighed. She moved over so they could sit an appropriate distance apart and then she patted the seat. Felice slid back and even kicked off her heels.

"I hate these things," she mumbled. She spread her legs across Nellie's lap and smiled seductively. "Is this okay?"

Nellie laughed. "Sure. Now tell me how you know Jacques."

"It's not important."

"It is to me."

Nellie stroked her feet and massaged her toes. Felice closed her eyes and her mouth dropped open. "Ah. What are you doing?" she managed to ask.

"I've dated a few auto models who worked the trade shows. All of them have liked foot rubs better than sex."

"Fools," Felice mumbled, "but this is *incroyable*."

"And I'll keep doing it as long as you answer my questions. Why does he want to talk to me?"

Nellie increased the pressure of the rub and she moaned softly. "Um, well, he said he needs your help."

"For what?"

"He didn't say." She leaned forward and with a look of sincerity asked, "Will you please meet with him? Don't let me fail. It will not be good for me."

They stared at each other, as the car glided down the road. Nellie had always been a sucker for a damsel in distress. She thought about how easy it would be to drown in Felice's green eyes. How gorgeous and supple her skin would be to touch.

"When can he meet with me?"

"We can take the jet and go tomorrow."

She thought about the tree line in front of Black Lake. She didn't have a backup plan, and she had a sneaky suspicion Jos had acquired a better view and would have superior pictures. Nellie couldn't imagine *Auto Monthly* was that well connected. Someone was helping Jos and Nellie needed to learn who that was. But that could wait. She was curious about Jacques Perreault. She regarded him as one of the scummiest carmakers in the world, but perhaps meeting him would give her some answers.

"Fine," she said.

Felice sat up, stunned. "You'll go? Really?"

"But only because I don't want you to get in trouble."

Relief washed over her face. She pulled Nellie into a deep kiss and climbed into her lap. Her short dress rode up and she took Nellie's right hand and set it on her naked butt cheek. No underwear. Nellie's resistance melted away. She caressed her rock-hard bottom, conscious of the lacy red garters trailing down toward her nylons. The front of her dress had a long zipper. Her hands already preoccupied, Nellie broke the kiss, gripped the zipper between her teeth and pulled it down as far as her neck would allow. Felice laughed and finished the job for her. A red bra held her breasts captive and was a perfect match for the garters.

She buried her face in Felice's cleavage and kissed the soft flesh. It wasn't enough. She grabbed the hem and struggled to pull the dress up. Felice laughed and freed herself from it.

Nellie slowly drank in her soft, nubile white body. Felice cupped her chin and thrust her face upward. "Take back what you said."

Nellie's mind was a fog, trapped in a haze of lust that demanded to be satisfied. It took a moment to remember her previous comment made with the common sense she'd possessed just a few minutes prior. Where had it gone?

"You're old enough to be with me," she said quietly, knowing as she said the words that she didn't believe them. She'd be ashamed later. But that was later.

Felice's seductive cat smile returned. She pulled herself up and leaned against the glass separating them from the driver, her feet propped against the seat. If they were in an accident or hit a bad pothole, she'd career into the footwell or on top of Nellie. She spread her legs as wide as she could and thrust her pelvis in Nellie's face. She was clean-shaven and nothing was left to the imagination. Her wet clit glistened and her pungent femininity overtook the smell of the intoxicating French perfume.

She slid her left leg over Nellie's shoulder and drove her fingernails into Nellie's scalp, pushing Nellie's face into the center of her desire. Her tongue went deep and Felice gasped, sending a wave of pain through Nellie's scalp. But it was good pain. They found a rhythm and Felice took control until Nellie gave her exactly what she wanted.

"Women are much better lovers than men," Felice proclaimed as she crawled off a naked Nellie.

"I have no idea," Nellie said. "I'm a gold star."

"Indeed," Felice said. She checked the time on her phone and knocked on the glass. "We need to get back."

Nellie yawned and wiped the sleep from her eyes. "We've been driving around for at least two hours. Do you think the driver suspects anything?"

Felice adjusted her bra and pulled the dress over her head before she answered. "He doesn't suspect. He knows exactly what we're doing."

Nellie chuckled and reached for her clothes. "You were awfully sure of yourself. What if I'd stuck to my original answer?"

Felice zipped up her dress and adjusted the garters. "Then I would've thought myself a failure, but I knew that wasn't going to happen."

"Why? Because you're irresistible?"

Felice faced her with a sweet smile. Nellie sensed this was her real smile, the one she offered to a salesclerk after making a purchase or to a waiter bringing her a glass of Bordeaux, if she was actually old enough to drink.

"I've heard you are a lover of beautiful women. If I'd failed to seduce you, then I wasn't beautiful enough."

She reached into her purse and pulled out a gold cigarette case and a lighter. She offered a cigarette to Nellie, who declined, and quickly lit up. She expertly blew a smoke ring and opened the back window an inch.

"How old are you?"

"Twenty-one." Nellie groaned and hung her head. Felice patted her leg. "It's all right. I've been twenty-one for almost a month."

Nellie leaned back and watched the landscape while Felice checked her email and sent texts. She imagined one of those emails was to Jacques Perreault, telling him she'd shagged and snagged the notorious auto spy Nellie Rafferty.

She wondered what Jos was doing. She started a text to her and then deleted it. They weren't at a place where they could talk to each other via text. She wanted to see her. She needed to see her. She'd admitted copying the journal. It was an important step for their relationship.

Relationship? Where did that come from?

Nellie knew the only way Jos could've connected with Justin Juniper was by reading the journal. When she'd gone to retrieve it after the trip to Nevada, she noticed the false back in the glove box in backward. She originally dismissed it as a mistake on her part—until Jos showed up on Patton Road. Since the journal was still in the Jeep, she knew it hadn't been stolen. Then she remembered Jos had pulled up at the Honda shoot. She certainly had access to the Jeep while Nellie sat out in the desert waiting for the shot. More than likely she'd been following Nellie. She thought of Caress. How much had Jos seen?

Since that realization, Nellie's mind and heart had struggled between attraction and betrayal. There was something unusual about this relationship. She'd thought a lot about Jos's observation regarding her relationships. Had she deliberately avoided a monogamous relationship because of her mother's influence? Had Willie encouraged her to stay single? She closed her eyes, remembering the afternoon in the shed and Jos's lips...

"Wake up, Nellie. We're back."

She sat up, disoriented. She was in the limo with Felice. Lucky's Place glowed in neon light and the Happy Hour crowd had left. Only a handful of regulars remained. The driver got out and opened Nellie's door.

"So, I'll pick you up in the morning at your condo and we'll go to the airport," Felice said.

"You know where I live?"

"*Oui*." She leaned over and kissed Nellie passionately. "There's a bed on the plane," she whispered. "It's very comfortable."

Although Nellie returned her smile, she was frowning by the time the limo drove away. What was wrong with her? Felice was practically a child. The more she thought about it, the worse she felt.

She climbed into the rented Malibu and stared into the dusk. It was past seven but it was still twilight, Nellie's favorite time to take pictures, and there was just the right amount of light. She loved wandering around her acreage, capturing the beauty of the desert. She didn't think she was very good at landscape photography, but she had an entire collection of stills only a few people had seen.

She started the car, and just as she was about to pull out, Lucy and Jos came out of Lucky's together. Nellie watched their body language closely. Lucy walked Jos to her own rented Malibu and Nellie chuckled. They thought alike.

Jos held out her phone and Lucy took it. Nellie guessed she was entering her address into the GPS app. Lucy handed the phone back and gave her a hug. Nellie counted the seconds until it ended. Ten seconds. They didn't move apart but stayed in an embrace. She frowned. They were practically the same height so they fit perfectly together. Lucy kissed Jos on her cheek before Jos disappeared inside the Malibu and drove away. Lucy watched Jos turn onto the highway. Once she was out of sight, Lucy pivoted sharply to her right. She stared at Nellie with her arms crossed before marching across the lot to where she was parked.

"Shit," Nellie muttered as she rolled down the window.

Lucy squatted and folded her arms across the open window. "How ya doing, Nellie?"

"Not as good as you apparently."

"Oh, I'd disagree. We just had a friendly hug. After you blew out, I convinced Jos to stay for another couple of beers. Nice gal. We both noticed you left with the blonde, and you were gone for quite a while."

"We didn't—"

"Cut the crap. Of course you did. You always do. That's why you're you." She stood up and started to walk away. She suddenly stopped and turned around. She was pointing as she said, "We're old friends, and well…whatever the hell else we are. Do the right thing and stay away from Jos. She's too good for the likes of either of us."

The comment angered Nellie, not only because she hated to be told what to do, but also because she knew her feelings for Jos were unique. She just couldn't put the puzzle together yet. She flung open her door and nearly strangled herself trying to get out. She'd fastened her seat belt already. When she finally managed to emerge from the car, Lucy was halfway across the lot.

"Hey! You've got no right to tell me what to do."

Lucy whirled around. "Don't start with me, Nellie. We've known each other too long not to be honest."

That was true but Nellie didn't care. "If she's too good for you, then I suppose you're not getting in your car and going to her motel room right now. You're not, right?"

Her shouting caught the attention of an older cowboy leaving Lucky's. His bowlegs ambled over to Lucy and he removed his cowboy hat. He was bald but he made up for it with a silver mustache that curled at the ends.

"Everything all right, Lucy?" he asked, his glare focused on Nellie. He turned to the side and Nellie caught the glint of a pearl-handled grip in his side holster. He was packing and wanted her to know it.

"I'm fine, John," Lucy said, patting his meaty shoulder. "This woman's actually a friend and we're just having a rather loud discussion. She's a bit stubborn and mule-headed."

John's gaze turned to slits as he eyed Nellie. "I see it."

Nellie stomped back to the Malibu. She deliberately peeled out of the parking lot, sending a cloud of dust everywhere. She laughed for a few seconds as she barreled down the highway but it quickly died away. She'd never fought with Lucy.

What the hell was Lucy doing with Jos? And what did she mean when she said, 'Whatever we are?' Did she want more? Her mind looped back to Jos's observation about her family. Was there something Nellie was missing?

And if Lucy wanted her, why was she hooking up with Jos? Were they really hooking up? Lucy had implied they were just being friendly and Jos had left alone.

"I don't care!" Nellie shouted.

She glanced at the speedometer. Ninety. She immediately slowed and pulled onto the shoulder. She turned on her hazard lights and took a few deep breaths. She'd never thought of Lucy as anything but a friend with benefits. She thought Lucy felt the same.

If she was honest, she wasn't upset about Lucy. It was Jos. The day they kissed in the Corvette was etched on her brain. She thought about it constantly, and that was strange. She never thought about the same woman for long. She loved watching women but the interactions were fleeting. Even with Lucy and

Caress. They only entered her mind at very specific times. But she couldn't get Jos out of her head. She remembered the way Jos had admired the old cars. She seemed so genuine. And the way she talked to her kids was great. Like they were little adults. She wasn't really a thief but something was pushing her to compete with Nellie. Her phone buzzed. It was Mai.

"Hi, is everything okay?"

"You need to talk to your father."

"Okay, but hey, I'm taking a little side trip to Paris. I should be home day after tomorrow."

"That's fine," Mai said casually. After a year with Nellie and Willie, she was accustomed to Nellie's ever-changing schedule. "But you need to figure out what Willie's saying. It's sounding serious. When I picked him up from bingo today, he was incredibly agitated."

She heard the phone being passed and Willie's mumbling as he fumbled with the unfamiliar cell phone. He regularly commented that the world needed to return to the rotary dial or at the very least, go back to the big push buttons.

"Nellie!" he cried, "you've got to do something!"

"Do what, Dad? What's going on?"

"We need to go to the media with what we know. Things are escalating."

"What's escalating, Dad? What is it we know?"

He ignored her questions, which wasn't surprising. He was completely in his own world. "People are going to die. People are going to die if we don't do something."

CHAPTER FOURTEEN

Milford, Michigan

The next morning Jos was on the road by eight thirty. Nellie had left a voice mail during the night. She wanted to set up a time to meet in the near future because they had things to discuss. She'd even joked about taking the Corvette out for a drive. Jos wanted to remain angry, but her playful tone was contagious and she found herself smiling by the time Nellie hung up. *Yes, we do have things to discuss.*

Her finger hovered over the delete option but she couldn't do it. She enjoyed listening to Nellie's voice too much. "What's going on with me?" she murmured.

Jos frequently thought about their afternoon in the Corvette. Nellie had left her sexually charged and Colleen had been available. Now she regretted it. She imagined Nellie was sleeping with the blonde. She'd slept with Colleen. How could she be angry?

"I'm a hypocrite," she declared.

She located the Dove Street house on her GPS and cross-checked the address with the section of Nellie's journal devoted to Milford, Michigan. The housing development sat on a hill overlooking the GM Proving Grounds. Once upon a time it had been a great place for car spies. In the journal Willie mentioned many different shots taken at the top. Jos imagined the carparazzi must have hated to see it turned into a subdivision, but such prime real estate rarely escaped development.

Her GPS led her straight to the community. The heavy iron gates slowly parted when she punched in the provided code. All of the houses looked the same: solid brick construction, large front windows and gabled roofs. Many owners had attempted to distinguish their homes with unique landscaping or lawn ornaments. Eventually she caught glimpses of the proving grounds behind the houses and she knew she was close. She came to Dove Street and turned into a cul-de-sac. Number 2759 sat in the center. Jos guessed she was at the highest point of what used to be the hill.

She looked between two of the houses and saw Black Lake. She grinned excitedly and grabbed the package and her gear. She checked her watch. It was precisely eight fifty-nine. Since she hadn't received a key, she presumed someone would be home to let her in. At the stroke of nine she rang the bell. A teenage girl opened the door before the bell finished chiming and Jos tried not to look too surprised.

"Hi," the girl said with an impish smile. She stuck her hand out and said, "I'm Erin."

"Jos." She handed her the package, noting the girl seemed to be expecting it.

"Thanks. Come on in. I'll show you where you want to set up."

Jos guessed Erin was sixteen or seventeen. Her dark hair, almond-shaped eyes and slight build suggested she was at least partially of Asian descent. Jos's thoughts immediately went to Bridget as a teenager. She hoped she would never allow strangers into their home.

Erin took her through the foyer into a great room. The back wall was a series of French doors that led to a wide balcony.

Artwork and pottery from around the world was prominently displayed on shelves and stands. Jos guessed that Erin's parents spent time out of country. She wondered if they had any idea that their daughter was such an entrepreneur. Her question was answered when a distinguished Asian gentleman in a suit and tie appeared.

"Jos, this is my dad, Henry."

They shook hands as he said, "Hello, Jos. I just wanted to stay long enough to meet you. Can't be too careful these days."

"Dad," Erin said, rolling her eyes.

"No, Erin," Jos agreed, "I'm with your dad. I have a nine-year-old daughter. I totally get it."

"Nice to meet you," Henry said. "And just so you know, the house is outfitted with cameras. They're not in the bathroom, of course, but you are being filmed. Periodically during the day I'll check the footage until Erin tells me you've left. You seem like a nice person, and I hope you understand."

"I do," Jos said emphatically. "I would probably do the same thing," she added, although she doubted she would ever allow Bridget to chaperone complete strangers in their home.

He kissed Erin, grabbed a briefcase Jos had failed to notice and left with a wave. Erin led her to the balcony, which provided an unobstructed view of the giant track a hundred yards away. An inviting wicker patio set with comfortable chaise lounges sat in the corner. She glanced up at the sun. If the testing didn't start within the hour, it would be incredibly difficult to get the shot.

Erin went to the far side of the balcony and put the sun to her back. "Okay, so you'll want to angle your camera this way. It's hard to tell whether they'll run the test clockwise or counterclockwise, but you want to snap just as they hit that curve right there. The one that's perpendicular to that building." She spoke with her hands like she was directing a film. "There's no other place. When GM figured out the carparazzi had a friend in the neighborhood, moi," she said, pointing proudly to herself, "they got smart and started moving the testing times around. It's usually still before lunch, but sometimes they wait until three or four o'clock in the afternoon when it's really hard to get a good shot."

Jos nodded and started unpacking her gear. She thought it might be like this. Fortunately she was patient and had brought a book.

"Would you like some coffee and a pastry?"

"Sure," she said. "That would be great."

By the time she'd set up her tripod, Erin had returned with a tray and two cups. She sat down on one of the chaise lounges and said, "Okay, ask me your questions."

Jos was surprised. She did have questions, but she hadn't intended to probe for answers. She sipped her coffee and joined her on the chaise lounge. "Okay, so I have a daughter a little younger than you. Why aren't you in school?"

She smiled. "Usually I have very good attendance, so if I'm absent once in a while, it doesn't hurt my grades."

"What year in school?"

"I'm a junior. One more to go."

"How did you get involved in this?"

She glanced at the track in the distance and stretched out on the chaise. "That's a creepy story. I'm guessing they were watching me for a while. One day I was out at the mall going to the movies. I was waiting by the parking lot for some friends, and this guy comes up to me. He looked like a normal guy. He wasn't wearing sunglasses or a trench coat or anything suspicious. He handed me his card. His name was Mr. Brent and he owned an advertising company. He told me he had a business arrangement for my family if we were interested. He said it wasn't anything illegal, just an opportunity to make a lot of money because our house overlooked the GM Proving Grounds. Really he wanted to hire our house."

Erin grabbed a pastry and nibbled on a corner before continuing. "He said to call him and make an appointment. He emphasized that the amount of money he was talking about could pay for college. When I told my dad that part, he told me to make the appointment. We went to Detroit and met with him at his office. It was obvious he really was part of a downtown ad firm with multiple offices around the world. The deal was simple. He'd call us about once every two months and need to have the house available for a photographer to take pictures of the proving grounds when GM ran its tests. We learned that before our subdivision was built, this used to be a hill and a lot of photographers camped out here waiting for GM to test their cars. For allowing his clients to use our house, we'd be compensated. If at any time we felt uncomfortable, we could end the arrangement. My dad's a lawyer and he checked it out, and since it was legal we decided to do it."

"Have you ever told Mr. Brent no?"

She laughed and said, "Well, one time we almost said no. We were going out of town on a family trip. But the client wanted the pictures so badly Mr. Brent doubled the price. My dad stayed back and missed the first day of our trip. It's been a good deal for us. We've worked with him for about a year and most of my college is paid for."

Although Jos was curious to know the family's income from renting their house, she thought it improper to ask. "Do you have a specific college in mind?"

"I want to go to Caltech and study computers. I might change my mind about the location, but I'm set on the computer idea."

"That's great. I was a computer science major."

Her eyes lit up. "Awesome! Then you'll want to see this."

She jumped up and retrieved the package Jos had brought. She tore off the brown wrapping and packing tape. Inside was a RAM board surrounded by bubble gum.

Jos laughed. "That's pretty ingenious. Instead of packing peanuts, he uses Double Bubble."

"It's my favorite," Erin said, holding up the board. "Take a look at this. I'm building a supercomputer and this is the next piece."

"That's gonna be some computer," Jos said, figuring the board was worth several thousand dollars.

"When Mr. Brent found out I was into computers, he started adding a computer part as part of the payment. Each time someone shows up, I get another piece."

They both admired the board a little longer and Jos said casually, "Do you remember the name of Mr. Brent's company?"

"Uh, I think it's something like Elevate," she replied as she studied the intricate wiring of the board.

"Who's Mr. Brent's client? Is it a magazine?"

"No, not a magazine. He works with different auto companies, obviously not GM."

"Do you remember which ones?"

"Um, I'm not sure. We never went back after the first meeting. There were some signs in his office…" Erin looked up and Jos could tell she was trying to remember. "There was Ford, Hyundai, Renault, Chrysler, Toyota. There might've been a few more." She shrugged and her attention returned to the board. "Wanna see my computer?"

"Sure. As long as I don't miss the shot."

"You won't." She grabbed a pair of binoculars from a shelf and went to the edge of the balcony. "They have a series of protocols they follow. The engineers come out and walk around the car with their tablets. Then the driver comes out. There's lot of joking around. As long as we check back every fifteen minutes or so, you'll be ready."

"Okay, let's look at your computer."

They went upstairs to her room and she showed Jos the partially built computer. Jos asked her several questions and she explained the design. The conversation convinced Jos that Caltech would be lucky to have Erin as a student.

She glanced through the window and thought of Nellie. *Where is she?* "Do any of your other neighbors allow photographers to set up on their balconies?"

"No. When GM realized what we were doing, they sent some men to go door to door throughout the neighborhood to all the homeowners who had a view of Black Lake. They convinced everyone to sign a good neighbor agreement and gave each owner ten thousand dollars. They didn't bother with us. They knew we wouldn't take the deal."

Jos did the math and said, "Ten thousand isn't very much."

"It's not," Erin agreed, "but these guys were persuasive and intimidating. Then as the houses went up for sale, GM bought them and gave them to employees. They also bought up a bunch of the condos on the other side of the track."

Jos peered at the row of white buildings and noticed six pine trees. "Why did they plant those trees?"

Erin shrugged. "I don't know. I think they're new. Weird."

Jos excused herself and resumed her post on the balcony while Erin stayed upstairs working on her computer. Jos popped a piece of Double Bubble into her mouth and leaned back on the chaise lounge, enjoying the quiet. Very rarely did she have an opportunity to sit and think. Working and parenting required all of her energy each day, and by the time Myles and Bridget were in bed, all she wanted to do was watch an hour of mindless television before she went to sleep.

She couldn't remember the last time she'd been this relaxed on a weekday. Her brain started connecting pieces. It was more than coincidental that Mr. Brent had orchestrated this opportunity and suggested how she could acquire Nellie's journal. Nellie hadn't been pleased to see her, was in fact surprised, and now Jos understood why. She'd thought this shoot was an exclusive.

She grabbed the binoculars and scanned the other decks. A few people were out enjoying the morning but none of them were Carparazzi, and Nellie was nowhere in sight. She followed the line of the GM track until she landed on the condo complex. Some of those balconies had a great view, except for the one behind the stand of trees. Something clicked in her mind and she remembered Willie mentioning a condo in Milford. If the one behind the trees belonged to the Raffertys, it would explain why, at Lucky's, Nellie had been so angry. Not only had she lost her exclusive, she'd lost her vantage point as well.

She put the binoculars down and resumed her pose on the lounge. Where was Nellie? Maybe the blonde had distracted her from the shoot. Or Mr. Brent. Assuming that was true, then Mr. Brent had deliberately pitted Jos against Nellie twice. That meant Jos was being used, and she didn't like that idea at all. She thought about their meeting at Lucky's. She'd seemed to care about Myles's problem with his coach, and she gave incredible neck rubs. If she hadn't run off with the blonde, Jos would've asked her to dance.

She took out her phone and tried to call her but it went straight to voice mail. She left a message, telling Nellie that she wanted to talk as well. She urged her to call back as soon as possible. She sighed and cracked her book, hoping to lose herself in the latest Marie Castle novel. A few shape-shifters were exactly what she needed to pass the time.

CHAPTER FIFTEEN

Paris, France

Nellie had never flown in a private jet so she wasn't prepared for the pampering and attention provided by the two flight attendants. She and Felice were the only guests on the plane. The attendants catered to their every whim, even whims Nellie didn't know she had, such as consuming expensive French champagne at thirty thousand feet. She enjoyed it immensely but she quickly recognized it was a ploy by Felice to get her into bed.

The jet belonged to Jacques Perreault, the CEO of Argent. Nellie imagined Felice was a regular in the king-sized bed that adjoined the more traditional outer cabin. While Felice continued to flirt and remind her of their liaison in the limo, Nellie found herself recoiling, her thoughts consumed by the phone message from her father.

After he'd proclaimed people would die, he'd handed the phone back to Mai who confirmed that no one was dying at the moment. He was obviously remembering something from his past. She wondered if the incident would be mentioned in his journal. She needed to check it out when she returned home. It would take hours, possibly days, to understand all of the notes and ramblings, something she'd avoided doing for so long. Then there was the reply she'd received from Jos. At least they were agreeing they needed to talk. Perhaps Jos could help her with the journal. She chuckled to herself at the irony.

Felice eventually stopped flirting and retreated to the lounger on the other side of the cabin where she furiously flipped through the pages of French fashion magazines to quell her sex drive.

Nellie imagined Jos was presently staked out, capturing the new Camaro's test run. Wherever she was located, Nellie doubted her view was obstructed.

She stood up and stretched, relieving the pressure on her sciatic nerve. Long plane rides were definitely aggravating her back. She pulled the letter from GM out of her pocket and reread the simple sentence. *Do you like our trees?* No, she didn't. Not at all. The message was disturbing for a few reasons. The relationship between the manufacturers and the carparazzi was professional but complicated. They needed each other to survive, just as celebrities thrived on the publicity and attention from the paparazzi.

She sat down and closed her eyes. She'd never been so brazenly taunted by an automaker. She couldn't wait to show the message to Willie during one of his more lucid hours. He'd be livid. She also couldn't help but feel that there was a force working against her—and for Jos. They'd been pitted against each other with Jos the victor more often than not. The situation with Lucy was proof. She'd given Nellie the exclusive on the Camaro. No one knew more about the inner workings of Milford than the Lucky family. If Lucy said it was an exclusive, it was. Yet someone had learned of the test and urged GM to plant the trees, thus thwarting Nellie's payday. Possibly that party had given the opportunity to Jos. Why?

Lost in her thoughts she didn't notice Felice until she'd practically crawled onto her lap. Just like a cat. She smiled politely and was about to tell Felice she needed to use the restroom, but Felice took Nellie's hand and placed it on her breast. She'd deliberately worn a tiny black leather skirt with a cream silk blouse and a black bra underneath. All of the blouse's buttons were undone and Nellie realized the bra was made of leather.

"The panties match," Felice whispered.

She licked Nellie's ear and trailed kisses down her jaw on the way to her lips. Nellie fondled her, enjoying the touch of the leather, as smooth and buttery as the interior of the Corvette. She imagined Felice straddling her in the Corvette's little bucket seat, naked and sitting on her haunches.

Then her conscience reminded her that Felice was twenty-one. She pulled away and attempted to button the silk blouse but her fingers were shaking. Felice grinned knowingly and grasped her hand. She licked the inside of her wrist, making swirls with her tongue.

Nellie felt her defenses wobble. Whatever resistance she had was wearing down quickly. It was nearly impossible to believe Felice was so young. Perhaps it was the French influence, but most women she'd known were not as skillful with their tongue as Felice.

Recognizing she'd cracked Nellie's resolve, Felice once again returned Nellie's hand to her breast. Her grin widened when Nellie reached around and unhooked her bra. She hopped off Nellie's lap and headed for the bedroom, leaving a trail of clothes along the way. By the time she reached the doorway, she wore only her stilettos and panties. As she'd promised, they were black leather as well. She leaned against the doorjamb and slid her hand down her belly under the leather panties. Her eyes closed and her mouth hung open as she writhed in pleasure.

Nellie couldn't move. She couldn't turn away either. Felice's show was both captivating and overpowering. Eventually Felice threw her head back and cried out in ecstasy. When she recovered, she wriggled out of her panties, strutted to Nellie in her stilettos and dropped them in her lap.

* * *

"This is the captain. We will be landing at Le Bourget Airfield in ten minutes. Everyone please return to your seats."

"Don't you dare stop!" Felice ordered. "Make me come once more." she urged.

They were sprawled on the king-sized bed, coiled in a sixty-nine position while fingers and tongues explored. They found a rhythm and quickly finished. In two minutes they were dressed and buckled into their seats. Felice returned to her fashion magazines while Nellie gazed at Paris below her. It was late at night and the City of Lights showed its beauty. She spotted the Eiffel Tower, its form impossible to miss against the night sky.

"Have you ever been to Paris?" Felice asked without looking up from an article on scarves.

"No," Nellie said. "Since there's not any testing done here, I haven't had a reason. Do you like living in Paris?"

The cat-like grin returned. "Of course. It's Paris."

"We're not flying into Charles de Gaulle?"

"No," she said with a disgusted look. "Jacques could never abide all the people. Le Bourget is for private jets only. It's where the Paris Air Show is."

As the plane descended nearer to the ground, Nellie closed her eyes. She was completely spent and landing was her least favorite part of flying.

By the time they stepped off the movable staircase, a Lexus 600hL had pulled up. Nellie's jaw dropped and Felice placed her index finger on Nellie's chin and playfully closed her mouth.

"Time to go to work," Felice said, and Nellie noted a change in her tone.

The driver took their bags and they slid into the back, two contoured leather seats with a console between them. Nellie studied the car's features, which included a DVD screen that dropped from the roof. She leaned back. It was as if the seat molded to her body. She glanced at Felice, who was checking her phone for emails. She tapped in a number, said something in French and hung up.

"How long will it take us to get there?" Nellie asked.

"Not long. We're not going to Argent headquarters in Boulogne. We're going to the Sixth Arrondissement on the Left Bank. This is a very private meeting."

"Why?" Nellie said uncomfortably.

"I cannot say. Enjoy the ride."

With those words Felice again tapped her phone and conversed in French with someone else. The woman who'd masturbated in front of her was gone. The Felice on the phone was closed, clipped and serious. While Nellie knew very little French, she understood tone. Felice wasn't speaking in a subservient voice. She was calling the shots. Perhaps she wasn't a model after all.

She paused from her conversation and leaned toward the driver, giving orders in French. When he nodded, she turned to Nellie. "We're taking the scenic route since we're early. He'll go past Notre Dame and the Louvre before he crosses the Seine."

"Great," Nellie said.

Felice blew her a kiss and returned to her conversation. Nellie gazed out the window, wondering what Jos was doing. She hoped the other carparazzo got the Camaro shot. If it couldn't be herself, she'd want it to be Jos. Nellie imagined her was on a plane headed home to her children, returning to her responsibilities.

And where was she herself? Willie was her responsibility and here she was halfway around the world. Jos had gone to Milford, done her job and quickly returned to Phoenix. So far all Nellie had gotten from the trip was laid. Did that make Jos a more responsible person? Was she a better person? *Yeah, but she copied my journal.* Nellie frowned. She realized she couldn't be upset with Jos for taking advantage. Someone told Jos about the journal. Someone had planned for her to get the Camaro shot. So she went for it. *I would've done the same thing.*

They slowly crawled through the streets of Paris and Nellie people-watched. The Louvre was easily recognizable with its white-light pyramid. When they drove past Notre Dame, Nellie opened the window and leaned out with her camera.

The two towers appeared to be awash in gold, and her zoom lens allowed her to see the intricate designs of the great French Gothic building. The driver slowed as much as he could until the honking horns forced him to accelerate.

It was nearly eleven when they crossed the Seine, but thousands were still out enjoying their Friday night. The Sixth Arrondissement was a wealthy residential area, a collection of apartments, shops and cafés. The Lexus pulled up at the curb of a multicolored five-story building that stretched the length of the block. Window boxes filled with flowers added bursts of color to the already festive exterior. A doorman greeted them and opened the car door for Nellie, who noticed that Felice made no effort to exit.

"You're not coming with me?" Nellie asked.

"No, Jacques insisted this be a private meeting. I think he believed I would be a distraction."

Nellie's gaze automatically drifted to Felice's cleavage and the black leather bra. When she again met Felice's green eyes, she was smiling.

"*Au revoir*, Nellie Rafferty. Until we meet again. Oh, and I left you a little present."

She kissed her cheek and returned to her phone. Nellie felt dismissed and slightly used.

A thought occurred to her. "What about my bag?"

Felice glanced up from her phone. "You won't need it for now. Gaspard will return and take you to your hotel after the meeting."

Nellie turned to Gaspard, her hand gripping the camera bag on her shoulder. "I don't leave this with anyone, anywhere."

Gaspard looked at Felice who nodded her assent. Nellie reached for the patient doorman's waiting hand and exited the limo.

"Oh, Nellie, if Jacques asks about the flight, there's probably something you should know."

"What?"

"I'm his daughter."

CHAPTER SIXTEEN

Sixth Arrondissement, Paris, France

Nellie was still reeling from Felice's revelation as the doorman led her through an opulent lobby with marble floors and matching columns. A circular oak staircase sat behind three old-fashioned elevators that looked like cages for humans. Nellie watched one descend, the elevator's floor coming into view with two passengers on board. At the lobby, the operator opened the accordion-like guard for the exiting guests.

She followed the doorman to a wooden door at the far end of the lobby. He unlocked it and Nellie realized it was a private elevator. He escorted her inside and shut the door before pulling the guard across the front. When he hit a button labeled *A*, Nellie assumed they were traveling to the *auvent*, the penthouse.

The private elevator was encased in paneling with soft lighting that cast shadows in the tiny box. She resisted the urge to pull out her camera and merely smiled at the doorman.

He smiled back and said, "Do you work at Argent?" Nellie noticed he said the *g* like an *h*.

"No, I'm a photographer." She patted her camera bag and he nodded.

"Photographie," he said.

The elevator opened to a small foyer and two enormous glass doors. The doorman rang the bell, and moments later a balding man in a suit greeted them.

"Mademoiselle Rafferty, welcome. I am Luc."

She extended a hand, and he drew it to his lips and kissed it. He gave the doorman a tip and dismissed him before showing Nellie inside.

In the living room, glass and steel tables surrounded white leather sofas, chairs and a chaise lounge. Nellie imagined Felice stretched out on the chaise, sipping red wine, her pale skin nearly matching the showy chaise. Tasteful art and vases added color, but Nellie immediately sensed that despite its decorative flair, no one really lived here.

In the middle of the coffee table sat three wineglasses and a decanter filled with wine. Luc held up one of the glasses and motioned at the carafe. "Might I interest you in a fine Bordeaux?"

"*Oui, merci*," she said, exhausting most of the French she knew.

He poured them both a glass, as well as a third, which indicated someone else would join them. She guessed it would be Jacques Perreault.

As he handed her a glass, a voice said, "I hope you're not toasting without me." Nellie and Luc turned to the hallway. Perreault strolled into the living room, his hand extended in greeting. "It is a pleasure, Mademoiselle Rafferty." He kissed her hand but continued to hold it. "You may not believe me, but I am actually a fan of your work, both yours and your father's."

"*Merci*," she replied.

He motioned to the couch. "Please, sit."

She set down her camera bag first and carefully lowered herself onto the edge of the couch, worried the red wine would splash all over the white leather. Luc sat on the sofa opposite her and Perreault took the overstuffed chair at the head of the table.

Perreault sat in the shadows like a specter. She'd only seen pictures of him at public events, such as the unveiling of a new car. He was incredibly handsome with dark, wavy hair, a strong chin and an angular face. She wondered if Felice had inherited her piercing green eyes from her father but the lighting was too dim to tell. She didn't know much else about him except that he had a legendary temper, and that he was ruthless. It was rumored he'd hurled a paperweight through a glass door after learning she'd scooped him a third time.

He tugged at the cuffs of his shirt and smoothed out his jacket front before accepting a glass of wine from Luc. For the moment he was smiling and happy. He raised his glass and said, "Here's to new friends and prosperous opportunities."

She toasted and took a sip. The French Bordeaux was exquisite and she imagined it was the most expensive wine she'd ever consumed.

"It is good, no?" Jacques asked.

"It's spectacular," she said honestly.

"Excellent. I'm sure you would like to know why you're here."

"I'm very curious."

He leaned back in the chair and swirled the wine like an expert. When he looked up and met her gaze, his smile was gone. "I want to hire you. I'd like you to become Argent's official photographer."

She nearly spewed her wine across the table. She pursed her lips to prevent a huge laugh from escaping. "I'm very surprised. Why would you want to hire me?"

"It is clear you are better than my security team. Three times you revealed my designs before they were announced. It is true, no?"

She chose her words carefully. "I'm not sure it's a matter of being better than your team, but I'm a good planner and sometimes I get lucky too."

He smiled. "You are humble. You're the best, Nellie Rafferty. I want the best on my team. It's that simple. What do you say?"

He raised his glass and Luc immediately thrust his into the air as well. Nellie set hers down.

"Wait. There's a lot more that goes into a deal like this. If you want me to seriously consider this offer, I need to know my salary, my job expectations—"

"Of course."

He nodded at Luc, who reached for an envelope on the sofa table behind him. He handed it to her and she withdrew a single piece of paper. Clearly the French were far less verbose than Americans when it came to contracts. There was no small print, no forms in triplicate or places to initial. Four sentences spelled out how she would lead her life while employed by Argent.

The deal was simple. She would be paid one million American dollars each year for the next three years not to photograph any model made by Argent except when explicitly requested to do so by Argent officials. She would be on call to photograph all Argent PR shoots. The contract went into effect the moment she signed and ended three calendar years from that signing. The last sentence stated that if during that time, any unauthorized pictures of an Argent vehicle were sold to a magazine, the deal would be forfeited and she would be required to return all monies received since the signing.

She reread it three times. Once she was sure she understood, she looked up. Luc was holding out a pen. She held up her hand and shook her head.

"So, you're paying me not to do my job, and if anyone else manages to get a shot and sell it, you're also holding me accountable for that as well?"

Luc shrugged. "Within reason. We will expect you to do your best and use all of your contacts to our advantage."

Perreault continued. "You may spy on other vehicles and scoop their publicity." His smile broadened and he added, "In fact, we would appreciate you doing so. But when it comes to Argent, you will be loyal to us. We will not see our cars on the cover of *Car and Driver* before we want them on the cover."

His sharp tone suggested he was reliving the last time. She'd scooped Argent's SUV, the Aventure. That was supposedly when the paperweight went through the door.

"So, to be clear, I won't spy on Argent, I'll prevent everyone else from spying on Argent, I'll spy on everyone else, and when you need pictures taken, you'll call me and I'll be your main photographer."

Perreault nodded. "That's it exactly. And for your efforts we will pay you one million dollars a year."

"Plus health benefits," Luc added, "for you and Willie."

"What if there's a conflict? What if you want me here in France and there's a different job elsewhere I want to take?"

"Then you come to us," Luc answered. "We are first."

Perreault glanced at his watch. Clearly this meeting had passed his allotted time for it. She sensed he was agitated that she hadn't just accepted the pen from Luc and signed immediately.

She studied them carefully. Luc's left leg was bouncing uncontrollably. He was nervous. Perreault stared at her. He was used to getting his way. People were easily intimidated by him. People that weren't Nellie.

"Why?" she asked.

"Why?" he repeated.

"Exactly. Why now? Why me? I appreciate your faith in me, but most auto manufacturers wouldn't hire a member of the carparazzi. In fact, none of them have."

He leaned forward, expertly weaving the stem of his wineglass between his fingers. The movement was so fluid and natural that Nellie found herself momentarily fascinated.

"That should be obvious to you. You are the best, at least for now," he repeated. "You have beaten me and I'm tired of it. Instead of fighting you, I want you to join our team. It's that simple."

"Would this offer have anything to do with the new proving ground in Arizona?"

He sipped his wine unhurriedly, savoring the taste and unwilling to sacrifice its sweet pleasure to answer her question. Eventually he said, "Perhaps. It certainly would be convenient to have you so close since I foresee many photo opportunities in the future."

"Are you working on a new prototype?"

He studied her before he said, "I will answer that question after you accept my offer. To tell you more before you are a member of the Argent team would be foolish. I'm sure you understand."

"I do."

He set his glass down and leaned forward. "I will assure you, Mademoiselle Rafferty, that if you join Argent, you will be a part of one of the most exciting releases in the history of the automobile—"

Luc coughed loudly and Jacques abruptly recoiled. He held up his hands and said, "I get carried away. Fortunately Luc looks after me." He nodded at his number two, and Luc refilled their glasses.

Nellie's curiosity was piqued, but she wanted to verify his comments with her sources. "I appreciate your very generous offer, but I'll need some time to think about it."

Perreault stared at her. "How much time?"

"I'll let you know by the end of next week. Again, I very much appreciate the offer and your hospitality, but this would be a significant change for me."

"Because you are used to doing things your way, no?"

She nodded. "Yes. I'm a freelancer."

"How has that been working out for you lately?" Luc asked casually.

Suddenly Nellie was on edge. She sat up straight like an animal in danger. "What do you mean?"

The two men exchanged a glance and Perreault said, "I heard there were some trees planted in front of your condo in Milford." He chuckled. "That's unfortunate."

"And we've heard of another woman in the carparazzi. Jos Grant? Do you know her? There's a rumor that she has the Rafferty journal. That must have been quite a shock."

Nellie felt the room shrinking. It was like she was in a cage. "What are you telling me? Did you plant those trees?"

Both men laughed heartily. Luc said, "I assure you, mademoiselle, we don't plant trees." The laughter died away and he finished with, "But we do pay people to plant them. And sometimes we also join forces with our auto colleagues to stop carparazzi."

Perreault added, "Jos Grant seems like a lovely woman. A mother with children to feed, looking to make her mark." His face was hard when he said, "I think you've met your match in her. We will help you or we will help her."

Nellie set her glass down in fear that she might hurl it across the room. "You're threatening me?"

"No," Luc scoffed. "Not at all. Just stating facts. We want to help you. You are Argent's choice, but in the event you don't want to help us, we will find another way."

Perreault finished his wine and suddenly set the glass on the table with such force that it broke the stem. He dropped the remains and stood. Light washed across his face and confirmed Felice had inherited her piercing green eyes from her father. "You've humiliated us three times, Mademoiselle Rafferty. It will not happen again. We will expect your decision soon. *Bonne nuit*," he offered before disappearing down the hall.

She gently set her wineglass on the table to make a point. Luc saw that her hands weren't shaking and she wasn't rattled by Perrault's histrionics. She looked squarely at Luc and said, "Anything else?"

"No," he said.

He stood and she followed him to the door. With his hand on the knob, he said, "Be smart, Mademoiselle Rafferty. We are offering you an incredible opportunity."

He opened the door and she was surprised to see the doorman standing by the elevator. She guessed Argent had no trust in her ability to exit the building without photographing something.

By the time the doorman had escorted her to the street she was deep in thought. She slid into the Lexus and closed her eyes. She tried to sort out the tangles of what had just occurred as they drove through the streets of Paris, but her mind was sluggish. Perhaps she was in shock or maybe it was the high alcohol content of the Bordeaux. All she could conclude was that everything was related. Jos and the journal. GM planting the trees. The package Lucy gave to Jos.

Lucy. She glanced at her watch. It was seven p.m. in Milford. Lucy wouldn't have much time to chat. "I shouldn't be selfish," Nellie mumbled quietly so the driver couldn't hear her. "I shouldn't be, but I am," she said as she tapped at her phone.

Lucy answered on the fourth ring. Nellie could hear the murmur of the bar patrons in the background. "This better be important, Nellie. I have a full bar and only two hands."

"You have great hands," Nellie said seductively.

"Are you drunk?" Lucy spat.

"Don't hang up on me," Nellie pleaded. "I'm sorry about the other night. I shouldn't have yelled at you."

"Apology accepted. Are we done?"

"Did you ever want a relationship with me?" she blurted. When Lucy said nothing, she repeated, "Did you?"

Suddenly the bar noise evaporated and Nellie knew she'd gone into her office. "Why are you asking me this? Why now? We've been pals for twenty-five years."

Nellie could hear the anger in her voice, and she didn't want to press her too hard. "What you said last night in the parking lot. It made me think you wanted more."

Nellie heard several gasps of frustration before Lucy could speak. "Leave this alone, Nellie. Whatever we might've had is long over. There's no point in bringing it up now."

Suddenly Nellie's Bordeaux-induced buzz was gone. "Bring up what? Why—"

"Leave it alone, Nellie," Lucy pleaded.

"I need to know."

Lucy sighed. "Do you remember the second time you visited Milford, around December of nineteen ninety? You were twenty-two and I was twenty-six?"

Nellie clearly remembered the first time they'd met. The conversation went on for much of the night and ended with a drive to the woods in Lucy's Oldsmobile. They'd tested the backseat for several hours. That image was clear to her, but there were a few dozen visits over the last two and a half decades. Bits and pieces of memories she couldn't separate. She finally said, "I'm not sure…"

"You and Willie came up for some GM unveiling. We joked about the idea that I should come back to Phoenix with you. It was so damn cold and you said I needed a Phoenix winter."

Nellie recalled that conversation. They'd had sex at the house of one of Lucy's friends. The friend was away and it was too cold to lounge in the Oldsmobile.

"You said you couldn't come back with us," Nellie summarized.

Lucy chuckled before she said, "That would be the way you remember it."

"What do you mean?" Nellie pressed.

"Are you sure you want to go there?"

"Yes!" She realized she was shouting and said, "Sorry. Please tell me."

The Lexus driver glanced at her through the rearview mirror but quickly returned his eyes to the road. Nellie found the switch that raised the privacy partition.

"Okay, so here's what happened," Lucy said. "You asked me to go to Phoenix and I said that sounded great. You weren't leaving for another week and we kept talking about it. We even started to make plans for me to stay indefinitely. I actually sold a few things, like my guitar and my bike. Do you remember now?"

"I do," she said. Her memory suddenly had enough information to fill in the details. "We'd made the plan, but the day before we left, you showed up at the condo and said you couldn't go. I remember being so disappointed and we both started to cry. But then you kinda brushed it off and said that we could still have fun whenever I came to Milford."

"That's right," Lucy said quietly. "Then the phone rang. It was your dad saying that he and my dad were stuck in Detroit because of a snowstorm and they wouldn't be back until morning. We had the condo to ourselves for a whole night."

"Yeah, that was really convenient."

"Not really," Lucy said. "I think your dad wanted us to have one more night together. I think he wanted to assuage his guilty conscience."

Nellie closed her eyes. She dreaded the next question since she was rather certain she knew the answer. "Why did he feel guilty?"

"Do I really need to say it? He was the one who asked me not to come. Said it would break your mother's Catholic heart to see us carrying on. He knew we were in love and it was obvious to anyone who spent five minutes around us. We'd never be able to hide it from her."

Anger bubbled in her gut. "Why didn't you tell me that?"

Lucy groaned. "I don't know. Probably because Willie was like a second father to me. He was family. I loved you but I couldn't cause a rift in your family. If I'd told you what Willie said, you would've confronted him. You were younger and I was a little older. I knew your relationship with your parents was more important than what we had, especially since you wanted to take his spot in the carparazzi."

"You had no right to make that decision for me."

"Probably not, but I figured we'd each find someone else eventually."

"Well, we didn't," Nellie snapped.

"Uh, actually that's not true. There was someone really special to me for a long time, and now I've met someone else."

Nellie couldn't believe this. She shook her head. "So, you screwed around with me while you were with someone?"

"No," Lucy explained. "You don't have a great sense of time, Nellie. Sometimes we don't see each other for two or three years, and just because we see each other, doesn't mean we hook up. I've always been faithful when I've been involved, which is why I wasn't going to sleep with Jos. I'm devoted to Robin. Besides," she said with a pause, "I think Jos is taken."

Nellie felt the hair on her neck stand up. "What did she say? Is she getting back together with her ex?"

"Whoa, whoa," Lucy laughed. "I was talking about you, dummy. She wants you and I think you want her. It's time to stop running, my friend. Gotta go."

She hung up before Nellie could reply. Nellie gazed out the window at the Eiffel Tower. She suddenly remembered they were on their way to the hotel. She had no desire to spend another minute in France. She needed to process everything Lucy had told her, including her feelings for Jos. Perrault's words echoed in her mind. I think you've met your match in her. We will help you or we will help her. There was also a new emotion, one she'd never experienced. She was furious with Willie.

She lowered the partition and said to the driver, "Take me to deGaulle Airport now."

"But mademoiselle—"

"Now!"

CHAPTER SEVENTEEN

Mesa, Arizona

Jos pulled up to Colleen's townhouse but hesitated before she shut off the van. Colleen had called and asked her to come right over. They had things to discuss but she wouldn't say what those things were on the phone.

Her thoughts swirled. She was sure Nellie was with the blonde. Jos had awakened Sunday morning to her phone buzzing. Still half asleep when she answered, she'd had a short conversation with Nellie, who was desperate to talk with her. When Jos suggested she come right over, she stammered that she couldn't. When pressed for further details, Jos learned she was in the Paris airport waiting for a return flight to Phoenix, having just visited Jacques Perreault. It turned out the blonde, Felice, was his daughter. How convenient.

She flipped the ignition off but didn't emerge from the van. She visualized Nellie approaching Felice at Lucky's Place. There had been palpable hostility. Then Felice melted Nellie's anger and led her away like a puppy following its master. Jos was sure they'd had sex, which would account for Nellie's incoherence every time Jos mentioned Felice.

Perhaps sleeping around was common among carparazzi members. She kept that thought in the forefront of her mind as she strolled to Colleen's door and pressed the button. She glanced back at the street, noting that Kelly's Land Rover wasn't there. She usually parked on the street since it was a gated community and Colleen rarely kept the garage clean enough to house two cars. *Good. We'll be alone.*

Colleen opened the door dressed in workout attire. Her body shone with perspiration and her hair was plastered against her head. "Hey, come in," she said, out of breath. "Just got back from a run."

Colleen shut the door behind her and pulled her into a smoldering kiss. "I've missed you."

"Me too," Jos said automatically. Although Colleen smelled a little ripe from her run, it still felt good to hold her.

Colleen pursed her lips and Jos grew wary. It was one of her tells, and it signaled she was about to say something Jos probably wouldn't like. Jos raised an eyebrow. "What?"

"I told Kelly about us."

Jos was stunned. "You did? How did she react?"

Colleen tightened her grip around Jos's waist and kissed her neck. She whispered in her ear, "She's upstairs in the tub waiting for us."

"Us? Colleen—" She stepped away from the hug.

"Jos, c'mon. Give it a try. Before I left you suggested an open relationship. How is this different?"

Jos glanced at the stairway to make sure Kelly wasn't in earshot. "There's a big difference between two people and three. Remember, I had a threesome in college. I know how complicated it can become."

Colleen rolled her eyes and pulled Jos back into her arms. "That was college. We're all older and more mature."

"How old is Kelly?"

"She's twenty-nine." Colleen held her face between her palms. "I know how lonely you've been. I've missed you a ton, babe. This might actually be our answer," she said sincerely.

"I don't know…" Jos was unsure but Colleen knew her well enough to know she was on the fence. Colleen just needed to push her off.

Colleen took her hand and led her up the stairs. "Just try it once."

Jos had never seen the condo's upstairs, so her gaze flitted about. Colleen led her into the oversized master bedroom where a little pile of workout clothes sat near the foot of the bed.

"Get in here," Kelly called. "The jets are so relaxing."

Colleen stripped off her shorts and tank top and entered the bathroom, but Jos lingered in the doorway. A bubble bath had been drawn and Kelly lounged in the Jacuzzi tub, her breasts floating on the top of the foam.

"Hi, Jos," she said warmly.

"Hi," Jos squeaked, not sure where to focus her eyes.

Colleen crawled into the foam and cuddled next to Kelly. Jos remained in the doorway, feeling like an intruder. Kelly was certainly as beautiful as Felice and probably just as smart. Colleen had said she was in line to be the first lawyer at the firm to make partner before she was thirty. Kelly broke their kiss and fixed her gaze on Jos.

"Join us," she said, motioning to the empty spot next to her.

Her bright blue eyes invited Jos to the party. She slipped out of her clothes while they both watched and climbed into the tub. The water was perfect and the jets instantly soothed her. She locked eyes with Colleen and that was enough. Her anxiety disappeared as she settled next to Kelly, who seemed entirely at ease sitting between two women who had shared children and a life.

"Kiss me," Kelly said to Jos.

Jos obliged. Kelly's breath smelled like peppermint. The kiss continued and she pulled Jos onto her lap. Colleen floated behind Jos and caressed her breasts.

Kelly shifted just enough to slip a finger inside Jos. Her tongue matched the rhythm and Jos started to rock against

Kelly's leg. Colleen pinched her nipples, reaching the border between erotic and painful. She tried to let go but she felt claustrophobic sandwiched between the two of them. Despite the touching, licking and stroking, Jos's motor died. She didn't know what to do. She couldn't imagine pushing them away without making a scene. "Think of Nellie," she murmured.

"What did you say?" Colleen asked.

Jos blinked. Her worst nightmare had come true. She'd always known her incessant talking to herself would get her in trouble.

"Who's Nellie?" Kelly asked with a grin. "Should we call her? Foursomes are even better than threesomes."

"I can't," Jos said, pushing them both away. She floated to the opposite side of the Jacuzzi. "I'm sorry, but I don't think this is going to work."

"Don't give up so quickly," Kelly said.

A small metal box sat near a tall pillar candle. Kelly withdrew a match and lit the candle. She reached back into the box and withdrew a joint she lit with the burning candle. After taking a long toke, she handed it to Colleen who did the same and handed it back to Kelly.

"Care to partake?" Kelly asked. "It might loosen you up and we could try again."

Jos looked around. "Where are the kids?"

"They're with your mom at the Science Center until four," Colleen replied.

Kelly floated to Jos and put the joint between her lips. "Smoke up. It's a great buzz."

She took a hit and passed the joint back to Kelly. She immediately felt the effect and the room started to spin. Kelly and Colleen chatted about work, but Jos was content to lean back in the tub and forget about everything for a while. At least she tried to forget about everything. She wondered what Nellie would think if she knew about the threesome. She'd told Colleen the truth. It wasn't her first threesome. There'd been one in college and another with her first roommate and her girlfriend. Neither of them was great, but she wasn't quite as sheltered as

Nellie might think. After all, Jos's mother hadn't even bothered to marry her father.

Eventually Jos's thoughts led back to Felice. It wasn't that she considered Felice a threat. Quite the opposite. Felice was a reminder of what Nellie was—a player. And a reminder of what Nellie wanted—a good time.

Jos looked around the bathroom. Kelly and Colleen had discarded the joint and were going at it as if she weren't there. Their hands were busy under the foam while their lips and tongues made loud slurping noises. She was definitely the odd woman out. She stared at them and realized it was completely and totally over with Colleen. Maybe she belonged with Kelly and maybe not. But it was no longer Jos's concern.

She sighed and pulled herself from the tub. She dried off and pulled on her clothes just as Colleen cried out and screamed for more. She headed downstairs and out the door. Neither of them called to her. They didn't even realize she'd left.

She climbed into the van and reclined the seat, still too stoned to drive. She thought of Nellie and what it would be like to be with her in a Jacuzzi. A smile came to her face just before she fell asleep.

* * *

"Do you think she's dead?" a young voice asked.

"No, she's just sleeping," an adult replied.

Jos blinked and looked at Myles, Bridget and her mother. She remembered the threesome and the joint. She suddenly sat up and plastered on her mom face. "Hi kids. How was the Science Center?"

"It was fun," Bridget said. She eyed Jos warily. "Are you okay, Mom?"

"I'm fine, sweetie. Just taking a nap. I wasn't feeling well so I rested a bit before I tried to drive."

She kept her gaze focused on her children. She knew if she looked at her mother, she'd crumble. She couldn't lie to Delia Delaware Benton—ever. Bridget cocked her head to one side. "Why are you at Mama C's house?"

Myles made a face. "Yeah, and why do you smell funny?" He looked at Delia. "She smells…what's that word you taught us, Grandma? The word that described the smell at the Grateful Dead concert?"

"Acrid?" Delia offered.

Myles nodded his head. "Yeah, you smell acrid, Mom."

"Pungent also works," Bridget suggested.

"Good choice, B.," Delia agreed.

Jos glared at her mother who grinned back in return. "Kids, Mama C was burning a candle and apparently it's not a good one if it smells acrid and pungent. I'll let her know."

The front door swung open and Colleen and Kelly strode down the walk, dressed in fresh clothes and makeup, completely sober. Bridget and Myles ran to Colleen and Delia leaned on the open window. She wore black pants and a flowing white shirt. Her long blond hair was knotted in a bun and she looked forty instead of fifty-nine. Often when they went out together, people mistook Delia and Jos for sisters, a fact that pleased Delia immensely.

"You want to tell me what was really going on?"

Jos shook her head. "No, I don't want to discuss it. And it doesn't matter anyway because it will never happen again."

Delia squeezed her shoulder. "I'm worried, Josie. You're not happy. I thought you and Colleen were done."

"We are," Jos confirmed adamantly. "I just don't know what's next so I'm replaying the past."

Delia gazed at her lovingly. "Where's your plan? You always have a plan." Jos's eyes filled with tears and she shook her head. "Okay, I'm stepping in. Let me just go tell Colleen and life-size Barbie that we're out of here. Move over. You're in no shape to drive."

Jos crawled over the console, not wanting to get out of the car and face Colleen or Kelly again. Delia returned and they waved goodbye to the kids.

"Where are we going?" Jos asked.

"Where we always go when we need to talk."

Jos slowly navigated the maze of gardens in her mother's front yard. No one ever used the front door except missionaries and salespeople, but most of them found the jungle-like courtyard too daunting and just skipped the small historic house in central Mesa.

She struggled to keep her balance as she followed Delia down the cobblestone path to an old shed that her mother had claimed as her studio years before. Colorful metal sculptures were everywhere, made from upcycled cans, car doors, bedsprings—anything metal. While the shed looked as though it would collapse during a light breeze, her father had added interior supports and drywall so it was habitable. He'd offered to build her mother a new place, but she liked the rustic-looking exterior. Jos and her father just shook their heads and didn't argue.

There was no point in arguing with Delia Delaware Benton. At various points of Jos's life the studio served different purposes. It was where Delia wrote her great American novel, practiced the violin and did yoga. An only child, Jos kidded her that the shed was simply a refuge from Jos during her formative years. Some mothers hid in the bathroom to get privacy. Delia locked herself in the studio.

Once Delia envisioned something, she set out to make it a reality, like her metalworks business. She'd never worked outside the home, but after Jos's father was killed in an accident on U.S. 60 when Jos was twenty-two, Delia realized she needed something to do. She'd received a large settlement from the pipe company whose load had been strewn across three lanes of traffic and caused Doug Grant to smash into the center barrier. So while she had money, time was her enemy.

She became interested in welding after visiting a neighbor who was a professional welder. He gave her a few lessons on using a blowtorch and she set out to make beautiful objets d'art from scraps the neighbor brought home from his various jobs. She designed animals, flowers, pieces of furniture and children's toys during the summer. Then she sold her wares at the various craft fairs throughout the winter when the snowbirds appeared.

Jos plopped onto Delia's "thinking sofa" while her mother ambled behind the workbench and put on her welding gloves. She picked up a metal rat whose eyes were made of steel ball bearings.

"Will someone actually buy that?" she asked.

"They already have. I've been commissioned to create a Cinderella scene for the library."

"Really? I'm impressed. That's awesome."

"Thanks, honey," she said with a smile. She continued to work, moving about the studio, her welding mask perched on her head.

Jos watched Delia scrub the rat with a ball of steel wool, admiring her mother's intense focus on a task. Tenacity was in her genes. She'd inherited her own easygoing attitude from her dad. All in all, she'd been very lucky to have them as parents, despite the fact that they had never married. When she'd come out to them during high school, they weren't surprised. But they cautioned her to be careful since the East Valley was a Mormon stronghold. They wanted her to be herself but they also wanted her to be safe.

"What's going on?" Delia asked. "Did you get the shot in Michigan?"

"I did," Jos said.

Her mother glanced at her quizzically. "And?"

"I've done something bad to another person. Somebody I might care about. It's not bad like murder bad, but because I think I care about her, I feel guilty. And she knows I did it so I'm sure she's angry with me. And there's something weird going on between us other than the bad thing. I think we're both being manipulated by an outside force. That's the part we really need to talk about, but I'm not sure we can get past the bad thing I've done. We've made a plan to see each other, but I don't know if I can face her."

Delia didn't respond immediately. She just stared at Jos objectively. This was why Jos had always confided in her mother. She never judged. She always listened and she only gave a sliver of advice. It was as if she'd pulled the best kernels of wisdom from all the parenting books and thrown the rest away.

"What's the first step?" she asked.

"I guess talk to Nellie. That's her name," she added.

She smiled. "And you're interested in this woman?"

"Yeah." Jos could feel her cheeks redden. It was always easier acknowledging her feelings with her mother. "She's carparazzi too."

"Hmm."

She knew what her mother was thinking. "You're wondering why I started up with Colleen again when I'm interested in Nellie."

Delia shrugged but kept buffing her metal rat.

"I'm done with Colleen, and a part of me thinks I should just put Nellie out of my mind. Maybe I just need someone a bit like Colleen, someone who wants a family."

Delia gazed at her thoughtfully before she asked, "How important is it to you that you find someone and go back to being a family under one roof? Is that how you define family?"

Jos hadn't considered that part. "I just want Myles and Bridget to be happy, to feel loved. I don't care how that's achieved."

"Can you put Nellie out of your mind? Is she easily forgettable?"

Jos laughed. "Nellie Rafferty is anything but forgettable. She's exciting and laid-back at the same time. And she has this amazing car collection!"

Delia grinned and Jos realized she was shouting in the tiny studio. She had her answer. She couldn't push Nellie aside, or the feelings that surfaced whenever they were together. She had to explore. She had to know.

"Anything else you need from me?" Delia asked.

Jos jumped up from the sofa and put her hands on her hips. She felt refreshed and invigorated. "How do you do it?"

"How do I do what?"

"How do you make parenting look so easy?"

Delia's smile broadened. "Practice," she said. She flipped the welding mask back over her face and grabbed her blowtorch.

CHAPTER EIGHTEEN

Nellie threw her pen across her home office and watched it bounce off the bookcase. She cradled her head in her hands. She'd been tense since her return from Paris yesterday. She'd spent the entire flight trying to recall that day in the condo with Lucy twenty-five years before. The details were fuzzy and it was impossible to remember the exact words spoken. They'd cried, hugged and Nellie had left. She frequently remembered something happened on the flight home...something sexual. Had one of the flight attendants flirted her? Another passenger?

She hadn't shared that fact with Lucy on the phone. It represented something Nellie had learned about herself during her adult life—very few situations left an indelible imprint on her. She didn't remember incidents or people deeply. Emotions were fleeting, and with the exception of a few memories, such as the day her mother died, few events stayed with her after they occurred. She was already moving forward to whatever happened next.

Upon arriving home from Paris, she'd found Willie in bed, sick with a fever. He was now asleep, snoring softly, a blanket pulled up to his chin and his spindly arms across his chest. He was so frail. She imagined this was what he would look like when he died. All of the questions she wanted to ask and the confrontation she'd rehearsed fizzled away at the sight of him.

She rubbed her eyes and returned to the journal. Paper surrounded her—on the desktop, at her feet and taped to the walls nearby. After a cleansing breath she got up and retrieved the pen. She stared at the mess. She'd copied Willie's journal several times once she recognized that a single story or anecdote was often mentioned in different places using various details. She put the related pages together, creating paper caterpillars all over the office. She realized the journal was documentation of his fading mind. His final entries were nearly two years old and most were incomplete and nearly illegible. It looked as though he'd forgotten how to make some of the letters in the alphabet.

She knew those pages would be of little use, but the majority of the journal, specifically the stories, might provide clues to his recent agitation and belief that people would die. She glanced at her yellow legal pad. She made a list of the odd things he'd mentioned over the course of the last two months. Meetings. People dying. Ralph.

He'd known so many members of the carparazzi and auto industry throughout his life. He'd meticulously listed names and private phone numbers because getting past secretaries was his forte. He'd charm them with his good looks and friendly attitude. He'd always said to her, "Nell, remember the secretaries, janitors and security guards deserve as much respect as anyone else, more so if you want something from them. And in this line of work, you always want something." He didn't need to list those names. Up until the last decade, his mind was sharp and he never forgot a face. His love of people was evident.

Why couldn't you love me enough to let me have a girlfriend?

A teardrop hit the yellow pad. She automatically backed away and closed her eyes. "Don't let it get to you."

She steadied her emotions and strolled around the room, examining its nondescript contents as if she were touring the Louvre. It was hard to believe she'd driven by the Louvre just two days ago. Maybe someday she'd go back and really see the beautiful sights. Several times during their drive to the Left Bank, she'd wanted to jump out of the Lexus with her camera and play tourist.

Luc already had left a voice mail, wondering if she'd reached a decision. She glanced into the living room. Willie sat in his favorite chair, Chevy at his side, with his head between his paws. Nellie and Mai had grudgingly allowed him to return to his chair in the living room now that his fever had broken.

If she took the job with Argent, everything would be so much easier and she could spend more time with Willie. They would certainly have enough money to live, and she'd take only a few side jobs to keep things interesting. She was tired and her body certainly didn't move the way it did when she was thirty. She remembered the day in Death Valley, sitting among the creosote bushes trying to get an Internet connection, racing against Jos, a woman fifteen years her junior—all for a damn picture.

It would be an easier life. But could she work for Argent? The memory of Perreault smashing his wineglass on the table seemed to be the coda each time she thought about the offer. She'd called Luc back and said she needed the entire week to decide, and if that meant Monsieur Perreault needed to take the offer off the table, then so be it. Luc had told her he was sure Monsieur Perreault would understand.

Nellie snorted. She doubted Jacques Perreault understood or ever exercised patience of any sort. She wondered what he was like as a father. If he treated Felice the same way he treated others in the auto world, she'd need a ton of therapy. Perhaps her unquenchable sex drive was tied to a lack of love.

She shook her head. "Not my problem." She stared at the printouts. She needed to whittle down the paper, but it was impossible to discern what might be important. Willie rarely commented or editorialized in his notes. It was more like a planner than a journal, a way to keep track of events and possibly link those events together if necessary. He didn't include words like 'important' or use exclamation points to note a key meeting. It seemed as though everything and everyone was equally important, and there wasn't a single reference to anyone named Ralph.

She glanced at her watch. Nine twenty-four. She'd been up since dawn drinking coffee and trying to decipher the journal. She felt her heart pounding. She wasn't sure if it was because she was over caffeinated or because Jos would arrive in six minutes.

She glanced at the mess, unsure if she should discuss the journal with Jos. A part of her was still hopping mad that Jos had copied it. She had a right to doubt her. A part of her was also relieved because she saw new possibilities with Jos. She'd never shared certain aspects of her life with the women she dated, women who lived in different parts of the United States. It ensured intimacy was impossible.

"Maybe that's the point," she whispered.

Only Caress and Lucy knew about her life. They were her best friends, confidantes and lovers. Yet, they'd never visited or seen the shed except in pictures. Flirting and pillow talk bookended the amazing sex, and while Nellie was completely free when it came to new positions or erotic lovemaking, she realized she was closed when it came to discussing her family.

"Apparently my father wanted it that way," she muttered.

There was more to think about but the doorbell rang. She heard Mai introducing herself to Jos. Nellie strolled into the living room as Jos greeted Willie and Chevy. Chevy put his paw up to shake while Jos cooed at him.

When she saw Nellie watching, Jos whispered something to Chevy who seemed to understand.

"Hey," Nellie said.

"Hi."

It was awkward between them, but Nellie knew it would be. They'd ended their conversation in Michigan at a weird place.

"You all going to the auto show today?" Willie asked.

Jos turned to him and said, "I don't think so. Which one's going on right now?" she asked, as if his sense of time were completely normal.

He scratched his cheek covered with morning stubble and said, "Think it's Chrysler or maybe Ford."

He rambled on while Jos listened and Nellie enjoyed the view. Jos's sleeveless button-down shirt was tucked into dark blue walking shorts. She carried a brown accordion file under her arm.

Willie pointed at Nellie and said, "If you get me my journal, Parnelli, I can double check."

At the mention of the journal, Jos looked away. Nellie felt her cheeks flush.

"You know, Willie," Jos said, "I don't think Nellie and I are going to have time to stop by Chrysler today. We've got some business to take care of but maybe next time. And maybe you could come with us," she suggested.

Willie's face brightened. "I'd love to. I haven't been back to the office in months." He laughed and said, "I wonder how Chet is doing." He licked his lips and sat up.

Nellie knew there was no way to avoid this story. It was one of his favorites. She motioned for Jos to take the armchair closest to Willie and she dropped onto the sofa and pulled out her phone.

"Chet Myers was the Chief of Engineers at GM all through the fifties and sixties until he retired. Wasn't afraid of anything, especially admitting he was wrong." Nellie looked up in time to see his gaze shift from Jos to her. She crossed her arms, the phone forgotten. Although she'd certainly heard this story before, she sensed he knew the double message he was sending to them.

"See, Chet worked on the new Chevelle. Prided himself on some changes to the engine...I can't remember what they were," he said with a wave. "But two days in a row the driver comes back from testing the car on the highway and says he's hearing a noise in the back every time he decelerates, a high-pitched vibration. First day, Chet doesn't believe him, but when the driver comes back on the second day saying the same thing, Chet decides to test it. He asks for the keys, and the curious driver watches him go to the back, open the trunk and get in. He hands the keys back to the driver and says, 'Let's go.'"

Jos laughed and Nellie smiled. She could watch Jos all day.

"So, did Chet hear the sound when they got on the highway?" Jos asked.

Willie nodded, "You betcha. But the driver was sweatin' bullets when he let him out of the trunk. He thought he'd get fired."

"Why?" Jos asked. "He was just the driver."

"Yeah, but you gotta understand drivers are the bottom of the food chain. They're treated like scum. More than a few guys got fired by engineers just because they didn't like the message. They'd get angry and fire the messenger."

"But Chet didn't do that?" Jos suggested.

"Nope. He appreciated what the driver was telling him. But he was one-of-a-kind. Not a lot of engineers would've crawled into that trunk in the first place." He paused and took a breath. While he was telling the story, he'd looked exclusively at Jos, but now he looked at Nellie. "Fortunately, Chet wasn't prideful. He admitted his mistakes. Knew a good thing when he saw it." He nodded. "Yup. A good guy, that Chet."

Willie leaned back in his chair and seemed to float away. Nellie fought the urge to bring him back. She'd learned it was better to savor these moments rather than try to push his memory. It just resulted in temper tantrums.

Within two minutes he was asleep and snoring. Jos got up and retrieved his blanket from the floor. She carefully covered him while Nellie watched.

Jos turned toward Nellie, her hands on her hips. "That's quite a story."

She stood up and stuck her hands in her pockets. "It was. Some of it I'd never heard."

"Oh?" Joss cocked her head to the side. "Which part was new?"

Nellie chuckled and said, "All of the parts where it sounded like one of Aesop's fables."

They drifted closer but neither wanted to be the first to touch. Nellie breathed in the fresh scent of Jos's soap.

Jos said, "So, the part where he talked about admitting mistakes, that was new?"

"Yeah."

Jos handed her the accordion folder. She peeked inside and saw the journal pages.

"I'm sorry," she said, her eyes full of tears. "I never should've copied your journal. I don't know what I was thinking." She paused. "No, that's not true. I know what I was thinking. I wanted to be the best. I want to be the best but I'd be happy to share being the best with you."

Nellie's gaze locked on her mouth and the wonderful way her lips moved to form words. As she took a breath to start another paragraph, Nellie kissed her. Jos dipped her chin and fell into Nellie's embrace. It was still new to them and each kiss was long and languid. Want quickly turned to need but fortunately Willie's snoring snapped the momentum.

They both giggled and nuzzled noses. "I accept your apology," Nellie said. "Let's take a ride."

CHAPTER NINETEEN

Verde Valley, Arizona

Jos accelerated the classic Corvette to one hundred ten. She whooped in excitement and glanced at Nellie, who was laughing hysterically. It seemed like the car was flying, skipping over the little dips on the highway. Periodically it tapped the asphalt before surging ahead. She'd only driven a convertible a few times, never exceeding the speed limit. The Corvette drove itself and she was just along for the ride.

After a few seconds of experiencing the rush, she lifted her foot from the gas and decelerated to ninety. While she wasn't comfortable driving really fast like Nellie did, she wasn't settling for sixty miles an hour either.

There were very few cars on this stretch of road, a favorite among test drivers because of its isolation. Highway patrol rarely bothered with it. They knew the test drivers used it the most and giving them tickets was just a hassle and bad for relations with the car manufacturers, especially if they expected a deal the next time they bought a fleet of cruisers.

Nellie leaned over and said, "Slow down just past that patch of low brush."

Jos nodded and decelerated further. Her heart sank. It was like the end of a great carnival ride, when she'd catch her breath and wait for the carny to let her off. She just wanted to go again and she was tempted to hit the gas once more. "I can live dangerously," she muttered. "Just not for very long."

Nellie leaned over the console and asked, "What did you say?"

"Nothing," Jos said. "I was just talking to myself. Bad habit."

Nellie chuckled. "No worries. I do it all the time. It's natural for carparazzi. We spend too much time alone."

As they passed the low brush, Nellie indicated a turnoff. They were now on a paved forest access road that extended for several miles around the mountains. Nellie pointed at a crossroads and she took a left.

"Slow down to ten," Nellie said.

The Corvette seemed to crawl along until it came to a dead end, a turnaround in the middle of nowhere. Directly in front of them was a padlocked gate.

"Where does that lead?" Jos asked.

"Back behind the mountain, I think. Go ahead and kill the engine."

Jos did as she was told and the silence was overwhelming. Since much of Arizona was part of the state land trust, thousands of acres remained pristine and undeveloped.

"It's unbelievable here at night," Nellie said. "You can see the stars perfectly because we're so far from Phoenix's light pollution."

Jos scanned the desert, a landscape for an Arizona postcard. Dozens of saguaros saluted and a roadrunner caught her eye. She slowly got out of the Corvette and inched closer. When it sensed her presence, it quickly scampered away.

Nellie's door opened and her boots clicked across the asphalt. A tingle went up Jos's back in anticipation. She welcomed Nellie's arms circling her waist and turned to face her. Their kisses were tentative, each wanting to please the other. The stronger the desire, the bolder they became until their bodies molded together. Jos felt the wetness between her legs. There would be no distractions out here. No children calling her, no Willie yelling for Nellie.

Nellie caressed her breast and her lips strayed to Jos's neck. She let herself go and thought of nothing except Nellie's touch. Her head lolled back when Nellie's tongue drifted to her cleavage. One, two, three, shirt buttons came undone.

"We can't do this here," Jos managed to say, but she didn't recognize her own voice. She buttoned up her shirt and stepped out of Nellie's reach. "We need to talk first. I think I've been used and I think you're being used too."

"I agree," Nellie said. "I'd like to propose that we share what we know and we try to work together. I'm all for being the best with you, not against you."

"I really am sorry about the journal."

Nellie nodded. "How did you know about it?"

"This man named Mr. Brent. He started calling me right after I met you. First he told me about the journal. Then he gave me the lead on the Camaro testing, including a place to take the shots."

"Where was that?"

"He rents a house in the subdivision that used to be the hill where Willie took pictures. I think the house sits at the very top and has the best view."

Nellie nodded and Jos could almost hear the gears of her brain turning. She was gazing out at the desert, thinking.

"Does any of this mean something to you? Do you know Mr. Brent?"

Nellie shook her head. "No, I don't know him. But Jacques Perreault offered me a job."

Jos stared at her. "What?"

"He strongly suggested I should work for Argent because if I don't, he'll make my life miserable in the carparazzi. I'm guessing he occasionally works with Mr. Brent. It's no accident that Mr. Brent has set you up for success and I've struggled recently."

Jos closed the distance between them and wrapped her arms around Nellie's neck. "You don't think I had anything to do with that, do you?"

Nellie's expression softened. "Of course not."

She pulled Jos to her for a reassuring kiss. They held each other in the quiet of the desert. Jos closed her eyes and listened to Nellie's steady heartbeat. It soothed her frazzled emotions. For the last several months she'd felt so lonely, adrift. She had never imagined how difficult single parenting really was and she still didn't feel she was a truly skillful member of the carparazzi. She started to cry softly and Nellie hugged her tighter.

"Hey, we're allies now," Nellie whispered.

Jos tilted her face up and kissed her, salty tears washing over their lips. Nellie took charge. The shirt buttons unbuttoned again and her hands roamed freely over Jos's breasts and buttocks, shifting Jos's emotions from melancholy to excitement.

Nellie broke the kiss and met her gaze as if she were coming out of a trance. "No one would see us. This road is hardly used. We're parked in the shade," she added, as though she were reciting a list of persuasive arguments.

Jos regained enough of her senses to say, "Take me back. Take me someplace private."

She opened one eye. Nellie was staring at her. "Get in. I'm driving."

Jos's legs seemed to have lost their joints, but she managed to stumble around the car and collapse in the passenger's seat. Nellie took them back to the main road and they retraced their path. Jos looked down and realized two more of her shirt buttons were open.

They headed straight back to Wittman. There were no further scenic stops. Nellie was on a mission, left hand on the wheel and right hand on the gearshift as the Corvette reached one hundred. Periodically she would glance sideways, and Jos knew she was sneaking a peek at her lacy black bra. She saw how effortlessly Nellie drove the Corvette and wondered if she herself would ever drive that fast without having an anxiety attack.

Once the Corvette was parked inside the shed, Nellie said, "Hand me my camera, will you, please? I want to take a few more shots of you sitting in the Corvette."

Jos opened the bag at her feet that Nellie had tossed in at the last minute. Sometimes prototypes just appeared and great shots happened by accident. You had to be ready. She frowned. "What's this?"

She pulled out a pair of leather underwear and Nellie's face turned pale. "Um, I'm not sure how those got in there."

Jos raised an eyebrow. "I'm guessing these belong to Felice?"

"Um, well, maybe," Nellie hedged.

"That's a mood killer," Jos stated as she buttoned her shirt. She exited the Corvette and headed out of the shed.

"C'mon, Jos!" Nellie called. "Don't be like that."

Jos pushed the panic bar and opened the shed door. She was instantly blinded by the summer sun. She trudged back toward the house, not looking forward to seeing Willie again. She was numb. She didn't know how she felt, but for some reason, everything had changed when she saw the underwear.

She spied a side gate without a padlock and sighed with relief. It opened to a path that led to the front driveway. She climbed into the van and searched for her keys, suddenly realizing she'd silenced her phone. She had two messages, one from Colleen and the other from an unknown number. She suspected it was Mr. Brent.

She glanced at the gate she'd just closed. She wanted Nellie to appear, rushing toward the van, pleading with her to stay. She counted to three, and when the gate remained shut, she gunned the engine and sent the brakes squealing. Already she missed driving the Corvette.

She hit speaker and turned onto U.S. 60. "Hey babe," Colleen said happily. "I get to call you babe now, don't I? I've got some news, but I don't want to leave it in a message. Call me back."

She shook her head, dreading the conversation with Colleen. There would never be another tryst or threesome. Then she smiled. She was finally ready to move on. She felt Nellie's arms wrap around her again—but then she pictured the underwear in the camera bag. She deleted Colleen's message and played the second one. It was Mr. Brent at yet another number, but his message was always the same.

"Jos, please call me."

He never left his name, and he'd stressed that when she received a message she needed to call him back quickly. He disposed of the phone almost immediately, which was why each number was always different. He didn't want to leave a phone trail, a thought she found unsettling.

She pressed the call back number and he answered on the first ring. "We need to meet ASAP. Where are you?"

"I'm on the west side, heading home."

"Good. You're close. Can you meet me at Washington Park near the tennis courts?"

"Um, sure. When?"

"Now. I'll meet you in twenty."

He hung up and she tossed the phone onto the passenger seat. She felt a stabbing pain in her stomach and wondered if her ulcer had returned. She'd acquired one at the height of her stress with Colleen. Once they'd broken up and she'd made a few changes to her diet, the ulcer disappeared.

"And it feels like it's back," she said, reaching for the antacids in the glove compartment.

The ulcer was a sign she needed to heed. This was the second time she'd driven back from Wittman an emotional wreck. Perhaps Nellie was an infatuation and nothing more. Perhaps it meant she belonged with someone like Colleen. Not Colleen specifically, but someone stable who wanted a relationship. She thought about how wonderful her life with Colleen was in the early years and after they'd adopted Myles and Bridget.

"Those were good times," she admitted.

The only thing that had changed was her job. She needed to figure out the balance, as her mother would say. She sat up straighter and announced, "I accept that I'm a single parent. I'd like a partner, but I'm okay being alone." She popped another antacid and pushed aside thoughts of her personal life.

It was only a ten-minute drive to Washington Park. Early September was still too hot for the retirees to play tennis during the day and the students were back in school, so the park was a ghost town. She parked the van but kept the AC blowing. Always careful of her surroundings, she glanced through the side windows and noticed a man with an Afro sitting in an old sedan several spaces away. He appeared to be reading messages on his phone. She hoped he wasn't the elusive Mr. Brent. She'd pictured him driving a much snazzier car.

He wasn't due for another five minutes so she pushed back her seat and let the antacid work. Maybe she'd overreacted at Nellie's. She'd wanted her so badly, but the sight of Felice's underwear had driven her away. Why? "I'm the one who almost had a threesome," she reminded herself. Yet faced with the reminder that Nellie bedded many women, she couldn't handle it.

"Stop being a hypocrite," she said to the steering wheel. She picked up her phone and started to compose a text.

Before she could hit send a different text arrived. *I'm between the courts and the community center.*

She pulled the seat upright and peered through the windshield toward the location. The African-American gentleman from the old car sported a sling on his right arm and was talking to a nattily dressed man in a suit carrying a computer case. That had to be Mr. Brent. Tall, styled blond hair and broad shoulders. He wore the suit well. She approached him with a new wariness, conscious of his manipulative tactics.

The men stopped their conversation and both acknowledged her with a pleasant smile. Mr. Brent stuck out his hand. "It's a pleasure to finally meet you, Jos Grant. This is Robert Keller."

Robert waved his good left hand. Mr. Brent led them to a nearby picnic table and booted up the computer. "Robert has a story he'd like to tell you."

She sized up Robert. He was dressed in jeans and a polo shirt that didn't quite cover up a Semper Fi tattoo on his left bicep. Ex-military, thin, probably in his thirties.

He cleared his throat and nodded. "I'm a driver for Argent."

At the mention of the French automaker, she found herself sitting up straighter. She glanced at Mr. Brent, but his gaze was fixed on Robert.

"They hired me away from Toyota with a much fatter salary. Normally drivers don't get paid much."

She remembered what Willie had said: Drivers are scum.

"It was all legit. Argent honored my confidentiality clause with Toyota. They weren't trying to get me to give up Toyota's secrets. But I didn't realize they have some secrets of their own."

"What secrets?"

He leaned forward and whispered, "Their new car has serious problems."

"I didn't know Argent has a new car," she said to Mr. Brent.

"It's called the Folie. In French that translates to madness. It's a sports coupe unlike any other. And the most important feature is that it's being built with superior computer technology. The Folie will be the first self-driving car on the market."

Her eyes widened. "Seriously? I've seen the self-driving cars made by the computer companies, but I didn't realize any of them were ready for mass production."

"Well, it's not. That's why we're here. But let's go back a bit. I assume you're familiar with the advancements in auto technology. Many cars now have features that help a driver make decisions."

She nodded. "You're talking about things like the Lane Departure Warning that tells drivers they're veering out of their own lane. And there's the Frontal Collision Warning that can actually stop the car if you're sitting at a red light and your car starts to roll into the car ahead of you."

"Yes," Mr. Brent agreed. "Those are two examples. Up until now these features assisted drivers, such as telling them whether it's safe to turn right and making decisions for drivers, like the Frontal Collision Warning you mentioned."

He shifted on the bench and cued up a video on the screen but didn't hit play. "Argent has made the next significant advancement. The greatest challenge faced by self-driving cars is human judgment. The self-driving car always follows the rules of the road, but nothing has been invented to help the car's computer recognize human error soon enough to adjust. Watch."

The video began at a four-way intersection. Four cars approached at the same time, each from a different direction. Jos recognized three of the cars as Argent sedans. The fourth car she'd never seen but it reminded her of a cute British MG of yesteryear. Mr. Brent pointed at the little car. "There's the self-driving car." It reached the stop sign first by a second and clearly had the right of way. It started to go forward but one of the sedans darted into the intersection. Jos cringed instinctively, fearing the collision that was about to happen. Instead of being crushed, the little car immediately stopped and the larger car crossed in front of it.

"Two years ago this would've resulted in an accident, but that car," he said, pointing at the cute little one, "was built with a safety ring around it, so it responds to the actions of other drivers in one one-hundredth of a second. It can literally read human judgment. No other manufacturer, including the computer companies, can duplicate this feature."

He clicked another button. "Meet the Folie."

She watched the cute sports coupe spin on a showroom platform. "Wow," was all she could say.

"That's why Argent is here in Arizona," Robert continued. "It's a hotbed for computer technology. The land is cheap and the taxes are low."

She was still trying to understand why they were sitting in a park discussing this. "Do you want me to take pictures of this car? Is that why we're meeting?"

"It's bigger than that, Jos," Mr. Brent said seriously. He turned to Robert and nodded at him to continue.

"So, I started doing the Folie's test drives around the track. Sometimes I drive, sometimes the car drives. It's unlike anything I've ever experienced. And Jacques Perreault has spared no expense. Normally a prototype costs one to five million dollars. The Folie probably cost fifteen million. This car is beautiful. Nobody has anything like it."

"And I'm guessing it would be really expensive for a consumer to purchase one?"

"Almost two hundred grand," Mr. Brent replied. "Expensive but not unaffordable for the uber rich. This will be Argent's foothold in the luxury car business and the future."

"So, what's wrong with it?" she asked.

"The first week goes fine," Robert continued. "I'm putting the car through its paces and everything seems to be great. The second week is about endurance. I drive it all day in the heat at sixty miles per hour. Around and around the track on cruise control."

She glanced at Robert's sling. "And how did it do?"

Robert snorted and said, "Fine, until I tried to decelerate."

"What?"

"It wouldn't give me back control," Robert explained. "If I tapped on the brake to end the cruise control, it lurched and continued to accelerate back to the chosen cruising speed. I tried turning the cruise control on and off, but it kept going. I drove in circles while the engineers figured out what to do. It was almost comical. I'd zoom past them, but the next time I cruised by, the group had grown by two or three more people, all of them standing around with their tablets arguing about what to do. The amount of engineers outside kept increasing. They radioed ideas to me. Try this or try that. Since it's more computerized than most cars, they had me doing some ridiculous stuff like running the windshield wipers while I turned the lights on and off."

"How did you finally stop?"

"That time they had to change the computer codes from the main system and take control of the car remotely. The *computer* told the car to stop."

"The computer could stop the car but the human being couldn't," Mr. Brent summarized.

"Exactly," Robert said.

Jos pointed at his sling. "How did you hurt your arm?"

"I'd unbuckled my seat belt while they were having me try all of these ideas and I just forgot about it. When the computer stopped the car, it literally *stopped* the car. Tires squealed and the whole system locked up. I smashed forward into the steering wheel. Fractured my arm and also broke two ribs."

"That's horrible," she said. A thought occurred to her. "You said *that* time. This has happened more than once?"

The men glanced at each other, their expressions grim. Robert prepared to respond, clearly trying to choose his words carefully. "The issue is always a little different and to the credit of the engineers, these problems are happening less frequently."

"What does that mean?" she asked, confused. "Does the cruise control work or not?"

"Yes," Robert said, but then he added, "most of the time." He leaned forward to explain further. "The engineers have succeeded in correcting the problem for probably ninety-five percent of the drivers."

"I still don't understand," she said.

Mr. Brent held up a hand. "Here's how it works, Jos. When auto manufacturers design cars with safety features, they are expected to meet minimal standards, which will account for almost every car buyer's driving habits. There are many habits that are similar to millions and millions of people. But there are always a few outliers, people who, for example, because of their occupations, where they live or how they drive, are out of the norm. In those cases, a certain feature may not perform as expected."

"And it's usually not just one characteristic in isolation," Robert said. "It's usually two or three anomalies put together. An example would be a driver whose daily job requires him to accelerate and decelerate frequently at high speeds while on a steep grade. The likelihood of all of those characteristics in one driver on a daily basis is very slim when you're talking about a sports coupe. The automakers develop cars for the majority of drivers," Mr. Brent summarized. "If car manufacturers had to tailor their vehicles to every person's life, they'd never put out an automobile."

"So if I'm understanding you correctly, you're telling me that the Folie's cruise control is going to work most of the time, probably all of the time for most drivers. However, there could be an anomalous group of drivers who, because of their driving characteristics, could find themselves unable to end the cruise control and ultimately not stop. And that's just a maybe. It might not happen at all."

"Yes," Robert said.

"How do I know if I'm in that group?"

Mr. Brent chuckled. "You don't. And if we'd never had this conversation, you'd never know such a group existed."

She felt the acid in her stomach churning again. "But stopping is the most important thing a car does, more so than going forward."

The men both nodded and Mr. Brent said, "But Argent has decided that the risk is insignificant. They've invested too many millions in the Folie to turn back, especially for a problem that may never surface."

"But what if it does?" Jos argued. "I don't understand what's exactly wrong with the Folie, but we're talking about speed and deceleration, not whether or not the Bluetooth is going to work. If even one car can't stop, dozens of lives could be in jeopardy."

Mr. Brent nodded vigorously and touched her hand. "We completely agree with you. Which is why we've asked you here today. There are more cruise control tests scheduled with the prototype. They're still trying to fix the problem. We want to get some video of that test. There's an opportunity for a spy to infiltrate the proving grounds just like the old days. If the fixes work, and there's nothing wrong with the Folie, then great. Let it be produced."

She sensed she knew what was coming next. "And if there's still a problem, you're going to release the video."

Mr. Brent nodded but refused to acknowledge the truth out loud. Instead he explained. "The self-driving car is cutting edge but it's still too new. It's not ready and Argent is rushing to production in order to be first and overtake Renault as the leader in the French market."

Robert added, "And there's talk that Jacques Perreault is being considered for a position with an American company."

"As CEO?" Jos asked.

"Yes," Mr. Brent said. "We think that's another reason to expose Argent."

They both stared at her, waiting for an answer.

At the rumble of a car engine, she gazed toward the parking lot just as the cute Argent Amour pulled into a space. The Amour was currently the tiniest of the Argent fleet and it reminded her of a Fiat. A woman got out and pulled her seat forward in order to extract her daughter from the car seat in the back. She locked the car and headed to the nearby playground.

Jos thought of Myles and Bridget. If Argent was willing to cut corners on one vehicle, why not do the same with another? She'd actually test driven the Bijoux, the Argent minivan. Given what she'd learned today, she was glad she hadn't purchased it.

She sighed and asked, "What do I need to do?"

CHAPTER TWENTY

Mesa, Arizona

As Nellie waited in line at the front gate of the Argent Proving Grounds, she felt a pang of anxiety. Perhaps she was making a mistake. She was a person who liked to watch events unfold before she committed to action. Patience often pointed to the right direction and the decision became easy. But nothing yesterday had been easy and she wasn't sure of this decision at all.

She'd spent the morning walking the acreage with Willie and Chevy, listening to more of Willie's stories and enjoying a coherent conversation with him. She told him about the offer and he asked some good questions. She almost asked about the situation with Lucy all those years ago, but found herself unable to pose the question. She wanted to keep the conversation pleasant. That it was normal drove her to tears. She thought it was a sign to take the job.

There wouldn't be too many more of those mornings and she didn't want to miss them. She was tired of flying all over the globe for a photo. No more long layovers, back pain, terrible airline food or rude taxi cab drivers. She could easily give up being chased by engineers, having her Jeep vandalized and enduring the childish behavior of security personnel. She remembered a guard who'd successfully kept her from the shot at a proving ground in California. As she'd started to drive away, he'd turned around and mooned her.

She would have few regrets, but a major one would be not seeing Jos. Giving up the spy world would mean they would seldom run into each other, if at all. Jos had made the chase fun again. Although Argent's contract allowed her to freelance, she doubted she would do it. She was content just living off her million a year. She'd already contacted her financial planner for investment advice. She hoped to make the three million she'd collect stretch for a lifetime.

One of Willie's questions stuck in her mind. He'd asked, "Can you give it up?" She imagined that was the same question he'd asked himself when he moved to General Motors. In the end the answer had been no and he'd left. As her Jeep rolled up to the Argent security shack, she wondered how she'd feel in a year.

"Name?" the guard asked.

"Rafferty. Nellie Rafferty here to see Felice."

He nodded and raised the gate's arm. Nellie was in. It felt odd to be invited inside a proving ground. She'd only been invited once before when an old friend of Willie's had slipped them inside a cold weather proving ground in Alberta. They'd been so bundled up no one recognized them.

She chugged along at fifteen miles per hour toward the inner sanctum, beyond the ten-foot high gray concrete walls that bordered the entire facility. As she neared the five buildings that housed the Argent brain trust, she passed six Argent automobiles lined up like a welcoming committee. It was not uncommon for automakers to leave cars out in the sun for years, subjecting them to one of their greatest enemies: long-term heat. It was a science experiment that told the engineers how long it would take for the paint to oxidize, the windshield to crack or the rubber gaskets under the hood to completely disintegrate. She thought about pulling over just to peek in the windows, but she didn't think that would be the best move on the first day.

Each building sported a large red number to ensure no one got lost. Felice had instructed her to park outside Building Two and enter through the front door. Parking was ample and as she headed to the entrance, another security guard appeared to greet her.

"They're not messing around," she muttered.

She thought of Willie sneaking into the Big Three's headquarters again and again for decades. He wouldn't have lasted a day with all of the new surveillance technology. A twinge of jealousy hit her. Back then it was a game, one that was fun for everyone, even the automakers. They needed the carparazzi and the carparazzi needed them. Win-win. As she shook the guard's hand and followed him inside, she didn't feel good about her decision to join Argent. She felt like a sellout.

When Felice greeted Nellie outside her office, she was completely professional. Much to Nellie's relief, the cat was gone. After a quick peck on both cheeks, Felice motioned for Nellie to sit while she perched on the edge of her desk. "I'm so glad you're joining the team. Jacques was especially pleased."

She noticed Felice refrained from referring to him as her father. The comment made her stomach turn. "As important as your father is to you, my father is just as important to me. That's why I'm here. There's no other reason."

The smile faded and she nodded. "*Oui*."

"So how does this work?"

"Today we need to get you a badge, have you complete some paperwork and sign your contract. Then I thought I'd give you a tour of the facility and we can go to lunch at the C'est La Vie. My afternoon is open, and I'm not due back in Paris until tomorrow. I have an amazing apartment on Central Avenue I'd love to show you." Her smile became cat-like as she mentioned the last agenda item.

Nellie leaned back and crossed her arms. "I think we need to keep our relationship completely professional moving forward. I hope that's okay with you."

Felice's expression turned stony. "Of course. This is the workplace," she acknowledged. She headed for the door expecting Nellie to automatically follow. "Come. Let's get started."

Felice led Nellie to the third floor where HR lived. She disappeared for an hour and returned once Nellie was finished with the paperwork, just in time to see her sign the contract and receive her badge. "Now that you're official," Felice said, "I'm going to show you some spectacular things." Her eyes danced as they started the tour. She kept a quick pace, always taking the stairs instead of the elevator. She seemed to know everyone from the receptionist to the mail clerk. They all greeted her with a smile or a hug. Many asked about Paris or her dog, Bibi.

"What kind of dog do you have?" Nellie asked. She hoped to chip away at the cold shoulder Felice was giving her. While she didn't want them to continue as lovers, she certainly hoped they could be pleasant and cordial with each other.

Felice whipped out her phone and shared a picture of a French poodle with a bow in her hair. "Isn't she adorable?"

"She is," Nellie agreed.

Nellie found herself liking Felice more and more as the tour continued. She noticed Argent spent money on its employees. Each building housed a lounge, a game room and a kitchen area stocked with snacks. Couches were everywhere and a few people were napping. Nellie concluded the consideration for the employees was Felice's doing and not the brainchild of Jacques Perreault.

Felice pointed at a snoozing worker. "Unlike you Americans, we French don't work our employees to death. As you'll see with your contract, we provide exceptional health insurance and every employee is allowed six weeks of vacation, no exceptions."

"Six weeks?"

"*Oui*." She noticed Nellie's expression. "You are impressed?"

"I am."

"Good," she said as they entered yet another stairwell.

Nellie followed Felice down several floors. They reached a landing and she suddenly turned around, pressing against Nellie. The powerful kiss startled her and she grabbed the nearby railing to stay upright. Felice's hands found her bottom and her breast. Nellie gently pushed her away and did her best not to respond.

Felice looked down, ashamed. "I'm sorry. I just had to try."

"I understand," Nellie said gently. "It's worked every other time."

The green eyes looked into hers with resignation. "But not this time."

"No," Nellie said. "I'm hoping we can be collaborative colleagues. I don't have a lot of female friends. I'm hoping you could be one."

"Perhaps," Felice said honestly.

She headed down the stairs to the exit. They walked to Building Four and Nellie immediately noticed a shift in security. There were more cameras and the exterior lock required a thumbprint, not a badge swipe. Before Felice pressed her thumb on the pad she said, "You have been wondering why we've hired you. Now I can show you."

Nellie nodded and followed Felice past several testing areas to the back of the expansive building. An adorable red two-seater with a white stripe down the middle sat on a pedestal. Two men in lab coats leaned over the open hood, staring at the engine, which didn't look like a regular engine at all. She couldn't name any of the parts and it looked more like the inside of a computer than a car.

"Nellie, I present the next great automobile to you, the Folie."

Jos adjusted the wig a fourth time since she'd put it on. Perhaps she couldn't imagine herself a brunette, but the expensive disguise felt like a rodent dropped from the sky and onto her head. It didn't look right on her. She tugged and pulled before giving up. She donned the simple black frames with clear lenses that Mr. Brent had provided and stared at the full effect.

She wore a short black skirt, tailored silk blouse, a pearl necklace and matching earrings. She'd applied her makeup heavily, or at least, it was heavy for her. Normally she slapped on a little rouge and mascara, but he'd instructed her to go all out, the way most women did for a day at the office. The final touch was the blood-red lipstick.

She patted her lips together and stepped back. One thing was certain: she didn't look anything like her *Auto Monthly* photo. Mr. Brent assured her the key to infiltrating Argent wasn't the disguise, although that would help. Since most of the Argent employees were male, they would be staring at her face, her boobs or her legs. Like Nellie, Mr. Brent had complimented her on having the best legs he'd ever seen.

The key was Robert. He gave her credibility. The fact she was with him showed she belonged. Whereas security would be naturally suspicious of anyone unescorted in the facility, she was with someone who wore an Argent badge.

Each quarter Argent hosted a lavish luncheon for all the new staff hired during that time period. Since Robert had been hired three and a half months prior, he'd not yet had his luncheon. And he could invite a guest. This luncheon occurred during the workday. While everyone else was toiling away on a Monday, the new employees and their guests would be dining on steak, shrimp and champagne at the C'est La Vie restaurant that overlooked the testing grounds.

As the doorbell rang she glanced at the mirror one more time. She still wasn't pleased. Yet when she greeted Robert, his eyes grew wide.

"Wow."

She couldn't help but smile. "Thank you. Let me get my bag."

She showed Robert the purse and pointed at the gold emblem on the front.

"That's a camera?" he asked.

"It is. Mr. Brent has spared no expense."

She showed him her watch, which was really a screen to see the view obtained by the camera. He peered at the tiny face while she moved the purse back and forth.

"That's amazing," he proclaimed. "And a little scary."

In the car Jos tried to forget that Robert was constantly staring at her as they maneuvered through midday traffic.

"How will this work?" she asked as they cruised down U.S. 60.

"It's simple. When Argent built the restaurant, they made it so that it revolved."

"I've heard that," Jos said.

"The best views of the track are by the windows. For this luncheon those tables are reserved for the new employees. We're arriving a little early so hopefully we'll have our pick. If you think of the circular floor like a clock face, we want to sit at eight o'clock. Once we're seated, you'll prop your bag on the table, check the angle and leave it alone. Then we just enjoy lunch. From twelve to two, the engineers are testing the Folie on the track. Depending on the restaurant's view when we sit down, we'll know how slowly we need to eat."

"Because we want to make sure we're still sitting there when the restaurant spins around to the track," Jos concluded.

"Yes. There's only one potential snag," he said, his tone turning serious. "These luncheons are scheduled months in advance by the HR department. Engineering is supposed to talk to them and never schedule a test when outsiders are in the restaurant, but this is an emergency. They're trying to fix the Folie and they don't have the luxury of waiting. If the bigwigs knew that outsiders were going to be up in the restaurant watching the Folie unable to stop—"

"They'd go ballistic."

"Exactly. And it still might happen. Eventually the VPs and division heads will show up at the luncheon to greet us. They'll make little speeches and come around and shake hands. Since most of them are quite self-absorbed, they might not notice what's going on below them. But there's one in particular who's really sharp. If she shows up, she'll see it and she'll shut the testing down in a split second."

Jos frowned and faced him. "Her name wouldn't be Felice, would it?"

* * *

As Felice led her across the parking lot to the track, Nellie tried to digest everything she'd learned about the Folie. If Argent had successfully created a self-driving car that could predict human judgment and be mass-produced, the entire auto industry was about to change. *And Jacques Perreault will be an incredibly rich man. No wonder he could barely contain his excitement.*

They arrived at the track just as a sedan prototype sped past them while three engineers watched and took notes. Nearby two drivers performed statics on their respective vehicles. Statics were done throughout the testing period until a car reached the average amount of times a consumer would perform the same function. One driver opened and closed the trunk repeatedly while the other driver popped the hood and slammed it shut over and over. Nellie knew statics were by far the most tedious task for drivers.

"This is the new version of the Cherie," Felice said flatly, pointing to the car circling the track.

Nellie knew the Cherie was the most popular sedan in the Argent fleet. Suddenly one of the engineers started waving his hands and another was shouting into a radio. Nellie felt the hairs rise on the back of her neck and her heartbeat quicken. Only one thing sent engineers into a tizzy: carparazzi. She looked around and saw nothing. But then she heard the helicopter as it came over the track. She shielded her eyes as it approached and glanced at the Cherie, which was now headed for a hide shack ten feet off the course.

Every test track had at least one hide shack. When carparazzi was spotted, the driver cruised into a hide shack and dropped the shack's canvas flaps over the front and back until the offending photographer could be chased away. Nellie's gaze flitted from the Cherie to the chopper. It was going to be close as the chopper was overhead and the car still wasn't hidden.

Swearing in French, Felice ran toward the shack in her four-inch heels. The car finally drove inside and the waiting engineers lowered the flaps. The chopper flew away and Nellie smiled. They probably got the shot.

"Good for you," she muttered.

She wondered if Jos was in the helicopter and the image of her long legs filled Nellie's memory. She blinked and remembered she was on the other team now. She readjusted her smile into a frown before Felice rejoined her on the sidelines.

She continued to speak in French for a few more paragraphs until she ran out of steam. "Damn!" she shouted. "Do you think he got the shot?"

Nellie shrugged. "Hard to know, but your car was uncovered for a long time."

Felice whirled around and offered a cold stare. "You mean *our* car, Nellie, don't you? You work for us now. You need to get used to it."

She stomped away and Nellie followed. It was going to take some time to adjust to her new life. One she still wasn't sure she wanted.

CHAPTER TWENTY-ONE

Mesa, Arizona

They had just stepped inside the swanky C'est la Vie restaurant high above the Argent Proving Grounds when Robert's phone buzzed. He was gone several minutes while they showed Jos to a table against the window. The restaurant only needed to turn another forty degrees and she'd have the shot if the test started soon.

"Shit," Robert hissed as he sat down. "They bagged it."

"Why? What happened?" she whispered.

"Apparently carparazzi appeared while they were testing the new Cherie. Damn helicopter flew over the track. Felice Perreault actually witnessed the whole thing. She asked about the schedule for the rest of the day, and when she heard the Folie was up next, she threw a fit and told the engineers to cancel the test because of the luncheon. Too many outsiders up in the restaurant."

Jos slunk down in her seat. "What do we do now?"

Robert shrugged as the waiter approached. "I guess we enjoy lunch."

Nellie had seen a completely different side of Felice out on the track. She had no idea anyone could run like a demon in four-inch heels. Felice had actually passed one of the engineers running to the hide shack to cover the Cherie. Then after the helicopter retreated, she blew up again when the engineers told her the Folie was due to make an appearance. Nellie gave her credit, though, as she stopped short of calling anyone an idiot for thinking the Folie test was still a good idea. The woman had class even when she was angry.

"Let's go," she said to Nellie. "I need a drink."

They walked briskly toward the restaurant's elevator and Nellie gazed skyward at the round saucer-shaped structure.

"You know, helicopters are highly likely here," Nellie offered. "You're really close to the airport."

"I know," Felice said. "I've told the head of security the same thing three times. It had to happen before he believed me."

Nellie could hear the frustration in her voice. "I guess French women and American women have something in common."

Felice snorted and said, "It's worse for us. There is much more ego in Frenchmen. My father insisted on bringing Paul, the head of security, over from Boulogne. Even though I told him it was a bad idea."

They reached the elevator and she swiped her badge. The elevator doors immediately opened and they boarded for their ride to the sky. Felice couldn't stay still. She paced in the small space until the doors opened and they arrived at the restaurant lobby. In those few seconds Nellie realized the enormous responsibility Jacques Perreault had entrusted to his daughter.

Felice pulled her compact from her purse and checked her lips. "This will never do. Go get us a table and order a gin and tonic for me," she said coolly. She headed down a nearby hallway, passing a brunette with glasses.

Nellie watched the gentle sway of the brunette's hips as she rounded the corner. Her gaze traveled southward to her calves.

She knew those calves. *Jos? How?* She watched her return to a table where an African-American man ate dessert. When she sat down and Nellie could finally see her profile, she knew it was Jos in a wig.

The hostess appeared and blocked Nellie's entrance until she explained she was dining with Felice. Only then did she nod and lead her to a table in the bar. Nellie chose the chair that faced the main room and ordered their drinks. From her vantage point she had a clear view of Jos. Nellie glanced at the entrance. Felice was out in the lobby speaking to an employee, so Nellie took out her phone and sent Jos a text.

What are you doing here?

She watched Jos read the text and scan the room. When her gaze found Nellie, her eyes grew wide. She mumbled something to her companion who casually looked over his shoulder toward Nellie while Jos frantically tapped on her phone.

I'm on an assignment. What are YOU doing here? Don't tell me you took the job.

Okay, I won't tell you.

What?!!!

It's a long story. I would've told you if you hadn't run away.

Two words: leather underwear. But I'm sorry.

Me too.

Felice returned and Nellie put away her phone. The waitress brought their drinks and Nellie pretended to read the menu while she looked across the room at Jos. She looked good as a brunette. And that short skirt...

"Everything is superb," Felice commented. "My father relocated one of France's most promising chefs here. What people will do for money," she mused.

"Will you order the salmon for me? I'm going to call and check on my father."

"Of course," Felice said, checking her phone.

Nellie imagined Felice spent her life texting or reading email. She glanced at Jos and made her way toward the lobby. Jos followed her into the busy restroom, which included a sitting area.

They found a corner and Nellie said seductively, "So, going brunette?"

The look on Jos's face told Nellie she wasn't in the mood to play. "Why?" was all she asked.

"Argent made me an offer I couldn't refuse," she said simply.

Jos shook her head and a sliver of Nellie's soul enjoyed Jos's consternation. She was still angry with her for ruining their afternoon and this was her revenge. *No, revenge is too strong a word.*

Jos brushed a strand of hair from her cheek with a freshly painted nail and waited for two chatty women to exit the bathroom. Nellie noticed how comfortable Jos was as a femme. Nellie realized she couldn't stop staring. She wanted to touch her. She leaned closer and stroked the back of her arm. Jos jumped and gave her an exasperated look.

"Don't. Even though I'm sorry for running out on you, I'm still angry."

She adopted a pouty face but Nellie could tell her heart wasn't in it. "Are you really a lipstick lesbian at heart?" she teased.

The question seemed to surprise her. She made a face and said, "I don't go for labels. I love being a woman and I like having a reason to dress up, if that's what you mean."

"Who's the guy?"

The two women floated out the exit and Jos turned to Nellie. "Listen to me. The Folie is dangerous. That man sitting with me is a driver for Argent. He's my cover and we were here to get videos of the Folie test today."

"And who sent you? The elusive Mr. Brent? Jos, you've got to be careful around that guy—"

"I am," she said.

"Well, there's not going to be a test. Felice blew up when she heard about it."

"I know." Jos narrowed her eyes. "And it's nice to put a face with the underwear."

Nellie tried to take her hand but she pulled it away. "C'mon, Jos."

She jumped up. "We don't have time for this. I'm sorry I brought it up." She rubbed her temple as if she were getting a headache. "Have you wondered *why* Felice got so upset?"

Nellie shrugged. "I figured it was because the Folie is still a prototype and she's worried about carparazzi."

"That's not the reason." Jos abruptly stopped talking and stepped into the bathroom to check the stalls. When she saw they were alone, she continued, "In certain situations the Folie's cruise control doesn't work. It won't give back control to the human driver. They're trying to fix it, but according to Mr. Brent, they're going to release the car regardless since those situations are so unlikely to happen."

Nellie felt a knot growing in her stomach. It wouldn't be the first time a car manufacturer had cut corners. There were plenty of stories and rumors in the industry about death traps being produced. Still, driving was dangerous and risks could only be minimized, not eliminated. It would also explain why Argent was bent on hiring her. The freelancing Nellie never would've allowed such a rumor to swirl unchecked. But now Argent had her under contract. *Have I sold out? Was this the reason they hired me in the first place?*

"I need more information," she said, just as a group of women drifted into the bathroom. "Let me make some calls." She gave Jos's hand a squeeze before she exited. She trudged back to the table slowly. She needed to put her game face on or Felice would certainly know something was wrong. She smiled as she slid back into her seat.

"Everything okay?" Felice asked.

"For the most part. Sometimes my dad doesn't know where he is," she explained.

"That must be hard," Felice said kindly.

Their meals arrived and Nellie peppered her with questions about Paris, Argent and her father. By the time lunch was over, Nellie was convinced Argent was determined to become the premier French car company.

After they left the restaurant Felice dismissed Nellie. "If we're not going to my condo, then I'm going back to work." She smiled like the cat and said, "Last chance."

Nellie shook her head and waved goodbye. She hustled toward the parking lot before she could change her mind. She liked sex with Felice. It was fun. It was athletic. It wasn't serious. But she couldn't have sex with someone who manipulated her. As well as Felice treated her employees, she was there for a much different purpose.

She climbed into the Jeep and stared toward the proving grounds. What was she doing? After a single day of working for Argent, she felt as though a slice of her soul had disappeared. She checked her phone. She had four phone messages. Three were from Mai, telling Nellie that her father wanted to know when the meeting was happening, and another from Jos, who simply said, "Call me," in a very disapproving tone.

Then she thought of Willie. Today was just a tour. She wasn't expected to become a nine-to-five employee, but could she take their money? The more she thought about being manipulated, the angrier she felt. She saw the trees in front of Black Lake, the ones that ensured Jos got the best shot that day. She replayed the secret late night meeting with Jacques Perreault and his veiled threat that they would continue to thwart her efforts as carparazzi if she didn't join them. They were killing her love of the chase. She wasn't sure the Folie was dangerous, but she had no doubt that Jacques Perreault would do whatever was necessary to protect his new proving ground.

She turned onto the highway. "And what are you going to do about it, Rafferty?"

CHAPTER TWENTY-TWO

Mesa, Arizona

"Way to go, Bridget!"

Jos clapped as Bridget pumped her fist and high-fived several of her soccer teammates. She'd tied the score with the only goal for her team in the game so far. Bridget's gaze trailed along the sidelines, looking for Colleen and Kelly who were late—again. Her expression changed to disappointment but there wasn't time to wallow. The referee was already preparing for the kickoff.

Jos looked toward the parking lot for the tenth time just as Kelly's Land Rover pulled into a space. She shook her head and took a deep breath. She wasn't going to get into an argument with them in front of the other parents.

She scanned the players and found Myles in the midfield position. The kickoff sent the team running toward its own goal with Myles trailing behind. Perhaps this would be his last season. Maybe he could find another physical activity to satisfy her one rule: for every hour of screen time he wanted, he had to engage in a physical activity. She'd never dictated what that activity would be, and she'd encouraged his various choices over the last few years. Consequently, a collection of rackets, gloves, balls and a fencing foil had accumulated in the garage. She wasn't attempting to mold him into an athlete. He didn't have the competitive nature to be successful, except when it came to Bridget. He always wanted to be as good as or better than his sister at everything they tried together.

"What'd we miss?" Colleen asked as she set up her lawn chair.

"Bridget scored a goal," Jos said.

Colleen's face fell. "Shit."

Jos looked around. "Where's Kelly?"

"She's still in the car on the phone with a client." Colleen's attention strayed to the field. "Oh, Myles is playing too."

"Sort of," Jos said. While she was always upbeat when Myles was within earshot, she and Colleen candidly discussed their children's shortcomings with each other. Perhaps it was another reason Jos needed someone like Colleen, someone who understood the kids.

In the last few days, since she'd seen Nellie with Felice Perreault, she'd realized how much of a womanizer Nellie really was. She used sex as a weapon to get what she wanted. Jos didn't think she'd ever be able to do that. She was starting to wonder if auto spying was really the right career for her. She couldn't drive as fast as Nellie. She doubted she would ever be as conniving and she certainly wasn't as competitive. She and Myles shared that same trait. But she loved the chase. She looked around at all the other parents. They all had normal jobs—like computer programming.

"He's doing better at keeping up with the herd this week," Colleen commented, and Jos's attention returned to the game.

At that precise moment, Myles stopped running and stared at the grass in front of his feet.

"Your honor, I retract my previous statement," Colleen said as if she were in court.

Myles bent over and snatched something from the ground. He held it between his fingers and examined it. Jos imagined it was some sort of bug. Myles was always catching flies or scooping up lizards. He couldn't run but he had great reflexes.

"Myles, move your butt!" Coach Burns yelled.

Jos scowled. Myles constantly complained that the coach hated him. She thought Coach Burns's gruff attitude bordered on inappropriateness, but Colleen believed Myles needed a thicker skin. It was a balancing act and Jos had no idea if Myles's association with Coach Burns would scar him for life or help him grow into a man. Coach Burns was studying to be a PE teacher, but he seemed too cruel to be effective.

Myles looked up and Coach Burns pointed at the swarm of players near the goal. He dropped whatever he'd been holding and veered toward the ball. Suddenly it floated into the air and landed in front of him. He reflexively kicked it away like it was dangerous—toward his own goal. An opposing player sprinted to it while Coach Burns screamed at his team to catch up. The opposing player dribbled down the field while everyone, except Myles, followed behind. Jos pursed her lips, preparing for the worst. The player kicked it high over the goalie's head and into the goal.

The referee's whistle ended the quarter and Coach Burns stormed up to Myles, shaking his fist and pointing at the bench. Jos glanced at Colleen, who was checking her email and blithely watching the exchange. Jos sprang from her chair to intervene. Even she had limits. As she crossed the grass, a woman in a baseball cap stepped in front of Coach Burns. It took Jos a moment to recognize Nellie.

Whatever she was saying to him wasn't well received. His arms were crossed and he yelled at her. "Lady, I don't know who you are, but get off the field!"

"I'm somebody who knows a lot more about soccer than you do, buddy. You shouldn't be yelling at the kids, especially when it's your fault. If you'd spread out your team, you'd have better coverage."

He turned away and motioned for the referee just as Jos joined them. She looked at Nellie and said, "What are you doing here?"

"I had a little extra time and since you mentioned where they played, I thought I'd come watch…"

Nellie's sentence trailed off as the referee joined their huddle. "Tell this woman to get the hell off the field!" Coach Burns barked.

Several of the kids gasped, and one screamed, "You said hell!"

The referee looked at Nellie with compassion and said, "Ma'am, you're interrupting the game. Do you have a child on this team?"

"No, she doesn't," Jos replied, "but I do." She glared at Coach Burns and added, "Don't you ever speak to my son like that again. And if that's how you talk to kids, you have no business becoming a teacher."

He snorted and said, "I'm high school, lady. I'd never waste my talents on these crybabies." He threw his clipboard onto the ground and glared at Nellie. "You think you can do a better job? Have at it."

They watched him storm off the field. Bridget came running up to Jos. "Mom, does this mean we don't get to finish the game?"

Jos looked at the referee who shrugged and asked, "Is there anyone who can step in and coach?"

"I will," Nellie offered.

Jos was dumbstruck. "You don't have to do that. Can you do that? Do you know anything about soccer?"

A pleasant smile appeared on her face. "I'm the one who caused this, and yes, I used to play soccer in a rec league." She picked up the clipboard and went to the team's bench. She motioned for the players to make a circle and she got down on one knee. The ring of blue jerseys prevented Jos from hearing what she was saying, but she was smiling as she returned to a puzzled Colleen.

"Who's that?"

"That's Nellie Rafferty. She's carparazzi, or, at least she was. Now she's gone to work for the Argent car company."

"What's she doing here?" Jos noticed she now had Colleen's full attention, her cell phone abandoned in her lap.

"I have a meeting with her after the game. We have some business to discuss."

"Really? This wouldn't be the same Nellie I heard mentioned during a recent visit to my tub?"

She heard the sarcasm in Colleen's voice. "It is."

"Huh."

She felt Colleen's stare but she refused to make eye contact. She wasn't in the mood to answer her questions. The team returned to the field, but she noticed Myles and the goalie, Samantha, hang back for a private conference with Nellie. Eventually Samantha took off the goalie gloves and the gold vest she wore and handed them to Myles. She nodded to Nellie and ran to Myles's position.

"Oh, my God," Colleen said. "Is she really going to make him the goalie?"

"I think so."

Jos watched him walk to the goal with Nellie. She got behind him and pointed to the white line and whispered to him. He nodded several times, and before she headed back to the team, they exchanged a high-five.

A commentary buzzed through the parent spectators and Jos kept her gaze on the field. She knew what they were saying and she couldn't blame them. They'd watched him make mistakes game after game. The quarter began and Jos shifted her gaze between Myles, Bridget and Nellie. She wanted to watch all three of them at the same time. Nellie paced up and down the sideline, clapping and shouting encouragements. They'd spread out and indeed had much better coverage. They no longer looked like a herd. Once in a while she would call out to a child by his or her number, since she didn't know their names, and offer a suggestion.

Bridget flew up and down the field, expertly dribbling and passing. Within another minute, she'd scored her second goal. As the teams prepared for the kickoff, Nellie jogged down the sideline to Myles and gave him instructions. No doubt she was giving him a crash course on the special rules for goalies. When she crouched with her hands out in front of her, he imitated her and prepared for the kickoff.

"I hope your *friend* knows what she's doing," Colleen said, in a tone that clearly implied she doubted Nellie's abilities.

"She used to play soccer," Jos countered.

Colleen leaned closer. "Listen, about the other day when we were with Kelly—"

Jos held up a hand. "I don't want to talk about it, Colleen. Let's just focus on the kids." Out of the corner of her eye she watched Colleen consider the request before she leaned back in her chair and let it go.

The whistle blew and the kickoff sent the ball toward the other team. Jos tracked the ball, watching it move closer to Myles and then farther away. That was the story of kid soccer, four quarters of constant turnovers. Amid the jostling and swirling of arms and legs, a whistle sounded when an opponent hit the ground. One of Nellie's players had accidentally tripped him. Penalty kick.

Jos groaned. The game clock sat on a table between the teams. Three seconds left. The game would end in a tie if Myles couldn't block the shot.

"This is like the movies," Colleen said. "I'm expecting the music to crescendo at any moment."

Nellie was calling directions to Myles as the referee prepared the teams for the kick. Then he blew his whistle. The kicker did a quick two-step and sent the ball sailing. The arc was perfect and headed for the corner. Myles appeared to be in slow motion, unable to catch up to the ball. Then he stepped, jumped and swatted it away. The clock quickly went to zero.

Jos was on her feet cheering. She shouted at Myles who gave a thumbs-up before Bridget slammed into him with a body hug. Colleen threw her arms around Jos and kissed her hard.

When Jos stepped away, her gaze immediately went to Nellie, who was staring at them, her hands in her pockets. Jos wanted to scream across the field that the kiss meant nothing.

It wasn't a romantic kiss between lovers but a kiss between two parents who'd spent years trying to find something that interested Myles, something that showcased his talents. The kiss was just a byproduct of their joy. Their son had been successful.

Her knees went weak and she fell back into her lawn chair. Nellie was the one who had found his talent. Just twenty minutes before, Jos had decided Nellie had no place in her world. Now she gazed across the field at Nellie shaking a parent's hand and high-fiving one of the team members.

Jos looked over her shoulder. Kelly had finally appeared and Colleen was catching her up. Dressed in a silk blouse and designer jeans, her face in full makeup, she looked completely out of place among the ratty T-shirted parents. She tried to look interested, nodding and smiling as Colleen recapped the game, but her gaze focused on her expensive heels, which had sunk into the soft soil.

"Hey," Nellie called as she approached.

Jos gave her a big hug that probably lasted longer than it should have. She introduced her to Kelly and Colleen just as Bridget and Myles joined them.

"Can you believe it?" Myles asked.

Jos thought she was going to cry. She bit her lip and nodded.

His smile evaporated. "Aw, Mom," he said. "C'mon." He hated it when she cried.

Bridget looked at Nellie and said, "Are you going to be our coach from now on, Ms. Rafferty?"

Nellie's face struggled for the right expression. "Um, oh…"

"Bridge, we'll have to see," Jos said, pulling her daughter into a hug.

"Who wants pizza for lunch?" Colleen asked.

The kids immediately agreed and started to grab the lawn chairs. "Are you coming, Mom?" Myles asked. "And can Ms. Rafferty come?"

"That's really nice of you to invite me, Myles, but I have to be somewhere in a little while," Nellie replied. "But thanks for doing a great job as goalie." She offered him a fist bump before he followed Kelly and Colleen to the car.

Jos noticed Colleen taking a long look back at her and Nellie before she left.

"Thank you," Jos said with tears in her eyes. "How did you know he'd make a good goalie?"

"I got here right before he picked up that bug from the ground. He was so fast. He has great hands." She offered a seductive look and said, "Just like his mother."

Jos felt her cheeks warm and she looked away. They headed for the parking lot with the last group of parents. "So do you have time to talk business or do you really need to be somewhere?"

"I kinda made that up," she said, embarrassed. "I didn't think your ex wanted me to come."

The conversation died as they reached Jos's van. Once the lawn chair was stowed, Jos said, "Where should we go?"

"Well, I'm keeping you from your family. Can this wait?"

"No, it can't," Jos said adamantly. "It can't wait at all."

CHAPTER TWENTY-THREE

Tempe, Arizona

They headed to the Chuckbox for lunch. Located across from Arizona State, the Chuckbox was legendary in Tempe for its great hamburgers. Nellie arrived first and waited in the parking lot for Jos's van. She felt so good she wanted to dance. It had been one of the best mornings she could remember. Chewing out the jackass coach, helping Myles's self-esteem and winning the game were a collective trifecta.

Jos pulled into the lot and found a space toward the back. When she opened her door, Nellie hopped on the running board and kissed her. Jos pulled her closer and stroked her bottom. A car alarm chirped and they separated. They went inside and once they'd placed their order, Nellie leaned forward and stared at Jos.

"Well, that kiss answers one of my questions," Nellie said.

Jos raised an eyebrow. "Which was?"

"After your ex kissed you at the game, I wondered if the two of you were back together. But I know that's not possible after our kiss. It was just too hot." When Jos didn't disagree, she added, "So I don't think it's fair of you to be upset with me for sleeping with Felice when you're still seeing your ex, and possibly your ex's lover."

Jos nearly spit out her iced tea. "What?"

"I saw the way Kelly looked at you. She's after you, right?"

Jos swirled her tea and said, "Maybe."

"I knew it," Nellie said. "Threesome?"

Jos wanted to slink from the seat to the floor. "Maybe."

"So, are you going for it?" she asked casually.

Jos couldn't look at her. "It happened once. It was a mistake. I'm not sleeping with either of them ever again."

"And you should know I'm not sleeping with Felice ever again."

Their eyes met across the table, each woman assessing the other's honesty. Eventually Jos smiled tentatively and Nellie grinned. Then Jos's eyes pooled with tears. Nellie automatically reached across the table for her hand.

"What's wrong?"

"What you did for Myles…" She took a deep breath. "You're not who I thought you were, Nellie Rafferty."

Nellie leaned back and adjusted her ball cap. "Let me guess. You think I'm a womanizer who'll do anything to get the shot. I step on people to get what I want and I don't care who's left in my path of destruction."

"That was my original opinion," Jos admitted. "But I was wrong." She looked at the table. "There's other stuff, but we don't have to talk about it right now." Her gaze quickly met Nellie's before she looked away.

Nellie sat up straight in the booth like someone had slammed into her chest. She'd thought of some "other stuff" too that she wanted to talk to Jos about. Yet, she heard the hesitancy in Jos's voice. She wasn't ready. She needed more time. *And so do I.*

"Hey, it's okay," she answered. She saw the relief in Jos's eyes. "Let's stick to business right now. I did some checking on your friend Robert and his story."

"And?"

"He's who he says he is. A contact of mine who used to work for Toyota remembers him. He's legit. Known as a standup guy. If he's saying there's something wrong with the Folie, there probably is."

"That's what I thought too. He's very sincere."

She held up a hand and pulled her journal from the messenger bag. "Somebody who might not be on the up and up is this Mr. Brent. He's a PR guy based in Detroit. I'm not sure what his angle is at the moment, but he's the one who's at the center of all of this, right?"

She shifted uncomfortably in her seat. "Yes. He's the one who told me where your journal was. He got me the contact at Black Lake—"

"The place where a stand of trees suddenly appeared in front of my condo," Nellie interjected. "Sorry," she said quickly. "Didn't mean to interrupt."

Jos's eyes narrowed. "Wait. Your condo is behind those trees?" Nellie nodded. "I saw those. Wow, you probably had an awesome view. That sucks."

Nellie could tell Jos genuinely felt sorry for her. In that moment she realized Jos would never be at the top of the carparazzi regardless of how long she worked. She just wasn't ruthless enough. That was a good thing. She was so tenderhearted that to change her would ruin who she was.

"Argent suggested that GM plant a stand of trees, which would keep me from photographing the lake."

Jos sat up straighter. "Wait. *Argent* did that to you? The people you're working for now? Why would you go work for them?"

She sighed and shook her head. "I know it sounds crazy. But Jos, I'm tired. I've been chasing cars for twenty-five years. I've been spit on, shoved, threatened, cursed at, assaulted, and nearly run off the road. My back is in bad shape, and I've avoided surgery for a decade. I don't want to go under the knife. I just want to spend time with Willie. Argent is paying me a million dollars to sit around and take pictures once in a while. And," she added, "to thwart other members of the carparazzi from getting shots of Argent vehicles."

Jos crossed her arms. "I can't believe this. Argent has completely manipulated you. And me. I'm pissed. Why aren't you?"

"Maybe it's because I'm older," she admitted with a sigh.

Jos made a face. "Don't give me that."

"It's true," she argued, raising her voice. "You've done this for a year. I've done this my entire adult life. My perspective is a little different."

"So you're selling out. Giving up. Letting Argent use you."

She shook her head. How could she make Jos understand? Whereas her ethics could be somewhat flexible, Jos's were black and white. She sighed. "Call it what you want." She shoved her untouched hamburger away and stood to leave. "I'm not hungry anymore."

"What about the Folie? What if it's dangerous?"

"It's not," she snapped. "Leave it alone."

"But you just said—"

"I've changed my mind." She pulled out her wallet and threw a twenty on the table.

Jos gave her a hard stare. "I only have one other question for you. What would Willie say?"

Nellie leaned across the table until her lips almost touched Jos's cheek. "Willie doesn't even know it's Saturday."

She was numb by the time she got back home. But her appetite had returned. Willie was eating his lunch on the porch, so she decided to make a sandwich and join him. Jos just didn't understand, she told herself. Their lives were in completely different places. Her career was just starting and Nellie's was ending, or at least it seemed that way. Jos's comment about Argent using her stung, but it wasn't true. She was getting from Argent what she wanted: a way to spend more time with Willie. Feeling used was a matter of perspective. You were only being used if you believed what was happening to you was unjust. In this case Nellie knew exactly what was happening, and she was okay with it.

"And since I'm okay, I'm not being used," she said out loud as she headed for the porch.

Chevy was sitting next to Willie. Any other dog would be begging for food but not Chevy. He was listening attentively while Willie told a story. When she heard the name Ralph, she stopped and froze. She was still behind him so he couldn't see her. She wanted to know who this person was. She pulled her phone from her pocket and quickly found her tape recorder app. She set the phone just to the left of Willie but elected to stay out of his peripheral vision, worried that if he saw her, he'd abandon the story.

After he took another bite of his sandwich, he continued. "I didn't think it would be a big deal at first. I mean Renault was doing it and everyone loved the VW Beetle too. But they were smaller cars. This was supposed to be a cool six-seater, and boy, it was a beaut." He paused and nodded, as if Chevy were responding. Nellie leaned against the doorjamb, listening intently and hoping the recorder was picking everything up.

"But when Frank drove the proto, it flipped. That's when I knew the swing ax wasn't going to work. We went to Ed, all four of us. Me, Von, Frank and Charles. We told him it was dangerous. And it only took fifteen bucks to fix it!" he shouted. "In 1959, fifteen bucks was a lot more than it is now, but it wasn't a fortune when you're talking about a car."

He lifted his water glass with a shaky hand and Nellie took a step to help him, but she stopped herself. Mai came down the hallway, but Nellie saw her before Willie did. She waved her hands, motioning Mai to stay back. She nodded and returned to the kitchen.

The water glass managed to reach his lips and return safely to the table without an accident. "People died, including the Caddy Man's son. That was enough for me. I left, yes I did." He seemed to puff out his chest, his head nodding. "When Ralph came around, I talked. I told him who was making his life hell. Yes, I did. It was the right thing to do."

He pointed at Chevy. "You know who saved the day? Johnny D., that's who. Threatened to resign, he did, unless they coughed up the lousy fifteen bucks a car."

When he leaned back, his whole body settled in the chair, as if his joints had disintegrated. Nellie thought he was asleep until she heard a few notes of "Red is the Rose," her mother's favorite Irish song. She closed her eyes and saw her mother singing it to her at bedtime.

He warbled the last note and whispered, "I'll be joining you soon, my love."

Suddenly she couldn't breathe. She needed air. She grabbed her phone while his head was down and bolted outside. She didn't think. She just dialed. It went to voice mail. She hung up immediately and sent a text instead. *Jos, I need to talk to you. Call me. Please. I'm sorry about this afternoon.*

She hit playback and listened to her father's monologue. 1959. That was when he worked for GM. A prototype that flipped. Johnny D saving the day. She was rather certain she knew what he was talking about but she wanted to be sure.

She headed for the shed and the office behind the six beautiful cars. Her father had an extensive library of car manuals and books about cars. He'd grouped them by manufacturer. She went to the General Motors section and found what she was looking for.

CHAPTER TWENTY-FOUR

Beatty, Nevada

Jos couldn't help humming the old song "Route 66" as she motored through Kingman, a rural northeastern Arizona town that benefited from the tourists traveling along the famous road. She was headed again for Beatty, only this time it wasn't as an auto spy. She was acting as a photographer for *Auto Monthly*. She would attend an official photo shoot sponsored by Kia.

Andy had sent her with the directive, "Get a shot no one else will have." When she asked what that meant, he said, "I have no fucking idea, but according to my leadership seminar, I'm supposed to help each employee aspire to his or her own greatness. I'm figuring that if you get a shot nobody else got, you'll feel great."

She'd nodded but she was unclear how to accomplish such a feat, seeing as she'd be among a gaggle of photographers all waiting behind a rope for the unveiling. Once that occurred, they would contort themselves however necessary to capture the car from various angles while it turned slowly on a platform that reminded her of an old record turntable.

She checked her phone. No new messages. She sighed. Nellie had been calling her twice a day for the last five days, but she never called her back. Sometimes Nellie left messages and sometimes she didn't. When she did, they were all the same. She begged her to call saying she had something important to tell her. She'd figured out what Willie was talking about. Jos was certainly curious but she chose not to reply.

On her drive to Beatty she'd decided to spend some time working on herself. She needed to be alone while she found the balance between her career and parenting. She'd made a decision to cut off all communication with Nellie and all unnecessary or sexual interactions with Colleen. She'd cut Nellie out completely, believing that until she learned to turn off her libido, she couldn't even be friends with her. As for Colleen, she had to interact with her as a co-parent, just not in the bedroom.

She'd asked Colleen if she could stop by on her way out of town, but Colleen had misconstrued her meaning and opened her front door wearing only a silk robe. What was even more disturbing was seeing Kelly behind Colleen, stretched out on the couch wearing a black camisole top—and nothing else.

Jos stayed planted on the front doormat, afraid that if she entered, she'd be stuck there all day. She'd tried the threesome idea with them and it had done nothing for her. She tried to keep her gaze on Colleen while they spoke, but every few sentences she glanced toward Kelly. She'd started to pleasure herself and her moans served as background music for Jos's conversation with Colleen.

"I'm dialing back on everything," she explained. "I just need some time."

Colleen took her hand and attempted to tug her inside. "That's great. Start tomorrow," she said with a wink. "Have some fun with us today."

Jos shook her head and stepped backward. "No, it starts today, right now. I'm going out of town until Monday, but I'll be back in time to pick the kids up from school. Don't forget soccer practice tonight. It's Thursday."

"I got it," Colleen said. She parted the silk of her robe just enough to expose her left nipple. "She misses you. Come inside and give us a taste."

Jos took a breath and shook her head. "Don't you have work today?"

"Nope. We took the day off and you should too." Colleen licked her lips and blew her a kiss.

"Can't," Jos insisted.

Kelly panted and thrust her hips into the air, her moans intensifying. Colleen turned to watch. "Sure you don't want some of that?"

"Yeah, I'm sure. I gotta go."

She headed back to the van and heard the front door slam behind her. Colleen was mad. Jos hoped she changed her attitude before she picked the kids up from school.

"Maybe Kelly can put her in a good mood," she'd muttered.

Two hours later her mind was a blank space. Driving through the desert could do that to a person. The neutral shades of brown, endless tumbleweeds and lack of eye-catching scenery often hypnotized drivers.

"Probably why I talk to myself so much," she reflected.

One thing she hated about the spy business was the loneliness. When she was out on the road it came to her in little reminders. She missed Myles's running commentary while he tried to brush his teeth or Bridget's refusal to turn off her light so she could read just one more page. And she missed Colleen, or rather what she symbolized. Companionship. A lover. A partner. She blinked to regain control of her emotions.

Talking to herself countered the feeling of isolation. It often provided insight and epiphanies about life. Such an epiphany had occurred around Wickenburg earlier in the day. She wasn't going to press Colleen to be with Myles and Bridget. When she got home after this job, she'd talk to her mother about helping with the kids when she was out of town. No more begging Colleen to see the kids. If she wanted to see them, she'd make the effort and she'd get Kelly on board. Otherwise, Jos would approach parenting as if she were a single parent. Done. For good.

She found herself struggling to stay awake as she turned off U.S. 95 and approached Beatty. It was nearly four o'clock. She drove past the Sourdough Saloon and stared at the enormous Cadillac in the third space, right where Nellie and the bartender had made out the last time she was up here. Maybe she'd go have dinner there. During her last visit, the clerk at the Atomic Inn had mentioned the Sourdough's world famous hamburgers. At this point, since she'd skipped lunch, she'd settle for a halfway decent meal. She got checked in and hurried to her room.

A shower refreshed her and there was quickness to her step as she walked up two streets to the Sourdough Inn. The Caddy was still there but in the last hour the parking lot had filled with cars, many of them Kias. She guessed many of them were Kia people and carparazzi, here for the photo shoot. Country music seeped through the doors and the murmur of the crowd greeted her when she entered.

She wasn't prepared for the abundance of car memorabilia everywhere. After bumping into a waitress carrying a full tray of drinks, she realized she needed to watch where she was going. Once she sat down she could stare at the walls.

She edged her way to the bar and an empty stool on the side. A small group gave a loud cheer. In the center was a very large woman who Jos recognized as Caress, the bartender with three stars in Nellie's journal. She had her arms around two other women. They downed shooters while she shouted encouragement. When the shooters were gone, she gave each woman a long kiss, which caused another group of male onlookers to hoot loudly.

Jos rolled her eyes and slid onto the stool. The bartender, a man who looked to be nearly a hundred, chatted with a patron seated at the middle of the bar. She wondered how long it would take for him to notice her, so she was genuinely surprised when he finished a sentence, looked toward her and held up a hand. He reminded her of Willie when he was all there.

"What can I get you?" a female voice asked from behind. Caress ambled past Jos on her way behind the bar.

"Vodka on the rocks."

"Coming right up." She mixed the drink and Jos studied the many tattoos along her arms. Most were of female faces but some were artistic symbols and patterns. She also had a few tattoos of cars like the '66 Mustang.

"I like your Mustang," she said as the woman served her drink.

"Thanks. I'm Caress and this is my place. Is this your first time at the Sourdough?"

The question sounded innocent, but Jos couldn't help but feel as if Caress was coming on to her. It also didn't help that she was decked out in a leather vest and leather pants. Her enormous breasts strained the vest's buttons, which looked like they could pop off at any moment. Jos's gaze floated to the connect-the-dots tattoo on her left breast.

"Sugar, are you with me?"

"Of course," she stumbled. She took a hefty belt of the vodka and met Caress's stare. "I was just admiring your tattoo."

She traced the dots with her forefinger. "You mean this one?"

"Um, yeah."

Caress reached into the recesses of the bar and pulled out a marker. "Care to connect the dots?" She leaned forward, practically shoving her cleavage into Jos's face.

Jos sat there stupidly with the marker in her hand. "Really?"

"Go ahead. Don't worry. It washes off."

She steadied her hand on the bar and found the number one near Caress's areola. At this angle she had a side view of her nipple.

"Hmm," Caress said. "You have a very gentle stroke. And I notice you prefer to use the broad side of the marker rather than the slim side."

"Is that significant?"

"I think it means you're bold, not afraid to take chances. Only one other woman I know used the broad side. And she's a daredevil, oh, yes she is."

Jos followed the numbers and when the final line was drawn, she saw the outline of a giraffe.

"I take it you like giraffes?" She downed the rest of the vodka, and Caress reached for the bottle.

"I love giraffes," she said, filling up Jos's glass again. "Anyone who hardens my nipples the way you just did gets a round on me."

"Thanks," Jos said. She took a belt and felt the cares of her life drop into a heap on the floor.

Caress stepped away to check on the other patrons, but she came back carrying two shot glasses and a bottle of tequila. Jos had just finished her second drink and grew wide-eyed at the sight of the bottle.

"Um, I don't know if this is a good idea. I'm a lightweight."

Caress ignored her protest and filled the glasses. "Don't worry, baby, Caress will take care of you."

They clinked glasses and downed the liquid. Jos felt the burn from her tongue to the bottom of her stomach. Her eyes flew open and she realized what she'd forgotten to do—eat.

"Do you think I could get a hamburger?"

"Absolutely. Our burgers are the best." She signaled the cook, who nodded. She poured them each another shot. "How would you like to go home with me tonight? We could take a bath and you could wash this marker off my chest. I think it's the least you could do since you're the one who drew all over me."

Jos sat up straighter and said, deadpan, "Oh, I'm sorry. I thought you wanted me to draw on you."

Caress laughed, and Jos melted. Caress's smile was delightful. "I did, sugar. It's all good." She put Jos's hand on her breast, and Jos automatically started tracing the line with her finger. "So, how about coming home with me tonight?"

"Sure," she said automatically. She was transfixed by the image of the giraffe, and she didn't even realize she'd downed another shooter until the burn in her throat reminded her.

"You haven't told me your name, sugar. I've served you drinks, let you draw on my chest and see my boob, but you haven't given me anything."

Everything was starting to separate and float around the room. Jos leaned forward and took her hand. "I'm so sorry. How rude of me!"

Caress laughed. "What is it, sugar? What's your name?"

"Jos. Jos Grant."

Caress's expression shifted to disappointment. "Oh. I know who you are."

"You don't sound happy about that."

"I'm not." Caress grabbed a wet bar towel and rubbed it against the giraffe until it disappeared. "You don't get to play."

"Why not?" Jos asked, frustrated. She was completely turned on—and drunk.

Caress disappeared around a corner and Jos closed her eyes. Everything seemed to sway back and forth.

"Jos?"

She blinked and knew she was dreaming. Nellie was standing in front of her.

CHAPTER TWENTY-FIVE

Beatty, Nevada

"Are you real or a dream?" Jos slurred.

"I'm very real. I came all the way up here to talk to you."

"Why?"

"Because you wouldn't answer my calls." She turned to Caress with a scowl. "Damn it, Caress, why'd you get her drunk? I need her sober."

Caress put a hand on her hip. "How was I supposed to know who she was? Lighten up, Rafferty!" She expertly snapped Nellie's bottom with her bar towel.

"Ow! That hurt," Nellie exclaimed.

"That ain't the only thing that's gonna hurt, baby." Caress blew her a kiss.

"You two are luvahs," Jos said.

"What?" Nellie asked.

"She says we're lovers." Caress snapped her with the towel again before heading to the other end of the bar.

"Are you?" Jos asked.

Nellie sighed and leaned against the bar. "It's complicated. Caress is an amazing woman."

"I get that," Jos said. "We were going to sleep together until you ruined it." She opened her mouth and held the empty shot glass above her tongue, like a baby bird waiting for something to drop in.

"You drank it all," Nellie said sharply. The thought of Caress sleeping with Jos perturbed her. She'd never cared who else Caress slept with as long as she was careful. Yet for some reason, the idea of Jos being in Caress's bed really pissed her off—unless she was there too. "Come on, we're leaving."

Nellie tried to take her arm, but she pulled away. "Wait. My burger. I need to eat."

"Stay here and I'll go get it. Try not to pick up any more women while I'm gone."

"Funny," Jos said with a fake laugh.

Nellie couldn't help but chuckle and her anger disappeared. So this was Jos plastered. She was still adorable. She got her burger and returned to find Caress talking to her at the bar. Two more empty tequila shooters sat between them. Caress was stroking Jos's cheek and Jos was smiling.

"I thought you weren't going to pick up any more women while I was gone."

"I never agreed to that," Jos said. "And this is the same woman. In fact, I already told you on the phone that we needed to completely sever ties to each other."

"What? You never told me that. You never called me back."

"Well, I meant to tell you. I just hadn't gotten around to it."

"Great. We can talk about it in the morning. Right now, I need your help." She wrapped Jos's arm around her neck and helped her off the stool. "Say goodnight to Caress."

"Goodnight, Caress," Jos said in a sickeningly sweet voice.

"Goodnight, sugar. Maybe sometime later we can…" Instead of finishing her sentence, she made a V with her fingers and slowly flicked her tongue between them.

"Oh, yeah!" Jos proclaimed.

Nellie shot a withering look at Caress. "You are no help at all. None."

"I'm not happy. I'm going home alone without you or her. Together would be nice," Caress said, grinning. "What do you say to a threesome?"

Nellie opened her mouth to reply, but Jos said, "No more threesomes. It's just too crowded."

Caress's jaw dropped. "Knock me over." Once she'd recovered, she stroked Jos's cheek once more and said, "Honey, don't ever let one bad experience taint the entire well." She kissed her on the lips before she walked away.

"C'mon," Nellie said as they trudged toward the exit.

"I bet Felice would be into threesomes," Jos announced.

"I bet you're right," Nellie said as they meandered through the crowd. "But remember, I've stopped sleeping with her."

"Humph."

It took nearly twenty minutes to walk back to the Atomic Inn with Jos struggling to remain in an upright position. In the room she set Jos on the king-size bed and fed her part of the hamburger and some water. When Nellie stood to retrieve another bottle of water from her duffel, Jos fell backward and started to snore.

Nellie shook her head and checked her watch. Six thirty. Jos would probably wake up in a few hours once the tequila wore off. Nellie set up the information she wanted to show her before treating herself to the rest of Jos's burger and a beer.

She turned on CNN and climbed into the bed. She watched Jos sleep and gently stroked her silky hair. She was beautiful, almost regal-looking. Then she snored and Nellie chuckled. Such an unregal sound coming from someone so gorgeous.

She watched the news for an hour, her gaze straying from the screen to Jos's peaceful face. Eventually watching her wasn't enough. She discarded the empty beer bottle in the wastebasket and snuggled against her. She wrapped an arm around her middle and buried her face against Jos's neck. Jos stirred and pulled Nellie closer.

Nellie kissed her earlobe, the base of her neck and her jaw. When her lips met the corners of Jos's lips, Jos sighed and turned over, offering her mouth to Nellie. After a sweet kiss, she took Jos's cheeks between her palms and stared into her eyes, looking for permission. Jos pulled them together and she got her answer.

Nellie slid on top of her. Breasts collided, tongues explored. Jos tugged on Nellie's T-shirt. "Too many clothes," she whined.

They sat up and Nellie peeled off her shirt. Jos struggled with her buttons while Nellie's heart raced in anticipation. Her impatience boiled over and she took control of dispensing with her clothes. She cupped Jos's breasts together and tasted her nipples. Jos sighed as Nellie licked and nipped them to attention.

"What's this?" Nellie said, staring at two holes on either side of Jos's left nipple. "Do you have a nipple ring?"

Jos laughed. "Yeah, but I don't wear it. Colleen didn't like that other women noticed it." She frowned dramatically.

Nellie gazed into her glassy eyes. "Would you wear it for me?"

"Sure. Do you have a nipple ring?" Jos asked, cupping Nellie's small left breast.

"Nope. I'm sorry I can't give you quite the same delight you're giving to me," she said. "I'm not as well-endowed."

"You're perfect," Jos declared, kissing her again. She stroked Nellie's breasts, teasing them with her thumb and forefinger all the while. She dragged her hand down Nellie's belly.

Nellie broke the kiss and stared at her. "What happened to severing all ties with me?"

Confusion spilled onto Jos's face. They stared at each other while she unzipped Nellie's shorts and grinned. Every muscle in Nellie's body tensed as Jos burrowed underneath her boxers and between her legs. She slid through her wetness and went inside.

"Watch me," Jos commanded. "Watch me make you come."

Nellie did as she was told, giving up her precious control— and it turned her on more. Jos's fingers were magic, sliding in and out, picking up speed. Nellie's heart raced faster and faster. Jos thrust inside once more and pressed her thumb against Nellie's throbbing clitoris. She went over the edge, again and again. When she tried to pull away, Jos tightened her grip around Nellie's waist, pushing her fingers deeper inside her.

"More!" Nellie cried.

Jos gave her more until Nellie cried out one last time and collapsed on top of her.

"I think I'm having a heart attack," Nellie gasped.

"Seriously?" Jos asked.

"No, but it's certainly possible at my age."

Jos smacked her playfully as she rolled out of bed. "You're only forty-eight. You're still young," she shouted on her way to the bathroom.

"Not as young as you."

"So?"

Nellie didn't reply. She stared at the room's dingy popcorn ceiling and focused on her breathing. Did she really think she could keep up with a woman like Jos? She was so fit and beautiful. And thirty-four was young, regardless of what Jos thought.

When Jos returned from the bathroom, she wasn't smiling. She looked dangerous. She climbed on the bed and straddled Nellie. "I'm still horny. What are you gonna do about it, lady?"

"This."

Nellie pushed Jos backward and grabbed her fabulous calves, hoisting them over her shoulders. She trailed kisses up her thighs, inhaling the sweet smell of her longing. She parted her tender lips and slowly dragged her tongue the length of Jos's wetness. Jos moaned and thrust her pelvis higher. Nellie obliged and buried her tongue deep inside. Jos rocked her hips.

"Yes," she panted. "Keep going."

While her tongue played hide-and-seek, Nellie's thumb stroked Jos's clit gently, slowly, keeping time with the rocking of Jos's hips. The closer she came to climax, the faster she rocked. She started to thrash. She was on the edge. Just as she came, Nellie pressed against her center, as one orgasm turned into two and three. The waves of pleasure left her trembling. Nellie slowly lowered her onto the mattress and stretched out next to her. When she looked in Jos's eyes, she saw tears.

"Why are you crying?"

Jos shook her head and sniffed. "I can't tell you. You'll think I'm stupid."

She took her hand and entwined their fingers. "No, I won't. Tell me."

Jos stared at her. "I think you know but I'm scared to say it."

Nellie offered a little smile. So Jos felt it too. Nellie kissed her shoulder and snuggled against her. "You don't have to say it right now. But I feel it too."

"Okay," Jos whispered. "Did you really come all this way to see me?"

"I did."

The kiss they exchanged was the same as saying the words.

"What did you want to show me?" Jos asked.

"Not now. It can wait until morning," Nellie said drowsily. "Everything can wait until tomorrow."

CHAPTER TWENTY-SIX

Beatty, Nevada

Jos awoke to the door clicking shut. She sat up as Nellie brought in coffee and bagels. Her hipster hair was unusually messy, and Jos thought she looked incredibly sexy.

"Sorry. I didn't mean to wake you," Nellie said, handing her a coffee.

"It's okay. What time is it?"

"Only six-thirty. I'm used to getting up at five because of Willie. He's always been an early riser."

"Me too. Remember, I have two children. They're always up at the crack of dawn."

Nellie sank into a chair next to a small round table covered in papers. "That'll probably change in a few years when they turn into teenagers."

Jos rolled her eyes. "Don't remind me."

She realized she was completely naked under the duvet Nellie had covered her with at some point during the night.

Nellie stared at her as the conversation halted. Self-conscious, she pulled the duvet around her and headed for the bathroom.

"Aw, you're no fun," Nellie called to her. "I found your room key and went and got your duffel bag. It's in the bathroom."

Jos stopped at the doorway and dropped the duvet. Nellie's eyes seemed to pop out of her head. "I am lots of fun," Jos disagreed, "but you need to show me what you brought and I need to get ready for work. Otherwise, I'll be lounging on that bed and showing *you* how completely wet you make me just by sitting there and staring." She smiled and closed the door, pleased that Nellie's jaw had dropped.

A few minutes later, she joined Nellie at the round table and grabbed a bagel. Several index cards were in a line interspersed with a few blown up digital prints. What immediately caught her eye was a picture of a Corvair, which had been produced throughout the '60s.

"Why are we talking about the Corvair?"

"Let's start with the end of this story. I'm going to help you expose Argent."

Jos was stunned. "You are? That's great, but why? Won't you jeopardize your job? What about Willie?"

"Yes, if we do this right, I will definitely lose my job, but that's okay. And about Willie…" She pointed at the last card on the timeline. "For several months Willie has been increasingly agitated. Remember the day your Girl Scout troop was picking up trash by the highway?"

"Yes, he kept talking about missing a meeting with someone named Ralph."

"Exactly. And when I was up in Michigan, he said people were going to die. I had no idea what any of it meant until a few days ago. I overheard him talking to Chevy. I was there at the right time and I turned on my tape recorder app."

Nellie pulled out her phone and they listened to the conversation. It was difficult to hear every word, but Jos caught a reference to 1959, prototypes, the Caddy Man and the swing ax. She searched her memory and glanced at the picture. When Willie started to sing, Nellie stopped the recording.

"He's talking about the Corvair?" Jos asked.

"He is," she said, pointing at the top index card. "Time for a quick history lesson. In 1959 GM was looking to create a new and different six-seater, the Corvair. It was a beautiful car. They followed the trend of the VW Beetle and put the engine in the back. They used a swing axle, which was a type of suspension that allowed the wheel to move when it hit something in the road like a pothole. The wheel would curve depending on the irregularity.

"On a smaller car like the VW Beetle, that worked just fine. But the Corvair was bigger, so the problem was maneuverability. And when they put the engine in the back, the car was also tail-heavy. If a driver took a corner too fast, the car spun out. The tires literally folded in. Drivers were used to front-wheel drive and they didn't understand how to steer the car. The prototypes kept crashing. Some of the engineers figured it out, but the head of the division, Ed Cole, wouldn't budge. His answer was to inflate the tires at different levels. Then, when people had to oversteer to take a corner, they didn't spin out."

"But in those days automobile tires weren't supposed to be inflated at different poundage," Jos said. "That could cause a blowout."

"Exactly. It was unsafe. And what's even more ridiculous is that it would've cost fifteen dollars to change the car's suspension like the engineers suggested. But Ed Cole wouldn't spend the money. He couldn't or wouldn't understand that he was just trading problems by increasing the tire inflation."

"Wait. Was Willie one of those engineers who tried to change the Corvair?"

"He was. This was when he worked at GM." Nellie pointed to a picture of a group of men. Jos realized he was on the far right. "He was one of four engineers who begged to change the Corvair to front-wheel drive." She pointed to another picture. "Fast forward to 1960. The Corvair is named Car of the Year by *Motor Trend*. But then several accidents occur. Ernie Kovacs, a famous comic in the fifties, spins out and crashes into a pole, killing himself. The son of the head of the Cadillac division dies driving his Corvair."

"The Caddy Man's son."

"Yes. By this time, a young attorney named Ralph Nader starts to study the auto industry. He becomes interested in the Corvair and he finds someone on the inside of GM to feed him information."

"Willie," Jos concluded.

Nellie nodded. "So Willie has secret meetings with him. That's what he's been talking about." Nellie pulled out a tattered accordion folder, stained and covered in dust. "I found this on his shelf with all of his books. It's all of his notes that he shared with Ralph Nader. He couldn't stomach all the accidents. But when he shared the information with Ralph, he had no way of knowing that John DeLorean would eventually change the car. Remember, it takes a while for a book to be published. He just wanted the truth to be told because he wanted people to be safe.

"So John DeLorean takes over GM and demands they spend the fifteen dollars and change the car." Nellie pointed to a picture of DeLorean and then pulled a book from her backpack. "But then Ralph Nader's book comes out, *Unsafe at Any Speed*. He mentions several problems with various cars, but he gives an entire chapter to the Corvair."

"And that's the end of the Corvair," Jos summarized.

"It was," Nellie agreed. "Even though John DeLorean was willing to spend the money, it was too late. Once the public thought of the Corvair as a deathtrap, it was over."

"And that's why you're willing to help expose Argent," Jos said.

Nellie nodded. "Yes. I need to do it for Willie. First, I'm his daughter, and if even one person could be hurt by driving the Folie, then that's one person too many. I think it's what he would want me to do. The fact that he keeps talking about the Corvair, tells me it still weighs heavy on his mind. He probably wishes he'd done more before the accidents happened."

Jos jumped out of her chair and landed in Nellie's lap. She kissed her hard.

"Um, well, if I'd known that was part of the deal," Nellie whispered.

They kissed and groped to the point of distraction. Jos untangled herself and returned to her chair. "We need to stay professional. I have to go to the shoot in a few minutes. Do you have a plan?"

Nellie cracked a grin. "I do."

* * *

Just the thought of Jos made Nellie smile. They'd spent the entire ride home from Nevada in their separate cars talking on the phone like teenagers. Usually during the drive back from Beatty, Nellie fought to stay awake. She'd heard too many stories of people falling asleep at the wheel during a drive through the desert, so she always chugged an energy drink when she reached Flagstaff. It gave her a boost for the last hundred miles.

But the time flew by on this drive home. She and Jos chatted about all kinds of things—politics, family, religion, coming out, horses and cooking. She'd invited Jos and the kids over for a barbeque and a horse ride the next weekend. Perhaps their conversation was so lively because they were stoked on energy drinks, but it seemed only an hour or so had passed when she exited the freeway and Jos continued on to Mesa. She hated hanging up when she pulled into her driveway.

She glanced into the rearview mirror and saw her reflection—a smile. She hadn't really smiled in a very long time. It felt good to be happy, but it was a different kind of happiness. She'd always felt fulfilled and satisfied with her work, especially when it gleaned an enormous payday. It was proof of her worth in the carparazzi and it confirmed her love of the chase.

"We need to talk about some other stuff," she said to herself, repeating what Jos had said the night before. Sitting in the Jeep surrounded by the quiet of her acreage, she realized that her relationship with Jos wasn't about the chase anymore. It was about getting caught. And she liked it. She thought of Jos's soft skin pressing against her own, Jos holding her, kissing her. The image of her in that short pencil skirt, the one she wore to C'est La Vie, was imprinted on her brain. She had amazing legs. Amazing everything, really. She'd confirmed that fact once more after Jos returned from the Kia shoot. They'd had until noon to get out of the Atomic Inn and they used every minute of it.

"Whatcha smilin' at?"

She jumped in her seat. Willie and Chevy stood outside the Jeep. He had that twinkle in his eyes. She guessed he was remembering a time when he'd startled her. He loved creeping up behind her or one of her sisters and shouting, "Boo!" He always got the same reaction. They jumped and he laughed. Then they laughed. He always made them laugh.

She kept the smile but a tear rolled down her cheek. He patted her face with a palm made rough from years of hard work on the ranch and tinkering under the hoods of various automobiles.

"It's going to be okay, Parnelli. I promise," he said in a steady voice from her childhood.

"I know, Dad," she said.

He was the rock and he always made it okay. She'd grown up being her own person, unafraid of most anything because that's what her parents had taught her. Maybe that was why she wasn't afraid of her feelings for Jos. She'd never felt this way. She'd spent her life moving forward, speeding toward the next challenge. Maybe now it was time to stop, or at least slow down.

She climbed out of the Jeep and handed her camera bag to Willie. He asked, "Did you see your new friend? What was her name?"

"Jos," she said, grinning. "Yes, I saw her in Beatty."

He looked pleased. "You two make a good couple."

She was momentarily speechless. He'd pulled together all of the memories and concluded they were together. She wanted to ask about Lucy and the past but the words wouldn't come. *What good would it do?*

As they trudged toward the house, she said, "Dad, can you tell me about the Corvair?"

"Why, sure. What do you want to know?"

"Everything."

CHAPTER TWENTY-SEVEN

Nellie told Jos she wasn't willing to work with Mr. Brent until she got some answers. They all agreed to meet three days later at Washington Park. After Nellie had been introduced to Mr. Brent and Robert, they gathered around a picnic table in the shade.

"I imagine you have some questions for me," Mr. Brent said to Nellie.

"I do. I want to know how you knew where I keep my journal."

He sheepishly replied, "We have a connection at the senior center. He overheard Willie talking about it, talking about you." He paused and added, "I feel bad about using Willie like that. I apologize."

She nodded. It made sense that someone would hear Willie talking about the journal at the center. He didn't have secrets anymore and he loved to tell his stories. "Who do you work for?"

He looked at her sincerely. "You know I can't say, but I promise you that exposing the Folie is about saving lives."

They stared at each other. She suspected he was working for two different clients at the same time, and she was worried she and Jos would get caught in the middle. She'd seen it happen before and it didn't end well.

Jos touched her arm. "Why don't we at least hear what they have to say?"

Nellie shrugged and crossed her arms. "Okay, tell me what's wrong with the Folie."

Mr. Brent motioned for Robert to explain. He summarized the cruise control problem for her and ended by saying, "The car won't automatically slow down when the brake is tapped. It lurches and then returns to the original speed set on the cruise control."

"That could be a problem," Nellie said dryly. "What's the set of commands?"

"It's a little complicated to explain, but eight of the car's features must be used in a certain order while the car is at sixty or above. There's also a duration factor involved with some of the operations."

Nellie nodded. "It's like activating the Bluetooth, followed by turning on the back window defogger, followed by six more actions, one of which is using the cruise control," she summarized.

"And actually," Robert said, "You have to turn the cruise on twice during the series."

"I think it's amazing that you can even name the problem," Jos said. "Why is this happening?"

"They don't know," Mr. Brent said. "But Jacques Perreault thinks the risk is negligible and wants the Folie to move into production. The engineers calculate it as a less than one percent risk factor."

"But anyone in that one percent who performs those actions in that set order is going to be dead when they encounter a patch of traffic and can't slow down," Jos said.

"Exactly," said Mr. Brent.

"When is the release date?" Nellie asked.

He shuffled through his notepad. "November twentieth. Just in time for the holidays."

Nellie shook her head. "I just can't believe Argent isn't pushing it back."

"They've worked on this issue a lot," Robert explained. "They've defined the problem but they just can't fix it yet."

"There was even talk of ditching the cruise control," Mr. Brent added, "but Jacques Perreault insisted the feature remain. Cruise control is the middle ground between driving and a self-driving car. He believes if it's left out, the Folie will be less valuable than a regular car."

"It makes sense," Nellie agreed, "but still, he should pull it if it's not ready."

"Where does his daughter stand on the issue?" Jos asked.

At the mention of Felice, Nellie shifted uncomfortably. She'd told Jos she was done with her, but she still admired her business prowess. Jos's reaction had suggested she didn't want Nellie to admire anything about her.

Robert answered the question. "I heard some gossip from a female driver who happened to be around a corner when Felice took a call from another Argent executive. It sounds like she's trying to reason with her father, but he won't listen. He sees the Folie as his legacy."

"It still can be," Nellie argued. "Just not the way he envisioned."

Jos turned to her and asked, "How?"

"Argent has successfully addressed the greatest obstacle to the self-driving car: response to human judgment. That's the number one challenge the tech companies faced when they designed it. They couldn't teach the car to make split-second responses based on what human drivers were doing in the vehicles around them. The fact that Argent has done this is huge."

"But it's not enough for Jacques Perreault," Robert stated. "So on Thursday we'll be doing more tests with the cruise control on the track from ten to eleven." He looked at Nellie. "I've heard you'll be at the proving grounds photographing the Amour at eight thirty."

"That worked out well," Jos said.

"Sometimes it just happens," Nellie agreed, although she was somewhat unnerved that Mr. Brent knew her schedule.

The day before she'd gone to Nevada to meet Jos, Felice had sent a text arranging for her to shoot the retooled Amour. She'd told Jos she planned to poke around the Folie after the shoot. Mr. Brent's plan allowed them to skip a step. Sometimes luck was a critical factor in carparazzi work.

"So the timing works perfectly. You could slip out the back, go to the track and take some video," Robert said. He pulled out a map of the Argent Proving Grounds and drew a red line from the showroom where the Amour was housed to the hide shack on the track. "If you go behind the buildings and hug the exterior walls, you'll avoid the cameras. You'll wind up on the easternmost curve of the track. You can duck into the hide shack. As long as no other carparazzi appear, you should be fine."

Jos appeared to be studying the map, deep in thought. Her brow furrowed and her lips pursed.

Nellie touched her arm. "What are you thinking?"

She looked at her with concern. "I'm thinking this plan really exposes you." She addressed Robert. "How long will it take you to execute the commands to get the money shot, or in this case, the video?"

"Probably two minutes. I just have to get it up to speed, go through the motions, lock on the cruise control twice, and take it once more around the track. Then I'll tap the brake, which of course, should turn off the cruise control. You'll know it's not working if, after I tap the brake, it lurches and starts to accelerate. That's the money shot. Seeing the car jolt forward."

"If that played on a news channel with the proper voiceover, it would be the end of the Folie," Mr. Brent added. "Watching a car jerk around a test track doesn't do much for consumer confidence."

"Okay," Nellie said. "Sounds like a plan." Her palms were sweating and she wiped them on her shorts. Jos reached over and squeezed her hand.

They all got up and Nellie turned to the men. "Just so you both know—if at any point I feel like I'm going to get caught,

I'm bailing. Jacques Perreault isn't someone I want interrogating me."

They nodded, then headed for the parking lot while Jos and Nellie remained by the bench, holding hands. "Are you okay?" Jos asked.

Nellie's gaze followed the men as they left. She noticed they stopped at the end of the sidewalk and talked further. "Look," she said, "they're having the meeting after the meeting. I don't trust Mr. Brent. I want to know who he's working for."

"Who do you think it is?"

"Hard to say. Could be a competitor. Could be someone from the tech world who doesn't want the auto industry to succeed where they themselves have been unsuccessful. Whoever creates a self-driving car that can be mass produced is going to be very rich."

"I've heard eventually cars will just be black boxes that people step into and press a button. While the car drives, the passengers can do other things."

Nellie chuckled. "I can't picture Americans buying black boxes. Vanity is part of the American automobile experience."

"True," Jos conceded.

They watched Mr. Brent and Robert go their separate ways. Nellie wasn't surprised to see Mr. Brent slide into a Renault.

"I could follow him," Jos suggested. "See if he goes anywhere interesting. See who he meets."

Nellie shook her head. "Nuh-uh. Not gonna happen."

Jos looked indignant and folded her arms. "Why not? You're not the only one who can handle risky assignments."

Nellie glanced around the park. They were alone. She pulled Jos against her for a kiss. Just having her close fortified her resolve for what she had to do. "I know you can handle it. I just want to keep you safe."

"Don't you think I want that for you? I've read about some of the tactics Jacques Perreault's used against carparazzi."

She gazed at Jos's worried face and stroked her cheek.

"Nellie? Nellie, are you listening to me?"

"Every word," she said before she drew their lips together again.

* * *

Click. Click. Click. The camera captured shot after shot. Nellie moved around the Argent Amour slowly—climbing, kneeling and crawling over the interior to create a photographic scrapbook of every angle and every significant part. Amid the five or six hundred shots there would be twenty or thirty chosen for the website. Potential customers would scroll through them and decide whether they wanted to visit an Argent showroom. From a corporate perspective, the pictures were crucial: they determined Argent's profit margin for the next quarter.

A bead of sweat stung her eye. She stood up, backed away from the harsh lights and wiped her brow. She remembered a different shoot a year before—chasing the Amour through the backstreets of Boulogne. It was one of the three cars Nellie had scooped. Photos of its redesigned body were plastered on the cover of *Motor Trend* long before the PR department had planned for it to be revealed. As she crawled into the driver's seat to get some pictures of the dashboard, it seemed incredibly ironic that she was now taking the Amour's official photos.

Her heart raced but she knew it wasn't because of the Amour. Currently she was acting in her official capacity as Argent staff photographer. But once this shoot was finished, she'd sneak out the back door and head to the track. She took a deep breath to calm her nerves. This certainly wasn't the first time she'd trespassed, and technically it wasn't trespassing—yet.

She scrolled through the five hundred and sixty-four images, making sure she'd captured every inch of the car. She'd taken several photos of the same subject from multiple angles. Most of them were winners. She pictured Felice and Jacques Perreault arguing over the stills. If the decision-makers had a tough time deciding on the final choices, the photos were a success.

"Okay, guys, it's a wrap," she announced to the two Argent employees assigned to be her helpers. They started breaking down the lights and the backdrop while Nellie fussed with her equipment. Out of the corner of her eye she watched the security guard on the sidelines. Mr. Brent and Robert hadn't mentioned him. He stood between her and the back door. She couldn't just get up and waltz past him without being questioned. She glanced at the helpers, now on their knees rolling up the backdrop. Maybe he'd leave with them.

She pulled out a cleaning cloth and began to take apart the lens. This was a tedious activity, and perhaps they would grow impatient or another duty would pull them away. She worked slowly and eventually they'd packed everything up. They approached her, carrying the backdrop. She looked up with a smile.

"Thanks, guys. I'm just going to get some of this dust off my lens. I'll only be a few more minutes. Don't let me keep you."

"*Si,*" one of them said. She wasn't sure if either of them understood much English, but they were happy to leave without her.

That only left the security guard. She could feel her heart pounding. *What if this is a bust? What if I can't get out the back door?*

The security guard's radio squawked and echoed in the large building. The guard said, "Over," and quickly dashed for the front door.

Nellie was suddenly alone. "That was lucky," she said as she stuffed everything back into the camera bag and headed for the back door.

She opened it slowly and checked left and right. No vehicles. No traffic. She hugged the building and trotted toward the track. As she got closer, she could hear voices and the engine revving. She thought she heard Robert say, "Let's get moving," but she couldn't be sure.

She looked up at the security camera overhead. She had to wait for it to spin all the way to the right. Then she'd make a mad dash for the rear of the hide shack across from the track. This was the point where she was most vulnerable. If an engineer were looking out at the track instead of studying the Folie, she'd be caught. Robert's job was to keep the engineers occupied, but there were three of them and one of him.

The camera spun to the right and she was off. This time she sprinted, glancing over her shoulder at the engineers. They all huddled together studying something under the hood.

She reached the hide shack and squatted in the corner. Her legs burned and her sciatic nerve was on fire. The angle of the shack provided protective shadows that would keep her out of sight from the engineers. The only person who might catch a glimpse of her or her long telephoto lens was Robert. She wiped her hands on her shorts and checked the aperture. Stuck inside a dark little building, she wouldn't be able to capture the clearest video. It would be grainy but viewable.

She heard the car door shut. The test was about to begin. She knelt and focused the camera on the track. She prayed there were no other carparazzi in the area. If a helicopter appeared and the Folie zipped into the hide shack, she was in trouble. She'd called Caress, Lucy and a few other contacts to check. None of them had heard anything about a flyover at Argent.

The Folie started around the track. It was a cute little sports car, much cuter than the Google car. It picked up speed around the first turn and came toward her. She started snapping photos until it passed so she could check the lighting. She scrolled through the pictures. They were definitely grainier than she wanted, but they'd do. She changed the camera to video and resituated herself. She was ready.

Robert's plan was to disengage the cruise control as he approached Nellie. It was the closest he could get without arousing suspicions. The car whizzed by her again without any problems, finishing the second lap. It started around on the third and she placed her eye in the viewfinder. She tracked the car and hit the video button. REC flashed repeatedly as the car came toward her. She trained her eye on the Folie's hood, wanting to make sure if the car jolted, she didn't jerk the camera out of focus.

Suddenly the car seemed to lunge forward, once, then twice, before accelerating toward its previous speed. The engineers swore and one gave a guttural cry of the F-word.

"Turn the damn thing off," one of the engineers barked into his radio. Nellie imagined he was calling someone near the main computer. A screech of brakes stopped the Folie. Nellie hoped Robert had his seat belt on this time. His next task was to distract the engineers again so she could run back to the building.

She peeked around the corner. He'd already opened the hood and they were all clustered over the engine. The security camera was just spinning away from her. *Go!* She ran to the building wall and pressed against it. She took deep breaths to slow her galloping heartbeat.

"Almost there, almost there," she muttered, her leg on fire from kneeling in the shed.

She continued along the exterior until she reached Building Two where Felice's office was located. A staircase offered cover and she slid underneath it. There was another security camera between Two and One, but not a person nearby. She'd wait until the camera spun away and quickly hustle up a few stairs. If security was watching the feed, it would look like she'd just exited the second floor.

The camera spun away and she charged up the stairs—just as a woman came out.

"Nellie?"

She glanced up at the well-dressed brunette in her late twenties. It took her a second, but she remembered it was Felice's assistant.

"Hi," she said, hoping she looked confused. "I just finished shooting the Amour, and I was wondering if Felice was around. You know, give her an update?"

The assistant raised her eyebrows suspiciously. "Um, she's in France. I thought she'd made it clear to you that she only comes to the States every six to eight weeks."

Nellie nodded. "Yeah, she said that, but she'd mentioned on the phone that she might come back for this."

The assistant stood up straighter, somewhat offended. "She didn't mention it to me."

"It was probably just wishful thinking. But if she's not here, she's not here." Nellie looked at her watch. "I gotta get going, but what was your name?"

She extended her hand and flashed a wide smile. The younger woman blushed. "Kim."

"Nice to meet you, Kim."

They chatted until they reached the parking lot. Nellie started up the Jeep, waved at Kim and headed for the exit. Through the rearview mirror she noticed Kim remained planted where Nellie's Jeep had been parked, watching her, making sure she left the facility.

CHAPTER TWENTY-EIGHT

Mesa, Arizona

She sped toward U.S. 60 worried a security vehicle would come charging up behind her. It had happened once before. Although she was dying to see the footage, she vowed to be patient until she reached Jos's house. Years ago she'd made the rookie mistake of stopping at a fast food place near the location to check the photos. A group of engineers recognized her and dumped a soda over her camera as they exited.

She pulled into Jos's driveway and Jos ran outside to greet her. She gingerly climbed out of the Jeep and fell into a long hug.

"Your heart is pounding," Jos said. "And it looks like you're hurt."

"It's my back. It'll be okay." She started for the door. "C'mon. I want to see if we got it."

"Not we," Jos corrected her. "This was all you, babe."

Nellie suddenly stopped. "Babe?"

Jos's cheeks reddened. "Well, I…"

Nellie wrapped her arm around Jos's waist. "I like it."

Relief flooded Jos's face and they headed inside. They went to her office and downloaded the video to Jos's computer so they could play it on the oversized monitor. The first two minutes was the Folie making the laps. It was a very pretty car and Nellie cringed, knowing what was about to happen. Then it disappeared from the picture and reappeared making the turn at the top of the track.

"Here it comes," Nellie said.

They watched as it approached the hide shack. Suddenly it lurched and Jos gasped. As it picked up speed again, the expletives of the engineers were audible, including the loud F-word.

"Oh, my," Jos said.

"Yeah," Nellie agreed. "Oh, my."

They watched the video three more times and each time, at the moment when the Folie lurched forward, they both gasped.

"Imagine how the American public is going to react to this," Jos said.

Nellie dropped onto a chair and put her head in her hands. "It'll be the end of Argent."

Jos chuckled. "Yes. Poor Felice. I can just imagine the look on her face."

"This isn't a joke, Jos," Nellie shot back. "This could ruin a company that employs thousands of people. Even though Jacques Perreault is an asshole, those people aren't. Think about everyone in Phoenix who just got a job at the proving grounds. This is about them too. And to be honest, Felice is a great businesswoman. She isn't her father." She closed her mouth when she realized Jos's lip was trembling and tears were forming in her eyes. "I'm sorry. I didn't mean to get that upset. I just remember what happened in Detroit when so many autoworkers lost their jobs. It was horrible."

Jos turned away and busied herself with Nellie's camera. "No, you're right. That was a callous thing for me to say. Of course I don't want the whole company to go out of business. I was just thinking about *her*."

Nellie went behind Jos and wrapped her arms around Jos's middle. "I've told you. There's nothing between us anymore. You're the only one I want."

Jos turned and faced her. "Really?"

"Yeah."

Nellie pulled them together for a long kiss. When she started to unbutton Jos's shirt, Jos broke the kiss. "Sorry, we don't have time. My mother is bringing Myles home early for his orthodontist appointment."

"Okay," Nellie said. "I'll just hold you."

"I'll call Mr. Brent later. When do you want to meet?"

Nellie closed her eyes for a moment and steeled her resolve. Jos wasn't going to like what she was about to say. She pulled far enough away to look in her eyes. "I'm not giving the video to Mr. Brent, at least not right away."

Jos looked thunderstruck. "You're not. Why?"

She chose her words carefully, knowing that perhaps there wasn't any diplomatic way to say what she was feeling. "I want to give Argent a chance to do the right thing. Not for Jacques or Felice's sake, but for the company's sake. Maybe if they see a copy of the video they'll recognize what will happen if they release the Folie. I'm hoping they'll be smarter than GM was all those years ago with the Corvair."

Jos stepped away and moved to the other side of the room. She paced the floor and stared at the carpet. After a long time, her head shot up and she said, "What if they're not willing to stop production? What then?"

"Then we give the original footage to Mr. Brent and go to the media." She took a breath. "I'm not willing to sacrifice the safety of American drivers, but I'd rather the company do the right thing so safety isn't compromised and people aren't thrown out of work."

Jos folded her arms as if she were cold. She couldn't look at Nellie and she seemed to be floating farther away.

"Tell me what you're thinking," Nellie implored. "Please."

"I keep wondering if this is really about her. You don't want to hurt Felice. Yes, I'm sure you've considered the families, but the Nellie Rafferty I've heard and read about wouldn't miss a chance to claim the glory. If you give this footage to Felice, there's nothing in it for you. If you give it to Mr. Brent, you'll be famous. You'll make the talk show circuit. You'll be on the cover of all the trade magazines. Who knows? You'll have exposed one of the greatest auto scandals of all time. You might even wind up in front of a Congressional subcommittee."

Nellie slowly sank into Jos's large office chair and sighed. Her back was killing her. Her knees hurt and she felt a nagging pain in her shoulder. She looked up at Jos and tried to keep her temper in check. "Two years ago your summary of me would've been absolutely correct. But then Willie got sick and it was obvious his age had caught up to him. Hell, the man's ninety-three. How much more time does he have? I don't want to hit the talk show circuit. And I certainly don't want to spend God knows how many weeks sitting in front of a bunch of egotistical windbags giving testimony against Argent." She took a deep breath and exhaled. "Jos, I'm tired. My body and my heart are sending me the same message."

"And what's the message?"

"Hang it up."

Nellie watched Jos process everything. Her gaze flitted about the room. Nellie knew she wanted to say something but she was holding back. She looked nervous and chewed on a nail, a stress habit Nellie had never seen before.

"Give it to me," Jos finally said. "Let me be the one to expose Argent."

Nellie knew Jos could be competitive, and she'd come to realize how important it was to her to establish herself.

"I wouldn't mind being on talk shows or magazine covers," Jos admitted. "Frankly, I could use the exposure to bump my career. That orthodontist we're seeing today isn't cheap."

Nellie felt as if she'd been punched in the gut. "What about Argent? What about all the workers?"

She thought for a second before she said, "We could meet somewhere in the middle between treachery and sainthood."

Nellie shook her head. "What does that mean?"

"Mr. Brent can show the Perreaults the footage. If pride gets the best of Jacques Perreault, and if he decides to mass-produce the Folie, then we go straight to the media. I'll be the one who steps in the spotlight. However, assuming they decide to shelve the Folie, when Mr. Brent takes the footage to the media, he can sell the story as the big automaker does the right thing when faced with video from the carparazzi, as provided by Jos Grant. It's a win-win. Argent stays in business, although they take a little hit because they were strong-armed into behaving ethically. I still get the bump in publicity, albeit a smaller bump. Maybe they'll even let you keep your job if they don't think you were involved."

Nellie remained silent. She was processing Jos's sudden hunger for fame, trying to remember how she'd felt during her first years in the carparazzi. Of course, she'd never had two kids to feed, nor had she worried about her next meal or a place to live. She'd always had Willie.

She finally said, "I'm not worried about my job. Like I told you before, I'm prepared to lose it. More importantly, if we give it to Mr. Brent and he takes it to the media, we can't predict how it would affect Argent's standing in the industry. You're guessing if they own up to it everything would be okay. But any publicity could rock customer confidence and send them into bankruptcy. Sometimes believing a company is capable of doing something is just as bad as doing the deed. Look at—"

"Mom, I'm home!"

They heard the front door slam shut as Myles bounded into the office followed by an older woman wearing yoga pants and a denim work shirt. When he saw Nellie, a huge grin spread across his face. They high-fived and Jos introduced Nellie to her mother, Delia.

"Are you coaching us at practice tonight?" Myles asked. "Right now our coach is a gangster."

"Excuse me?" Nellie asked.

"Since their coach quit that day at the game," Jos explained, "the only one who's stepped up to help is an older brother of one of the players. From his chosen attire at last week's practice and game, it's somewhat apparent that he may have some unsavory connections."

"What's unsavory?" Myles asked.

"Not so great," Delia replied. She shot a withering glance at Jos. "However, we shouldn't judge people solely on their appearance." She looked at Nellie as if she were the judge. "Rodolfo was very pleasant to me when I took Myles and Bridget to practice last week. I'd like that to be noted."

Jos rolled her eyes before she said, "So noted, Mom."

"You should see his tats, Coach," Myles said to Nellie. "He's got sleeves up and down his arms and a teardrop under one eye."

"Sounds like an interesting guy," Nellie said. "Does he know a lot about soccer?" she asked, hoping Rodolfo was at least qualified to coach.

Myles scratched his chin. "Well, not much. I think he just watches the games on TV. That's why you should be the coach. You're awesome."

Nellie ruffled his hair. "Aw, thanks, Myles." She leaned over to be eye to eye with him. "I can't come to practice tonight, and I'm not sure about Saturday. Let me check my schedule. Now, I know you have an appointment and I don't want you to be late."

They said their goodbyes and Jos walked Nellie to the Jeep. "Don't feel as if you have to coach. It would be great, but I know you've got a lot on your plate."

Nellie caressed her cheek. "It would be fun but first I need to figure this other thing out."

"What about my offer?" Jos asked seriously.

"Let me think about it, okay? And to be clear, I would love to help your career. You know that, don't you?"

Jos nodded slowly. "I do. I know you want to help me."

She said the words but Nellie wasn't so sure she really believed them. Nellie gave her a quick kiss in case Myles was watching and drove away. As she waited at the four-way stop at the end of Jos's block, she glanced in her rearview mirror. Jos stood in the driveway, her hands on her hips, staring at the ground. She was deep in thought. In that moment Nellie remembered they'd downloaded the footage to Jos's computer.

"Damn," she said. Someone honked and she headed for the highway, thinking out loud. "Please, please, Jos, don't do anything we'll both regret."

CHAPTER TWENTY-NINE

Jos stared at Myles's orthodontia estimate. Four grand just for starters. If she looked at the average paydays she'd received for the shots she'd taken in the last year, his braces were at least three money shots. Except for Black Lake. That would've covered his whole mouth. Two potential buyers had gotten into a bidding war over the pictures of the new Camaro, and she'd made more than she ever thought possible.

She reminded herself that Nellie had been removed from the equation that day at Black Lake. Argent had deliberately sabotaged her view by planting those pine trees. Would Jos have been so fortunate had Nellie been able to shoot from her balcony? And how could Nellie be so worried about Argent's future with the Folie when Jacques Perreault had treated her so poorly? Jos wondered if Nellie had lost her edge. Most likely caring for Willie distracted her from the chase.

She reread the text Nellie had sent while she was talking to the orthodontist. *Jos, do us both a favor and delete that video footage from your computer. This is my call and my decision. I know*

and understand your position. If there's a way to help you, I'll find it.
Trust me.

Trust me.

Could she really trust Nellie? Could Nellie really trust herself? The woman was obviously stuck in a personal quagmire with her father, in addition to handling constant, chronic pain. She clearly had job burnout, which was certainly coloring her judgment about Argent.

Jos wanted to help her. Wanted to hold her. She knew she'd fallen in love but it was so different from when she'd fallen for Colleen back when she was twenty-four. It wasn't the gooey, chocolate-covered sweet love with hearts and flowers. This love was about support, friendship, laughter—and sex. Yes, the physical chemistry between them was electric. Colleen was an excellent lover but Nellie seemed to read Jos's every desire.

"Speaking of which," she muttered as she climbed the stairs to her bedroom. She checked her watch. The kids wouldn't be back from soccer practice for another twenty minutes. She burrowed through the drawers of her jewelry box until she found the nipple ring with the dangling diamond stud. She took off her shirt and bra and after a few tries managed to clip the rod in place. She fingered the diamond, imagining Nellie's mouth gently tugging and teasing. She closed her eyes and sighed. Just the thought made her horny. She strode to the full-length mirror and scrutinized her body. In a few years her boobs would start to sag, but for now they were assets.

She chuckled to herself, remembering a conversation with Andy a few months after she'd worked at *Auto Monthly*. "Grant, listen to me," he'd said. "Getting information from people and developing a network of contacts requires you to use all of your assets. And may I say with complete sensitivity and deference to my sexual harassment training, you have a great rack. Keeping that fact in mind, coupled with the fact that this business is ninety-eight percent male...well, you do the math." He'd been completely red in the face by the time he'd finished his little speech. He gulped some water and added, "And if I have in any way offended you, I apologize. I will never again make a comment regarding your amazing physique. So you won't need to report me to your supervisor." Then he looked up and laughed. "Of course, I am your supervisor."

She'd assured him she got it and she appreciated it. For a few months after their talk, she'd taken to wearing V-neck T-shirts with a thin, lacy bra—and her nipple ring. Men had noticed. Even some women had noticed the little round indentation on her chest. She increased her contacts and informants every day. Colleen had noticed as well and made her take it out—she felt threatened. Jos rolled her eyes, remembering their ten-decibel fight over it. She imagined Nellie wouldn't care. She'd probably help her pick out the most attractive V-necks.

She got dressed and went back to the computer. The orthodontia bill sat next to her keyboard. She logged in and pulled up the video from her desktop. She watched the Folie lurch around the track three more times. She wanted to trust Nellie. She really did.

Her phone chimed.

Jos, have you heard from Nellie? Did she get the video? Text me back ASAP. Want to meet tomorrow.

That was fast. She automatically started a text to Nellie. *Mr. Brent texted. Wants to meet. What do you want me to say?* Her finger hovered over the Send button. An image of Felice standing with Nellie at Lucky's Place flashed through her mind. *She's a good businesswoman.*

"Yeah, right," Jos whispered.

She heard a car door shut. The kids were back from soccer practice. Without hitting Send, she abandoned her message to Nellie and responded to Mr. Brent's text. She told him she had the footage and asked where they would meet. He replied immediately.

The park. 9 a.m.

The first thing Nellie did when she got back from Jos's house was make a martini. There was something about the process of creating a mixed drink that calmed her nerves. Martinis were especially therapeutic because of the opportunity to shake the liquors. She drank the first one quickly, made a second and went out on the patio to watch the sunset. Mai had left a note. She was picking up Willie from the senior center and they'd bring home a pizza. Nellie knew she had at least an hour to herself.

It had been a physically and emotionally draining day, beginning with a type of spy work she'd never attempted. Technology had created a physical distance between the autos and the carparazzi, a distance Willie had never known. He regularly trespassed and sneaked inside the proving grounds and headquarters. She couldn't imagine her heart racing every day as it had that morning when she'd sprinted to and from the hide shack. Yet, he had performed those stunts all the time—and rarely been caught. She raised her glass and said, "To Willie," and she meant it. She'd felt so anxious and nervous as if the pit of her stomach was pushing on her throat. She never wanted to feel that way again. It had been horrible.

The situation with Jos was nearly as bad. She wanted to further Jos's standing in the carparazzi, especially if she herself was going to bow out. But the difference between them was patience and time. It had taken Nellie years to earn her place but Jos didn't have that much time. She had her kids. Her house. Expenses. Nellie got it. She couldn't afford to have that much patience.

"Wouldn't be so bad if we lived together…" she mused. She blinked and stared into her nearly empty glass. "What the hell am I saying?"

She rose from the chaise and went back for another martini. She tried to wash away the idea with gin and vermouth but it morphed into an image of Nellie playing soccer with Myles and Bridget. Jos sat on the chaise next to Willie and they both scratched Chevy behind the ears and watched the soccer game.

It was quite the picture. She'd never seen herself with kids but Myles and Bridget were unique. They were like little adults, probably because they'd been through so much already. Jos and Colleen had done a good job. She fidgeted on the chaise and took another long drink thinking about Colleen. She was a woman with a college degree like Jos. A femme like Jos.

Probably far more skilled at understanding children, like Jos. Nellie crunched furiously on her olives. Realizing she was well on her way to getting plastered, she went back to the bar for a fourth. Just as she was pouring her drink, her phone buzzed.

Felice.

She quickly gulped the drink and answered the phone, trying not to slur her words.

"Hello, Nellie. We should talk."

Nellie noticed how calm Felice sounded, as if she were preparing to tell her about a wonderful movie she'd seen.

"Okay, what are we talking about?"

"Oh, no," she said quickly. "Not over the phone. We need to see each other in person."

Nellie shook her head. "I can't fly to France again—"

"I'm not asking you to," Felice interrupted. "I'm coming to you. I'll pick you up at nine tomorrow. *Au revoir.*"

Before she could ask any other questions, Felice hung up. Nellie froze and stared at her phone. She instantly regretted the four martinis. She needed to clear her head and she needed to formulate a plan.

She grabbed her camera bag and downloaded the video. She watched it from beginning to end several times. After she saved it on two different flash drives and her external drive, she popped the memory card out of the camera. She went to the gun safe in Willie's den and put the card inside on a shelf. Perhaps she was being paranoid, but she couldn't imagine any other reason why Felice was coming to Phoenix.

She had to know about the video. Nellie paced her office, fighting the hangover that threatened to overtake her. She had to think. The most obvious answer was Kim, Felice's personal assistant, the woman she'd met on the stairs. That had to be it. She stopped pacing and suddenly felt sick. There was one other possibility. The security cameras had caught her making a dash to or from the hide shack. She hadn't worn a disguise and the camera bag would be a giveaway for sure.

She'd decided on the drive home to share the footage with Felice, and her reaction would determine Nellie's next step. Jos was going to hate her for giving Argent a way out. Jos wanted Felice to suffer because she was blinded by jealousy. If the video was made public, Felice would certainly suffer, but so would thousands of workers. Nellie couldn't let that happen. Hopefully Jos would understand.

As Mai's car pulled up into the driveway, one more thought occurred to her. Felice was picking her up in her limousine. She thought about the last two times they'd shared transportation, the limo in Milford and the private plane to France.

"Crap."

CHAPTER THIRTY

Central Phoenix, Arizona

Jos knew it would be impossible to arrive at the park by nine. She had to drop off the kids at eight, and then drive across town in rush hour traffic. As she waited at a red light, she texted Mr. Brent to say she'd arrive around nine fifteen. Twice she checked her purse to make sure she'd put the flash drive in the side pocket.

"You're getting paranoid," she muttered.

She was also getting excited. It was thrilling to think about the media playing the video, exposing Argent's deception. She bit her lip and tried to push Felice's beautiful face out of her mind. But she couldn't. Felice was the face of Argent, not Jacques Perreault. Every time she thought of Argent she saw the blond vixen who'd trapped Nellie. She glanced down at the speedometer. Eighty. She looked in her rearview mirror, expecting to see flashing lights, but there were none. She smiled. Maybe her luck was changing.

* * *

Fortunately for Nellie, Friday mornings at the senior center included Memory Hour, a time when anyone could share a significant memory. Mai had already driven Willie over and Nellie wouldn't face questions about why a limousine was pulling into their driveway. Undoubtedly he would think they were going somewhere together.

Willie was a great storyteller and a senior center favorite so he rarely missed a Friday morning. Nellie had gone with him one day and stayed in the back to listen. The circle of gray-headed people had been captivated by his story of being chased off the hill that overlooked Black Lake. They laughed and nodded as he talked about the first Impala ever built and a young, angry engineer who raced up the hill to confront him. The engineer didn't understand the hill was carparazzi territory. He tried to explain while the engineer chased him all over the hill. As the story unfolded, the audience laughed harder with each detail.

That day at the senior center Nellie had witnessed the Greatest Generation's and the early Baby Boomers' love affair with automobiles. They all had a story about a car, whether it was their first car, the first time they made out in a car, a car that made a significant road trip, or their parents' car. It was different with Generation X and the Millennials. They exchanged their cars constantly. They didn't even bother to purchase cars. They leased and returned them a few years later for another one. It just wasn't the same. Nellie thought of Jos's comment about the black box being the future of the auto industry. She just couldn't see it. But maybe that was her own bias.

Her calls to Jos went straight to voice mail. She glanced through the front blind in time to see a sleek black limousine pull up. In a serious voice she said to herself, "Do not have sex in the limousine."

Perhaps the driver would let her sit in the front. But by the time she'd locked the front door, she could see Felice's trim legs covered by ivory stockings and her signature four-inch heels.

She slid into the backseat, preparing to be mauled by Felice's tongue, and she was surprised to see her engrossed in a webinar. She acknowledged Nellie with a slight nod but her attention immediately returned to her tablet. She took some notes, but what impressed Nellie was her commanding tone when she spoke. Nellie guessed she was leading a meeting, and although she spoke only French, it was clear she was the boss.

Nellie quickly noticed the glass divider between the front and backseats was down. She sighed in relief. No hanky-panky. The driver seemed to know where he was going, if in fact there was a destination. She realized they might just be driving around as they had in Milford, but when they turned south on U.S. 60, she guessed there was a specific destination. If he wanted to drive aimlessly, the desert was a much better choice.

She settled back and took out her phone. No message from Jos. She knew she had to take the kids to school, but her gut told her Jos was meeting Mr. Brent. If the video of the Folie made the six o'clock news...Nellie pictured the empty showrooms around the country. Production of the Argent fleet would stop if none of the existing inventory moved. She threw a worried look at Felice, who was entirely focused on her conversation. She needed to tell Felice about the video now. She wasn't sure if there was anything she could do to stop Mr. Brent. Maybe she could get an emergency injunction from a judge, but she'd need to get her legal team working immediately.

Nellie suspected Renault had hired Mr. Brent, and if not them, then most likely a tech giant, a company on the verge of achieving what Argent had already accomplished. She moved forward on the seat and waved at Felice to get her attention. She held up her finely manicured index finger and continued to listen and talk in French. She eventually muted the conversation and looked at Nellie.

"*Oui?*"

"I know you're busy but we have to talk. Something's happened and Argent is going to need to get ready for a sea of bad publicity."

Felice's reaction implied curiosity but not shock. "I have to finish this call. We will talk then." She offered the shy smile that melted Nellie's heart and squeezed her hand before she went back to the webinar.

Well, I tried.

She looked through the windshield. They continued south as U.S. 60 morphed into Grand Avenue, the main artery from Surprise to downtown. They joined thousands of other commuters going to work. Nellie leaned back and tried to enjoy the ride.

When Jos pulled into the parking lot, she immediately realized Mr. Brent hadn't arrived yet. She wasn't sure if Robert had been summoned, but his car wasn't there either. She glanced at her phone. It was nine twenty. Nellie had called while she was driving but hadn't bothered to leave a message. If she heard Nellie's voice, she might not have the courage to do what needed to be done. Nellie didn't understand. She was blinded by Felice Perreault's beauty. Argent had to be stopped. This wasn't about Jacques or Felice. This was about public trust. Safety. "Truth, justice and the American way," she muttered.

A minute later Mr. Brent's sleek Renault pulled into a nearby parking space. He was chatting on his phone, and he hadn't yet noticed Jos. She could tell he was unhappy as he made a fist and pounded the steering wheel. She took in the entire scene. A PR director yelling on his phone while driving a French car, one that was a serious Argent competitor and the leading car maker in France. She pulled out the flash drive and stared at it.

"What if I'm making a mistake?" she whispered. "Nellie could be right. What am I doing?"

She looked through the passenger window. Robert pulled up on her right. He held his phone to his ear. Their eyes met and she noticed he wasn't smiling. She looked left at Mr. Brent and then to Robert. They were definitely talking to each other and neither made an effort to leave their car. She suddenly felt trapped between them.

The limousine turned off Grand and headed east on Glendale Avenue. *Definitely going somewhere.* They made one more turn and the familiar parking lot appeared in the distance. She shook her head and glanced at Felice, who was starting to put her things away while she rattled off a list in French. Nellie guessed the call was ending as the limo slowed and reached the destination—Washington Park.

Felice signed off and put away her tablet. She turned and smiled at Nellie. "We have some things to talk about, no?"

Nellie nodded and opened her mouth, but she closed it when she saw Jos's van. She glanced at Felice with a worried look on her face. "What's going on?"

Felice didn't answer but offered her cat-like smile, one that Nellie suddenly associated with danger. She remembered the old saying, "The apple doesn't fall far from the tree," and the image of Jacques Perreault breaking the wineglass flashed in her mind. *You will help us or she will help us.*

The limo pulled into a space near a Renault and Mr. Brent opened Felice's door.

What is going on?

Nellie jumped out of the backseat and charged over to Jos's van. She saw her coming and rolled down the window.

"What are you doing here? What is *she* doing here?" Jos asked, pointing at Felice. Nellie could hear the panic in her voice.

"I'm not sure. Are you here to meet Brent?"

Jos hung her head. "Yes. I'm sorry I didn't listen to you. I just…I don't know."

Nellie whirled around and studied the scene before her: Felice was chatting with Mr. Brent. Robert had joined them as well. Everything clicked into place.

"Are we in danger?" Jos asked.

Nellie sighed in relief. Then she laughed uproariously. "No. C'mon, get out."

She took Jos's hand and they joined the group. When she locked eyes with Felice, she said, "Well played."

Jos looked completely bewildered. "Would someone tell me what the hell is going on?"

Felice stepped forward and extended her hand. "May I introduce myself? I am Felice Perreault. *Enchanté*, Mademoiselle Grant. You are indeed more beautiful in person than your little photo in *Auto Monthly*. I would suggest you demand a new one. And for the record, you are just as beautiful as a brunette." She kissed her hand and stepped back.

Nellie could see Jos bristle as the back of her hand met Felice's lips. She gave Jos a poke in the side and her demeanor changed. "Thank you. Now can you please explain what we're doing here?"

Felice looked at Nellie and nodded. She knew the truth would be more accurate coming from a native speaker. "In a nutshell, Felice hired Mr. Brent to spy on her own company."

Jos's gaze flitted around the circle. Nellie could tell she was the only one who hadn't figured it out. Jos turned to Felice. "Why in the hell would you do that?"

The cat-like smile trapped Jos's gaze. "To protect my father's legacy." She scanned the park and said, "There are too many of us standing here. Nellie, give me what you brought, and Mademoiselle Grant, give yours to Brent." She turned to Brent and Robert. "The two of you get going." A wave of her hand sent both men into action.

Nellie pulled the flash drive from her pocket and handed it to Felice, but Jos's hand remained in her purse. "Babe, you can give it to him."

"Why are you so sure?"

"Because only a fool would release the Folie," Felice said in an exasperated tone. "And I am not a fool. Unfortunately, my father is blinded by his pride."

"Do you get it now?" Nellie asked.

Understanding filled Jos's face and she handed the flash drive to Mr. Brent. "It was nice to meet you, Jos," he said before sprinting toward the car.

"Yeah," Robert agreed. He squeezed her arm and kissed her cheek. "You're a damn fine woman to have on my arm. You can pose as my wife anytime."

The comment made her laugh and she waved goodbye as he trotted back to his beater car.

Jos eyed her suspiciously. "You're really not going to release the Folie?"

"No." Felice deposited Nellie's flash drive into her purse. "Besides, I'm imagining that both of you have your own copy of the footage, no?"

"Yeah," Nellie acknowledged. "But if you're going to do the right thing, we don't have to," she said with a glance at Jos, who was studying Felice. "So your father doesn't suspect?"

Felice cracked a grin. "He thinks I'm too much his follower to suspect. You and I have a different relationship with our fathers. Mine is more complicated and the expectations much higher. He sees me leading Argent in the next decade, but he doesn't understand the Folie would take everything away from us."

Jos shook her head, clearly still shocked by the turn of events. "So you hired Mr. Brent and made sure the luncheon happened while the Folie was being tested. We would've gotten the shot that day, but you couldn't know the carparazzi would fly over the proving ground."

"Damn carparazzi," Felice joked.

"But you created another opportunity when I went to photograph the Amour," Nellie added. Another thought occurred to her. "And you made sure the security guard got a call so he'd leave me alone."

"Thanks to my highly trusted assistant. I wasn't there," Felice said. She raised her chin and added, "No one can prove I knew anything, especially my father. When I show him this video, he will blame Renault. That's as it should be. Then he'll cancel the debut of the Folie."

"This must have been hard for you," Jos said.

Felice's stoic expression cracked slightly. There were tears in her eyes and she looked away. "My father is a great man." She looked at Nellie with a wry smile. "Do you know anything about strong and difficult fathers, Nellie Rafferty?"

Nellie frowned. "I do."

"I don't always approve of his tactics," she continued, "and when I am in charge of Argent there will be changes in the way we do business. But first I have to make sure there is an Argent left to lead. He wasn't satisfied with his accomplishments. His name will be remembered as the man who made the most significant breakthrough in recent automobile history. That has to be enough, even if he doesn't agree." She'd raised her voice, and Nellie heard the strength of a leader.

"You must have been shocked when he decided to hire me," Nellie said.

Felice closed her eyes for a moment before she said, "That's when I knew I had to do something." She glanced at Jos and added, "I knew he'd manipulated both of you and he wouldn't stop until the Folie was released."

"Do you think you can fix it?" Jos asked.

Her face shifted into a tranquil expression as she pondered the question. "Perhaps someday. Perhaps not." She glanced around her and said, "I have to go." She kissed Nellie on the cheek and said, "You're fired." They both laughed and Nellie handed over her hardly used Argent badge. "But I intend to give you the first year's pay."

Nellie shook her head. "You don't have to—"

Felice put a finger to her lips. "You saved my company. It is the least I can do."

She turned to Jos and took her hand. She kissed it gently and said, "I'd love to take you for a ride in my limousine someday." She seemed to be feasting on Jos's cleavage, exposed by the wide V of her T-shirt. Nellie could clearly see the outline of her nipple ring, a fact not lost on Felice. "I have a nipple ring as well, although I hardly wear it. I'd put it on just for you."

Nellie rolled her eyes and Jos blushed before she glanced up at Nellie and said, "That's a very nice offer but I'm taken."

Felice laughed heartily as she walked back to the limo. "You Americans are so funny." Before she slipped into the backseat, she offered her beautiful smile and said, "*Bonjour*, my new friends. Until we meet again."

They watched her drive away and Nellie could feel Jos's eyes upon her. "Are you sorry you're not going with her?" Jos asked.

Nellie kissed her cheek. "Not at all." She stroked Jos's cheek and said, "I love you. I've never said those words to anyone. But I love you and only you."

Jos's blue eyes pooled with tears. "I love you too."

"Let's get out of here."

CHAPTER THIRTY-ONE

Wittman, Arizona

They headed back to the ranch and straight to the shed. Within ten minutes the Corvette was flying down the back roads. They waved at Justin Juniper as they hauled through the county island and the Hassayampa Wash, headed northwest toward the less-traveled state roads. Jos let Nellie drive, content with the view from the passenger's seat. She stared at her profile. Left hand on the wheel, eyes glued to the road while her right hand caressed Jos's neck. It was so natural for her. The amazing machine reached one hundred twenty and Nellie's pose and her expression never shifted. The landscape around them blurred, and Jos's eyes couldn't distinguish one feature from another.

Jos wondered if she'd ever be comfortable driving this fast. Of course it was difficult to imagine the van exceeding eighty, but even when she drove the Corvette, moving the red speedometer needle past ninety had panicked her. "Maybe I'm not meant to go that fast," she murmured.

"What?" Nellie asked, leaning closer to her.

Jos snuggled against her, allowing her lips to linger on Nellie's cheek. Eventually she whispered back, "I don't think I'll ever be able to go as fast as you."

She pulled away to check Nellie's expression. She was chuckling. She motioned for Jos to move closer again and responded, "I hope not."

When they reached I-17, approximately forty miles north of Phoenix, Nellie slowed the Corvette to the speed limit and enjoyed the stares, honks and waves from nearby motorists who wanted to gawk at the pristine piece of American history. Jos waved back, returning the thumbs-up given by the surrounding drivers. They returned to the shed just two and a half hours after they left. Driving over a hundred miles an hour substantially cut travel time.

Nellie bounded from the car, but when Jos attempted to open the door, Nellie said, "No, don't move. I want pictures." She disappeared into the back of the shed and returned with a very old Minolta 35mm camera. When she saw Jos's look of surprise she said, "I still have a darkroom and I love my Minolta, although the film is super expensive now." She squatted down to Jos's level and said, "Okay, give me a smile."

"You already took my picture, Nellie," Jos whined.

After several clicks, Nellie lowered the camera and said, "Not like this. Unbutton your shirt."

Her voice was like silk and Jos complied with her request. Then she sat up on her haunches and spread her arms across the Corvette's windshield, parting her shirt and exposing the pink lacy bra again.

"Oh, that's perfect," Nellie said. She crouched in front of the car's nose and snapped so vigorously, Jos thought she might break her finger or the camera from pressing down on the shutter button while Jos changed positions several times.

"How else would you like me to pose?" Jos asked seductively as she slowly opened the door and slid out of the Corvette. She casually dropped her shirt and wiggled out of her shorts. She had a plan but she wasn't sure Nellie would agree.

Nellie stood by the car, slack-jawed, clutching her camera. Jos smiled and stroked the hood lovingly. "I read that the hoods of the American classics were made of steel and could withstand nearly a ton of pressure. Is that true?" Nellie didn't answer. She seemed to be in a trance. "It's still a little warm. Do you have a blanket?"

Nellie nodded, her eyes wide, but she didn't move.

Jos grinned. "Do you want to go get that for me?"

Nellie scrambled to the back and reappeared with a blanket. She threw it over the hood and Jos stretched across it carefully, leaving her feet on the concrete. She wouldn't dare put a dimple or a dent in a classic car.

Nellie remained still as a statue, clutching her camera. "Okay," Jos said with a laugh.

She snapped several photos, and Jos rapidly changed positions, each one more sexual than the one before.

She sat up and turned her back toward Nellie. "Take this off."

It fell away and slid to the floor. Jos centered her bottom on the car's nose and leaned back carefully. She teased her nipples with the tips of her fingers and spread her legs as wide as she could without allowing her feet to leave the ground. Even in the midst of a seduction scene, she was conscious of the Corvette's fragility.

"Do you like my ring?" she asked, noticing Nellie's gaze had locked on her left nipple.

She didn't respond but instead took three steps back to get the full effect. Jos felt as if she were one with the most beautiful automobile ever designed. Her figure and the lines of the car became inseparable. The whir of the camera continued for several shots. She turned her head slightly toward Nellie.

"I only have one question. Why do you still have your clothes on?"

Nellie set the camera on a chair and stripped down to her boxers while Jos's hand burrowed underneath her panties. She stroked herself, her eyes closed and her mouth open.

She heard metal scraping on the pristine concrete floor. Dressed only in her boxers, Nellie dragged a small stool to the

Corvette and climbed the three steps. She held the camera over Jos and held the shutter button down. Jos continued to pleasure herself while Nellie took dozens of photos.

"You're going to miss out on the good part," she warned.

Nellie descended the steps and set aside her camera and the stool. She grasped Jos's busy hand and stared at her.

"Finish me," Jos whined. She shifted her hips back and forth to quell her aching need. "Now."

Nellie hovered over her, their faces nearly touching. "You've been a bad girl turning me on like this. You're going to need to wait a little longer." She joined Jos's hands together over her head.

Nellie kissed her quivering lips, her tongue darting in and out. When Jos moaned again, she trailed kisses down her neck and across her nipples, gently tugging on the nipple ring, sending waves of pleasure throughout her body. She traced circles on her abdomen and fingered the panty line of her briefs, slowly pulling them down until gravity sent them to the cement floor. Nellie knelt before her and kissed her creamy inner thighs. She parted her waiting lips and blew cool air on the intense fire raging within her core.

She moaned loudly and cried, "Please!"

Nellie flicked her tongue against Jos's wet center, once. Its power surged through her and she started to shake. Nellie did it again—with more pressure. Jos gasped.

"You're torturing me," Jos cried.

She sensed Nellie's nearness before fingers slid inside, filling her up. She writhed and undulated against the pressure, wanting Nellie deeper, wanting more. When Nellie pressed against her, she came. One orgasm rolled into another and another until she grabbed a handful of Nellie's hair and pulled herself up to a sitting position. Still, Nellie's fingers remained inside, her thumb massaging Jos's rock-hard clitoris.

She moved her hips and they found a rhythm. Nellie's lips suckled on her breasts. She was close again.

"Look at me," Nellie said. They gazed at each other until a scream burst forth and Jos fell against her.

Nellie held her, quietly whispering in her ear and kissing her cheek. When Jos looked up she glanced at the abandoned camera. "I may need to confiscate those pictures."

Nellie laughed and said, "Not a chance." Her expression shifted, and in the pale hue of the pendant light, she looked—hungry. "It's my turn," Nellie said, her voice rough and thick. "And I don't believe you've had the privilege of joining me in the bed of the '49 GMC truck."

Jos glanced at the monstrous green machine. She raised an eyebrow and asked, "How many women have preceded me?"

Nellie pulled her off the Corvette and held her tightly. "That doesn't matter, baby. I've saved the best for last."

POSTSCRIPT

One Year Later
Wittman, Arizona

"Move to the left," Nellie directed, and Bridget angled her feet in the correct position before she kicked the ball past Nellie toward the goal. Myles scooped it up and popped it over their heads in the opposite direction. They all exchanged high-fives and Nellie explained why it was important to use the goalie to move the ball downfield.

They returned to position to practice the move again and her gaze wandered up to the patio. Jos lay stretched out on one of the chaise lounges, reading the latest edition of *Car and Driver*. The cover featured one of her shots. Chevy was at her side. Nellie swallowed a huge lump in her throat and fended off the tears. They came less frequently now.

Willie had been gone for five months. She'd come to terms with his mistakes as a father. She'd never mentioned the incident with Lucy to him, just enjoyed the time they had left.

Felice helped her understand forgiveness was the right path. Ironically, they'd all become friends. Felice attended Willie's funeral and she often hired Jos to take Argent's publicity photos. She'd also helped market some of Nellie's still-life photography. Apparently the French had an enduring love for the desert. Everything had fallen into place.

Still, when Nellie was caught off guard, if she looked toward the patio at sunset, she expected to see Willie there next to Chevy. He so loved the sunsets. Suddenly four arms wrapped around her and a smile broke free of the tears.

"We love you, Nellie," Bridget said.

"We do," Myles confirmed. "We're here."

She ruffled their hair and hugged them back. "I love you too."

She glanced up at Jos. She lowered the magazine and watched them, a serene expression on her face. It was one of their "moments." She'd start to feel depressed about Willie's death, or concerned about her choice to leave the carparazzi or just frustrated by the events of the day, and then something would happen in their life. Myles would make a joke. Bridget would draw her a picture, or Jos would squeeze her hand. She'd be reminded of the love in her life. Right now it was four little arms wrapped around her middle. She smiled back at Jos, the woman she knew would join her in the chase for the rest of her life. They were just getting started.

Bella Books, Inc.

Women. Books. Even Better Together.

P.O. Box 10543
Tallahassee, FL 32302

Phone: 800-729-4992
www.bellabooks.com